At the end of the season the Little Bend *Guardian*, the local weekly, always published a special issue with pictures of all the players. Cody was at the Main Street Deli, picking up his after-work sandwich, when he saw the football issue in the rack. He moved toward the rack, wondering whether there'd be anything about him, going back and forth in his mind about whether to buy the paper or not.

Cody never got to the football article, because of something on the front page; something that got his heart beating fast, something, in fact, that woke him up and made him feel alive, as though he'd been in hibernation. Alive, but not in a good way: What Cody saw on the front page of the *Guardian* was a photograph of Clea. Over it, a big black headline read: "Local Girl Missing."

PETER ABRAHAMS

REALITY CHECK

HARPER TEEN
An Imprint of HarperCollins Publishers

To Peter and Peggy Rice

HarperTeen is an imprint of HarperCollins Publishers.

Reality Check
Copyright © 2009 by Pas de Deux
All rights reserved. Printed in the United States of America.
No part of this book may be used or reproduced in any manner whatsoever without written permission except in the case of brief quotations embodied in critical articles and reviews. For information address HarperCollins Children's Books, a division of HarperCollins Publishers, 10 East 53rd Street, New York, NY 10022.
www.harperteen.com

Library of Congress Cataloging-in-Publication Data
Abrahams, Peter.
Reality check / by Peter Abrahams. —1st ed.
    p.   cm.
"Laura Geringer Books."
Summary: After a knee injury destroys sixteen-year-old Cody's college hopes, he drops out of high school and gets a job in his small Montana town, but when his ex-girlfriend disappears from her Vermont boarding school, Cody travels cross-country to join the search.
    ISBN 978-0-06-122768-4
    [1. Missing persons—Fiction. 2. Social classes—Fiction. 3. High schools—Fiction.
4. Schools—Fiction. 5. Dropouts—Fiction. 6. Gambling—Fiction.] I. Title.
PZ7.A1675 Tro 2009   2008022593
[Fic]—dc22   CIP
                                                                                  AC

Typography by Jennifer Rozbruch
11   12   13   14   CG/RRDH   10   9   8   7   6   5   4
❖
First paperback edition, 2010

ONE

EXCEPT FOR FOOTBALL FRIDAYS, Cody Laredo's favorite day of the school year was always the last. Now, May 30, final day of his sophomore year at County High, he sat in the back row of homeroom, waiting for the teacher—a sub he'd never seen before—to hand out the report cards. As long as there were no Fs—even one would make him ineligible for football in the fall, meaning summer school, an impossibility because he had to work—Cody didn't care what was in the report card. He just wanted out.

"One more thing," the sub was saying. "The principal sent this announcement." The sub unfolded a sheet of paper, stuck a pair of glasses on the tip of his nose. "'County High wishes everyone a safe summer. Please remember . . ." And then came blah blah blah about alcohol and drugs, tuned out by some mechanism in Cody's brain, overloaded from having heard the same thing too many times. The sub thumbed through the report cards, called out names in alphabetical order, mispronouncing several. Cody was the only L. A minute or two later he was outside, crossing the student parking lot, warm sun shining down and the sky big and blue. Somewhere close by a horse neighed.

His car—a ten-year-old beater with 137,432 miles on the odometer, an odometer disconnected by the previous owner, one of his dad's drinking buddies—sat at the back of the lot, open prairie behind it and Coach Huff leaning against the fender.

"Hey, coach," said Cody.

"Close shave, son," said Coach Huff.

"Huh?"

"Ain't opened your report yet?"

Cody shook his head. The coach already knew his grades? What was with that?

"Waitin' for what, exackly?" said Coach Huff, a tall guy with a huge upper body and stick legs, varsity football coach and also teacher of health and remedial English. "Sign from above?"

Cody slit open the envelope with his fingernail, slid out the report card. *U.S. History—C–; Algebra 1—C–; Biology—D; English—D–; Shop—B.* D minus: close shave, no doubt about it. He looked up, feeling pretty good.

"Good thing Miz Brennan's a football fan," the coach said.

"She is?" Ms. Brennan was the English teacher, bestower of the D minus. Cody actually liked her, especially when she forgot all about whatever the lesson was and started reciting poetry, right from memory, something she did maybe once every two weeks or so. Somehow Ms. Brennan, an old lady with twisted arthritic fingers and a scratchy voice, had all this poetry in her head. Poetry in the textbook was a complete mystery to Cody, but in a way he couldn't explain, the murkiness all cleared up during Ms. Brennan's recitations, or at least he thought it did. Like: *Screw your courage to the sticking-place / And we'll not fail.* Cody was pretty sure he got that one, just from how she'd spoken the words, made his mind picture courage fastened deep to something that would never break, like a huge boulder. But he'd never seen Ms. Brennan at a football game.

"Either that," said Coach Huff, "or we're lookin' at a legit D minus. That the story? It's legit?"

Cody didn't know what to say, felt his face turning red.

"Just razzin' you, son. Nothin' wrong with your football IQ, that's for sure. We're all countin' on you in the fall." He pushed away from the car. The shocks squeaked and the whole body rose an inch or two. "Stay in shape this summer."

"I will," Cody said, thinking: *Is there something wrong with my other IQ? Does Coach Huff think I'm dumb?*

The coach got a squinty look in his eye. "Workin' with your dad?"

"Maybe," Cody said. His dad did landscaping in the summer. Landscaping wasn't bad, and Cody loved being outdoors, but he was hoping to find some other job, almost anything.

"Just remember—landscapin' don't replace liftin', so hit the gym."

"Okay."

"Upper body's important—put some zip on the ball."

"Why, coach? We never throw."

Coach Huff gave Cody a long look, then laughed, a single eruption of sound, close to a bark. "Sense of humor—I like that," he said. "Just remember there's a time and place for everything."

Coach Huff gave Cody a pat on the shoulder, started walking away. He met Clea Weston coming from the other direction, report card in hand, and nodded to her, but she didn't seem to notice. Her eyes were on Cody. The sun lit golden sparkles in her hair, and Cody thought: *The whole summer ahead of us!*

And what did he have at this very moment? A full tank of gas.

"Let's ride out to Black Rocks," he said. Black Rocks was an abandoned quarry near the bend in the river, the best swimming for miles around.

"I got a B in calc," Clea said.

"Wow," said Cody. There were two kids taking calc in the whole school, Clea—a sophomore like Cody—and some brain in the senior class. No one thought of Clea as a brain. She was just good at everything: striker on the varsity soccer team, class president, assistant editor of the lit mag; and the most beautiful girl in the school—in the whole state, in Cody's opinion.

But a real person, as he well knew, capable of annoyance, for example. When Clea got annoyed, her right eyebrow did this little fluttering thing, like now. "Wow?" she said.

"Yeah," he said. He himself wouldn't ever get as far as calc, not close. "Pretty awesome."

She shook her head. "I've never had a B."

For a second or two, Cody didn't quite get her meaning; he'd scored very few Bs himself. Then it hit him. "All As, every time?"

She nodded.

"You never told me."

She shrugged. "My father's going to be pissed."

5

"Come on."

"You don't know him."

Maybe not. He and Clea had been going out since Christmas but didn't spend much time in each other's homes. Clea lived with her dad and stepmom in the nicest house in town, a house that actually had a name instead of a number: Cottonwood. Cody lived with his dad—when his dad was around—in a one-bedroom apartment over the Red Pony, a dim downtown bar his dad—his parents, actually—had owned at one time, back when his mom was alive.

"Then don't tell him," Cody said.

"Don't tell him my grades? Are you serious? He'll ask to see my report card first thing."

"He will?" Cody's own dad hadn't seen any of his report cards in years.

"He keeps them all in his desk," Clea said, "going back to kindergarten."

"Whoa," said Cody.

"How did it happen?" Clea said. "I thought I aced the final."

For a moment tears shone in her eyes, and Clea wasn't a crier. He'd seen her cry only once or twice, and those had been mixed-up tears, partly, even mostly, happy. Cody couldn't stand to see her upset like this, especially about nothing. He handed her his report card. "Scan this," he said. "You'll feel better."

Clea ran her gaze over it. "Oh, Cody," she said, looking up, laughing a little laugh, like What am I going to do with you? She reached out, tousled his hair. Cody loved her touch, loved everything about her.

"What do you think my IQ is?" he said.

"Three thousand," said Clea.

○○○

They drove out to Black Rocks. The town they lived in, Little Bend, lay at the western border of hundreds of miles of flatland, the Rockies' foothills in sight. The quarry, abandoned after World War II, stood at the top of a long rise—the first suggestion of the mountains to come—overlooking the town, spread out from that perspective like an open book. Little Bend had a potash mine, owned for two generations by Clea's family, and now a year or two left before being worked out; an ethanol plant, just getting started, owned by investors from Denver and run by Mr. Weston; a base that the Air Force was always threatening to close; and a rodeo every summer that attracted ten thousand paying visitors, sometimes more. A pretty town in a pretty place: almost all the kids at County High hoped to end up somewhere else—Denver, Minneapolis, Seattle, California.

Cody followed the curving gravel road up the rise, parked

by a sign with a few bullet holes in it: ABSOLUTELY NO TRESPASS-
ING. ABSOLUTELY NO SWIMMING OR DIVING. He and Clea stripped
down to their underwear, ran to the edge, and jumped, holding
hands. They screamed their heads off on the long fall, then hit
the water, not too cold on the surface, icier and icier the deeper
they plunged. And darker and darker, too. Somewhere down
in the darkness they lost touch, kicked back up into sunshine
separately, and came together laughing. They kissed, their lips
and faces icy cold, their tongues warm.

"The whole summer," Cody said.

"Yeah," said Clea. "I just wish . . ."

"What?"

"Nothing."

"You're not still thinking about calc?"

Clea nodded, drops of clear water falling from the ends of
her hair.

"Stop," he said. "It's summer. No more teachers, no more
books. We're free—free at last!" He shook his fist in the air.
Clea laughed.

They swam to a rocky ledge that jutted out from the steep
quarry walls, climbed onto it, lay down. The black stone soaked
up the sun's heat, soon warmed them up. It was quiet and peace-
ful, the only sounds their own breathing, and the quarry water
they'd disturbed still lapping at the walls. Cody felt a change

8

in the atmosphere, like the air pressure was rising, bearing down; a change he felt in his stomach, and lower. He reached out, touched Clea's leg, could tell that the change in the atmosphere was affecting her, too—maybe it was just their own little private atmosphere. Cody moved his hand higher, the world shrinking very fast around him. Willpower, judgment, all kinds of other cerebral things started shutting down, like fuses shorting out in a fuse box. Then, very faint, he heard a car engine. He took his hand away.

"Someone's coming," he said.

"I don't hear anyone," said Clea, taking his hand, drawing it back to where it had been.

Cody sat up, heard the car again, coming up the slope, no doubt about it. He rose, pulled Clea to her feet. She had a funny little pout on her face, the kind of look her teachers didn't see; maybe no one else got to see it, no one but him.

"There's never any space," she said.

"That's the thing about Big Sky country," Cody said.

Clea smiled. A beautiful, private kind of smile. "I like how you think," she said.

"Me?"

They followed the steep path that corkscrewed up the side of the quarry pit, headed for the car. Another car, kicking up a dust cloud, was coming up the road, two or three curves from the top: a black-and-white car, with blue lights, not flashing, on the roof. Cody and Clea hurried to Cody's car, started throwing on their clothes. They were just about done, Clea slipping on her sandals, when the cop drove up and stopped beside them, his window sliding down. His gaze, not friendly, went from Cody to Clea, back to Cody.

"Sign too small? You missed it?" He pointed his chin at the sign. Cody and Clea said nothing. "Who wants to read it for me?" They remained silent. "How about you?" the cop said, pointing his chin again, this time at Cody.

"We weren't doing any harm," Clea said.

The cop turned to her. "Was I talkin' to you?"

Clea shook her head.

"Read the sign, boy."

Cody read the sign in a low voice. "Absolutely no trespassing. No swimming or diving."

"Left out that second *absolutely*," the cop said. "Any reason for that?"

Cody thought: *Absolutely*. He said nothing, just shook his head.

"This your car?" the cop said.

Cody nodded.

"Let's see some ID." Cody handed over his license. The cop glanced at it, handed it back. "Weren't fixing on swimming down in the pit, were you?" the cop said.

Cody didn't say anything, but Clea had less experience with cops, actually none, and she said, "No."

The cop smiled. "Then how come your hair's wet? Some sudden shower happen up here and nowheres else?"

Silence. The wind rose, blew across the plain.

"Got some ID?" the cop said to Clea.

"I don't have my license yet," she said.

"What's your name?"

"Clea Weston."

The cop gazed at her for a moment; then his eyes shifted. Had he recognized that surname? "Get the hell out of here," he said. "And don't never come back." His window slid up and he drove slowly off.

"Goddamn it," said Cody. He kicked the nearest tire of his own car, hard enough to hurt.

Clea patted him on the back. "He's just an asshole," she said. Cody thought of his friend Junior Riggins, nose guard on defense, tackle on offense, and the biggest, strongest kid on the team, who said that human beings were all programmed to turn into assholes some time in their twenties—what other explanation was there? Junior was real smart, although no one in charge seemed to know, maybe proving his point. Clea patted him again. "Forget it."

11

But Cody couldn't, not just like that. His face was suddenly hot, burning red. He turned, and all at once found himself running toward the edge of the quarry pit—

"Cody, stop!"

—and diving off, headfirst and fully clothed. This time hitting the water reminded him of a moment halfway through the last season, the very first play of his first start as varsity quarterback, a quarterback draw—Coach Huff loved calling the quarterback draw—when the gap had closed in an instant and he'd been rocked from both sides by a pair of all-county 280-pound tackles, one of whom was headed for CSU on a full ride.

○ ○ ○

Down in the cold and dark, Cody remembered somehow bouncing up off the turf and saying, "Nice hit." He swam to the surface, treaded water. Clea was gazing down from the top, her face anxious; and then not. The sun had moved a little, no longer shining all the way to the water, leaving him in shadow, but it backlit Clea in a way that made her shine with her own light. Cody felt better.

TWO

CODY, SHIRTLESS AND BAREFOOT, wearing sweatpants he'd found under a pair of old cleats in the trunk of his car, drove Clea home. She lived in the Heights, the only really fancy neighborhood in Little Bend. The Heights weren't very high, just high enough to stand over the rest of the town. Cottonwood, a huge stone house at the very top of the top, and therefore with nice views of the river, had broad lawns cut like putting greens, lots of trees, two swimming pools—indoor and outdoor—and a tennis court. Cody pulled into the long circular drive. He cut the engine, turned to Clea. She was gazing at the house, the report card held tight in her hand. Sunlight glared on all the windows. Her mind was on something, exactly what he didn't know. Cody searched for words that might help out.

"Um," he said.

Clea turned to him. "Come inside."

"Huh?" said Cody. He'd been inside only once before, one afternoon not long after they'd started going out, when he'd come to pick Clea up and Fran, Clea's stepmom, had ushered him in to meet the family, meaning Mr. Weston and the two little stepbrothers. It had taken Mr. Weston what had seemed like twenty seconds to establish where Cody lived, who his father was, and Cody's future plans, which at that time came down to going to a D-1 college on a football scholarship, and still did.

"No one's home," Clea said. "Fran took the boys to Cowboy Town and my dad won't be back till late."

Cody didn't move. "He doesn't like me."

"That's not true," Clea said. They sat in silence. "He doesn't even know you," she added after a while. More silence. A little warm breeze sprang up, flowed through the open windows of Cody's car, ruffled the red roses in the Westons' flower beds. "Besides," Clea said, "*I* like you. I like you plenty."

Floral smells came wafting in.

"Come on," Clea said, touching his bare shoulder.

"I don't have a shirt."

"Lots of shirts inside."

Cody reached for the door handle.

They walked around the house until they reached a big glassed-in room the Westons called the conservatory, although Cody had no clue why. "This is never locked," Clea said. She opened the door and they went inside. The conservatory had a stone floor with a fountain in the center; water splashed from the mouth of a bronze frog. Clea led him to a door, around a corner, past the laundry room, a room almost as big as Cody's whole apartment.

"Just a sec," she said, darting into the laundry room and returning with a perfectly ironed button-down shirt, dark blue with thin white stripes. "Here," she said, tossing it to him. "Put it on."

Just from the feel of it in his hands, Cody knew this shirt was much finer than anything he'd ever worn. He checked the label: ANDREW TOTTEN, LONDON. And a smaller label stitched in gold beside it: MADE TO THE PERSONAL REQUIREMENTS OF WINTHROP WESTON. Mr. Weston had his shirts made for him? And in London?

"Go on," Clea said. "It's just a shirt. And you can keep it—he'll never notice."

Keep Mr. Weston's shirt? Out of the question. But with the A/C running it was a little chilly in the house—no A/C in the apartment over the Red Pony—so Cody put on Mr. Weston's shirt, too tight on him through the shoulders, too baggy everywhere else. Clea tilted her head to one side and studied him.

"A nice color on you."

"Blue?"

"That shade of blue. Navy blue." She took his hand—he noticed that she'd left the report card on the ironing board—and led him toward a staircase, kind of narrow for such a grand house.

"What's this?" he said.

"The back stairs."

They went up the back stairs, shadowy and smelling of old wood and wax—even a bit shabby, almost like it was a small leftover of some other house, not so grand, the kind of house Cody was more used to—and came out in a beautiful broad hallway lined with Persian rugs, the walls hung with paintings of the Old West. Cody knew nothing about art, but he wouldn't have minded lingering a bit; another time, maybe. This time, something was leading him along, and not just Clea's hand in his. She opened a door at the end of the hall.

"Ta-da!" she said.

Cody had been in only one other girl's bedroom before this—Tonya Redding's, almost a year earlier. Tonya lived in Lower Town, a few blocks from the Red Pony, where her mother worked as a waitress. Tonya's bedroom was kind of girly, with pink walls, dolls on the shelf, stuffed animals on the bed; despite everything, he'd wanted out of there pretty fast. Clea's bedroom was different: much bigger, of course, and beautiful, with a bank of windows on one side and French doors on another, but there was nothing girly about it. The walls were white, decorated with framed black-and-white photos of Clea on her horse, Bud; there were two bookcases, one filled with books, the other with trophies; the furniture was dark and spare. Clea's riding boots stood by the bed—a queen-size bed or even bigger, but it had plenty of space—and her riding helmet lay on the comforter, a comforter that looked like it might be made of silk.

Cody opened the French doors, stepped out onto a balcony. Below lay more gardens, the swimming pool, an acre or two of lawn, a barn, a corral, and Bud standing stock-still by a water trough, his white diamond-shaped blaze visible even at this distance. A perfect sight, very like a photograph, this one in color. Cody had a funny feeling, as though time had stopped for a moment. Then he felt Clea's hand on his back. He turned. She put her arms around him and they kissed. Clea liked to keep her eyes open when they kissed, and wanted his open, too. That had taken getting used to, the intensity close to painful. Clea had light-colored eyes, closer to green than anything else—a little surprising what with her hair being so dark, almost black—and during these kisses he seemed to sink beneath the green, down into something good and pure and giving that at all costs must not be harmed.

They went back inside and lay on the bed. Time grew erratic again, not stopping now, but instead becoming elastic, stretching and contracting, speeding up or slowing down, all depending on what was happening in Clea's bedroom. Cody sank into green waters, and knew without a word being spoken that something similar was going on with her. And there, so deep down, almost oblivious to anything else, he barely—just barely—heard Bud neighing in the corral. Some little corner of his mind grew preoccupied with the sound, worried at it, and all at once, Cody realized he'd missed something else, sensed but not absorbed: a faint crunch, the kind of sound a tire makes on a gravel driveway.

He sat up.

"What?" said Clea. "What's wrong?"

"Someone's coming."

"Impossible."

But she believed him and sat up too, holding the comforter—yes, silk—to her chest, all the way up to her chin. Cody started throwing on clothes and Clea did the same. It could have been funny, this repetitive dressing in hurry-up mode, but it was not. She was sitting on the edge of the bed, again fully

18

dressed, again slipping into her sandals, and Cody was standing by the French doors, sweatpants on, barefoot, fumbling with the buttons—there seemed to be way too many—on Mr. Weston's hand-tailored navy blue shirt with the thin stripes, when the door burst open and Mr. Weston himself strode in.

"Daddy? What are you—"

Mr. Weston made a chopping motion with his hand, a hand that held—Cody saw at that moment—the report card, and Clea went silent, her own hand frozen on a sandal strap. The room suddenly seemed much too small, and not because Mr. Weston was especially big. Mr. Weston was no taller than Cody—about six feet—and, while twenty or thirty pounds heavier, no more powerfully built. He had thinning reddish hair and a broad freckled face that had a funny way of looking warm and friendly from just below the eyes to the tip of the chin, like a smile could flash out at any second, but at this moment showed not a millimeter of friendliness. His gaze went to Cody's hands, still fumbling with the buttons, and then down to his bare feet. Nothing wrong with Cody's feet—strong, broad feet, size ten and a half—but now all he wanted to do was to somehow cover them up.

Mr. Weston's eyes—similar in color to Clea's but in no other way—rose slowly up to Cody's face. Did he notice that Cody was wearing his shirt? No way to tell.

"That your car in the drive?" he said, not furious, not even loud, but Cody's spine felt icy just the same. "I asked you a question," Mr. Weston said after a moment or two of silence.

Was it a serious question? Mr. Weston had seen Cody's car before, and besides, who else's could it be, an old banger like that in the Westons' circular driveway? "Yeah," Cody said, trying to look Mr. Weston in the eye, forcing himself to meet that gaze; and in it he saw, or thought he saw, that Mr. Weston didn't hate him, not exactly. It was more that he, Cody, wasn't important enough to merit Mr. Weston's hatred. Cody felt something catch fire inside him, a hot feeling that had come to him only once in his life, a few years before, the night his father punched him in the mouth.

"Look, Mr. Weston," Cody began, trying to keep the anger out of his tone, and maybe not succeeding very well, "Clea didn't do anything wrong. We were only—"

Mr. Weston held up his hand, the one with the report card. It shook. "I'm not interested in hearing from you on that subject, or any other, for that matter."

"Daddy!" Clea said.

Mr. Weston kept on, as though she hadn't spoken at all. "I'll let you find your own way out," he said.

The meaning of that didn't penetrate at once. Then it did. Was there any choice? Not that Cody could think of. He turned to Clea, still sitting on the edge of the bed, eyes wide, one sandal on, one sandal off. What to tell her? He couldn't come up with that, either. He just stood there, mouth open, turning red.

Clea rose, took his hand. "Go," she said. "I'll call you." She leaned forward, kissed him on the cheek.

Cody nodded. He turned, walked past Mr. Weston—now his mouth was open too—and out of Clea's room. The door closed behind him. He went down the hall but couldn't find the back stairs. Cody went the other way, trying one room and then another. It took him five minutes or maybe more to get out of the house, and by that time he was pouring sweat. He ripped off the hand-tailored navy blue shirt with the narrow stripes, flung it away, jumped into his car, and sped off, spraying gravel behind him and grazing a stone gatepost topped by a lion's head at the end of the driveway.

●●●

Cody was back at the apartment over the Red Pony, pacing around its small spaces, when Clea called. He could tell right away she'd been crying.

"I'm so sorry," she said.

"You? You've got nothing to be sorry for." Then Cody had a horrible thought. "Did he hit you?"

Clea sounded confused. "Hit me? Who?"

21

"Your father, of course."

"Oh, no," she said. "That could never happen."

"Good," he said. "Good. And I'm the one who's sorry. Sorry for getting you in trouble and everything."

She laughed, a sad little laugh. "It's not really you," she said. "More the B, like I told you."

"The B?" What was she talking about?

"In calc, for Christ sake," she said.

There was a silence.

"Sorry," she said.

"It's all right. I'm slow sometimes."

"No, you're not."

Another silence.

"It's so unreal," she said.

"What?" said Cody. "What happened?"

"My father is . . ." Her voice rose in anger. Clea had a temper, although it rarely showed, and Cody didn't mind when it did.

"Tell me," he said, "whatever it is."

She took a deep breath. It tickled his ear, like she was right there with him. "He's sending me to live with his brother," she said. "For the whole fucking summer."

Mr. Weston's brother? Wasn't he the one in Fort Collins? Not a terrible drive. "I'll be spending a lot on gas," he said.

"Huh?" Clea said.

"Your uncle—isn't he the Toyota dealer in Fort Collins?"

"That's Fran's brother," Clea said. "My dad's brother is an investment banker in Hong Kong."

Hong Kong?

"I leave tomorrow."

THREE

CLEA CALLED TWO DAYS LATER. "This is me," she said. "Saying hi from tomorrow."

"Huh?" said Cody.

"It's already tomorrow here."

"In Hong Kong?"

"Yeah."

"What's it like?"

"Weird. There's this restaurant where they serve snakes."

"You ate snakes?"

"Mmmm, good."

"Really?"

"Actually not bad. The restaurant was kind of amazing."

"Better than Golden Treasure?" Cody said. Golden Treasure was the only Chinese restaurant in Little Bend, and the only Chinese restaurant Cody had ever been to. Lots of people wouldn't go there on account of how dirty the kitchen was supposed to be, but Cody liked the pineapple chicken balls.

Clea laughed. The connection was good, and he could hear every little—nuance? was that the word?—in the sound. "Just a bit," she said.

Then came a pause, and in the background Cody heard a man speaking Chinese. "So," he said, "we can call and everything."

"Yeah," she said. "I got an international cell phone. Maybe I better call you, because . . . well, and also we can email and IM—that's free."

"Sure," said Cody. "Cool."

"How are things there?"

"You know. Good. Sunny."

"Sunny here, too."

"It's like, on the ocean, right?"

"Oh, yeah. It's an island, and my uncle's condo's on the penthouse floor of this huge tower. On one side we can see all these boats, and on the other there's China."

"Wow," Cody said. "Hey, guess what."

"What?"

"I got a job."

"Yeah?"

A good job—first of all, not landscaping with his father; second, it paid $10.75 an hour, not bad. But all of a sudden he wished he hadn't brought it up.

"What's the job?" Clea said.

"Uh, it's not that interesting."

Another pause. "Working with your dad?"

"No," Cody said. "Not that. This—" He stopped, hearing more talk in the background, this time in English.

"Cody? I've got to go. Talk to you soon."

"No problem," Cody said. And then, just popping out, very uncool, came: "Where you going?"

"On a cruise."

"A cruise?"

"Just in the harbor," Clea said. "To see how it all looks from there."

"Uh-huh," Cody said. "Well, later."

"Later."

Click.

Cody sat on a stool at the kitchen counter and switched on the computer—a five-year-old PC with a dial-up connection—and clicked on a link for Hong Kong pictures. The first one was still loading—bright blue bands descending from the top

26

of the frame, and then what might have been the top of a green mountain—when the door opened and his father came in.

Cody looked up. "Hey," he said.

"Yeah," said his father, setting a case of twenty-four on the counter. His hands—big and gnarled—were dirty, and he wore an old T-shirt with "Laredo Tree Specialists" on the front, meaning he'd been working. But not tree work: Laredo Tree Specialists—a side business back when they'd owned the Red Pony—no longer existed, had folded two or three years after Cody's mom died of cancer. Now his father mostly just mowed lawns, clipped hedges, weeded gardens; in winter he stuck a blade on his pickup and plowed for the county.

Cody's father ripped open the case, grabbed a can, snapped down the tab, took a big swallow. His gaze slid over to the computer screen. "What's that?" he said.

"Hong Kong." The frame was almost complete: mountain, almost covered with high-rises, big blue harbor, lots of boats, even a few Chinese junks. What Cody wanted to do now was examine it carefully, by himself, no distractions.

His father had another hit, wiped his mouth with the back of his hand. "What's so special about Hong Kong?"

Cody shrugged.

"Then why're you wastin' your time lookin' at the pictures?"

Cody clicked on shut down. The screen went dark.

"Didn't say you had to do that. It's your time to waste."

Cody got up, moved away toward the window. Down on the street, Tonya Redding was dropping her mom off for a shift at the Red Pony. Mrs. Redding walked toward the service entrance, putting on lipstick. Tonya glanced up, right at Cody's window, and drove off.

"I got a job," he said.

"Uh-huh," his father said. "What's it pay?"

"Ten seventy-five an hour." The summer before, his father had paid him $8.50.

His father tilted back his head, drained what was left of the can, tossed it in the trash. "Doin' what?"

"Working deliveries for the lumber yard."

"Beezon Lumber?"

"Yeah."

"Driving?"

Cody shook his head. "Riding shotgun. Loading and unloading."

His father reached for another can. "How'd you get a job like that?"

"Just went down there and filled out a form."

Another can got snapped open. Cody was highly attuned to that sound; it even caused a physical reaction, a cold feeling at the back of his neck. "Just filled out a form," his father said. He went over to the couch, switched on the TV.

"Yeah," said Cody, although it hadn't been quite that simple. He'd filled out a form, all right, but then Mr. Beezon had asked to see him, and he'd gone to the upstairs office, where Mr. Beezon, a tiny old guy with a big nose and hair growing out of his ears, had talked Rattlers football for five or ten minutes— Rattlers being the name of all the County High teams—and then offered him the job on the spot.

"Work hard and there might even be a raise in it for you," he'd said.

"Thanks, Mr. Beezon."

"And overtime, too, if this goddamn economy picks up."

Cody hadn't known what to say to that.

"Know what our problem is, Cody?" Mr. Beezon had said, leaning across the desk. His teeth were the same yellow color as the dinosaur fossil bones in the display room at the back of the Little Bend Public Library.

Cody had shaken his head.

"All those tax-and-spenders in Washington, that's our problem. What happened to this country, tell me that."

"I don't know, Mr. Beezon," Cody had said. "But, uh, I kind of like it."

Mr. Beezon had given him a long look. "Tomorrow

morning," he'd said. "Seven sharp."

"Okay."

"Know what seven sharp means?"

"Six fifty-five," Cody had replied.

Mr. Beezon's face, a mean old face not used to smiling, had shown just the tiniest hint of a smile.

Over on the couch, Cody's father clicked back and forth through the channels, TV light flickering on his tired face; tired, unhappy, and angry face would have been closer to the truth.

○ ○ ○

Cody went to work for Beezon Lumber. It turned out that Beezon Lumber did lots of business beyond Little Bend, had customers spread out all over the northeastern corner of the state, which meant Cody had plenty of time to absorb the opinions of Frank Pruitt, the driver. Frank was about the same age as Cody's father, and about the same size, too—meaning a few inches shorter than Cody—even had the same kind of huge, gnarled hands. The big difference was that Frank didn't drink. Frank believed that there was a right way and a wrong way to do every little part of the delivery job, and that we should use our nuclear weapons now—"at least one or two, for Christ sake"—while we still had the chance.

Cody made good money, forty-five hours a week at $10.75

and five to ten more at time and a half. He got a new transmission put in the car, also picked up a very cool set of rims, secondhand but in great shape. He hit the gym—where all returning varsity football players had half-price memberships—three nights a week, and grew stronger. His father met a woman from Pennsylvania or someplace, recently divorced and now living in the trailer park on the southern edge of Little Bend, away from the river, meaning Cody often had the apartment to himself at night. He bought a calling card and phoned Clea a few times, and she phoned him, too, but with the time difference and both of them being so busy—Cody working, Clea traveling a lot with her uncle—they kept missing each other. Email ended up working better.

hey, that guy frank I was telling you about, the driver? guess what—he can crush an apple in his bare hand— make the juice run out. eaten any more snakes yet? gym time. bye.

Hi, Cody. Sorry I didn't get back to you till now. We were in Bangkok—my uncle Bill advises the government there on investment issues. Investment issues—listen to me. Yeah, I'm on an all-snakes diet—and I got to ride on an

elephant. Her name was Britney—what else?—and
she makes Bud seem tiny! Miss you. xoxoxo C.

an elephant wow. the schedule was in the paper, we play
bridger in the very first game. so i gotta be ready. party
last night in river park. i didnt stay. cops busted it later I
heard from junior. he says hi—benched 305 yesterday
unbelievable! i miss you too. bye.

Just got my return ticket, Cody. I'm flying
back the other way, west. Dad and Fran are
meeting me in Paris for a few days and I'll be
home on Aug. 17. Having an awesome time but
can't wait to see you. I think about things—
things w/you, a lot. C.

i think about things and stuff too. 17th—not so long away
now. you wouldnt believe how hot it is here—two a days
are going to be crap. bunch of us went swimming at the
quarry to cool off. frank—the driver guy, remember?—
says there's lots of bodies down there from indian times.

That does it! I'm never swimming there again.
But I did some snorkling in Phuket—saw a

dolphin! Yo kong zai jian—that's Mandarin for
see you soon (I think). Love you. C.

Phuket turned out to be in Thailand. Cody found a picture online: a beautiful white sand beach with palm trees and strange rock formations—it looked like paradise.

● ● ●

Cody worked fifty-nine hours the week before Clea came home, making $501.65 after deductions, the biggest check he'd ever had in his hands. He went into Main Street Jewelers—the only jewelry store in town—for the first time in his life, and almost backed out when he saw Tonya Redding working behind one of those glassed-in display boxes. Of course she spotted him right away.

"Hey, Cody," she said.

"Hey," said Cody, as the door swung shut behind him. He glanced around, saw no one else in the store. "What are you doing here?" he said.

"Right back at ya," said Tonya. She was wearing some kind of low-cut top, had bright blue fingernails.

"Well," said Cody. "Um."

Tonya laughed. She had a very loud laugh, a fact Cody was aware of for the first time. "I work here," she said. "That's my excuse—what's yours?"

"I was just . . ."

"Let me guess," Tonya said. "You're looking for a welcome-back present for Clea."

Cody nodded: Little Bend was a small town, where everyone knew everyone's goddamn business. At that moment a curtain opened, and an old white-haired man came out, wearing a weird magnifier in one eye.

"Everything all right, Tonya?" he said.

"Oh, yes, Mr. Wexler," Tonya said. "I'm just helping this gentleman find something nice for his girlfriend."

Mr. Wexler removed the magnifier, gave Cody a quick scan. "Show him the heart pendants," he said, and then withdrew behind the curtain. Tonya made a face.

"Heart jewelry?" Cody said.

Tonya moved a few steps along the display case and pointed. Cody walked over, saw a row of gold hearts ranging from tiny to small, each of them with a red stone in the middle.

"What are these?" he said.

"Pendants, Cody. You wear them on a chain around your neck, sold separately."

Cody bent over the display case, examined the heart pendants one at a time, took his time. He had no idea whether he liked them or not. What were you supposed to look for?

Tonya lowered her voice. "Want a tip?" she said. "The heart

pendants—they're not her."

"No?"

"Not close."

"So, uh."

Tonya crooked a finger at him. He followed her down to the end of the case. "See these?" she said.

"Earrings."

"Yeah. Earrings. They're jade, done by a local woman who's really talented. And as a bonus, this jade comes from the Bridger Hills."

The Bridger Hills were twenty miles away. "We've got jade here?"

"Maybe not technically, but it's some of the best in the world. Asians are buying it all up as fast as they can."

Cody, a little confused, gazed at the jade earrings. They came in different shapes—round, square, rectangular, teardrop, and a few others he had no names for. Tonya went *tap-tap* on the glass with her bright blue fingernail. "Those?" he said, staring at a pair that seemed kind of oval with another smaller oval dangling down.

"She'll love them," Tonya said. "The coolest design, plus they'll remind her of home."

Cody bought the earrings—$299.95 plus tax—although it was more than he'd been planning to spend if he'd actually been planning, and although he had no idea why Clea would want to be reminded of home since she was going to be home when he gave them to her. But he paid for the earrings and felt good about it. Tonya put them in a velvet-lined box and wrapped it up in silver paper with a bright blue ribbon, same color as her nail polish. She walked him to the door, gave him a pat on the back, her hand possibly lingering a bit.

○ ○ ○

August 17 was a Sunday, a real stroke of luck since Cody didn't have to work. He washed and waxed his car, vacuumed the inside, buffed brightener on his new rims. Clea called on her way from the airport.

"Hi," she said.

"Hi." His heart beat faster, just knowing she was close.

"Coming over?" she said.

"It's all right with, uh, everyone?"

"Yeah."

"Okay."

"We're going through Arapaho Junction," she said. He heard excitement in her voice, even though Arapaho Junction was nothing but a gas station and a general store.

"Won't be long," Cody said. *Back to normal.*

She spoke softly. "Can't wait."

At the last minute, Cody realized that flowers might be

nice. On his way across town, he tried one convenience store, then another, finally finding a bouquet of pointy red and yellowish flowers. "What are these?" he asked the man at the cash register, who turned out not to speak much English. As Cody drove into the Heights and up Clea's street, flowers and earrings on the seat beside him, a black limo was going the other way. He turned into the circular driveway, parked in front of Cottonwood.

The door opened and Clea came flying out. She hurtled down the steps—how different she looked: hair, face, everything—and ran toward him. Cody had barely gotten out of the car, fumbling with the bouquet and the silver box, when Clea threw her arms around him. They squeezed each other tight. Clea made a little sound deep in her throat, a sound he could never describe but that said a lot. They kissed and hugged, then just held each other, quiet.

Clea pushed back a little, looked up at Cody. "You've grown so much."

"Almost an inch," Cody said. "Plus fifteen pounds."

She laughed, a laugh that got a little shaky, verged on tears. Then she noticed the flowers. "They're beautiful."

Cody held up the silver box from Main Street Jewelers. "Also there's this," he said.

Clea's eyes filled up. "There's something I have to tell you.

37

I wanted to say it in person."

"What?" said Cody, thinking: *She has a Chinese boyfriend.*

But it wasn't that. "They're sending me to Dover."

Cody made a baffled gesture with his hands, earring box in one, flowers in the other. "Dover?"

"It's a private school, Cody."

Cody had never heard of it.

"A boarding school," she said.

"Meaning you live there?"

Clea nodded. "It's in Vermont," she said.

FOUR

SHE WAS LEAVING ON WEDNESDAY. Cody called work first thing Monday morning. "I won't be coming in today," he said.

Mr. Beezon's niece Sue was the office manager. "You sick, Cody?" she said.

"No," he said, realizing too late that this might be one of those times when the truth was the wrong choice. "No, it's just, um . . ."

After a moment or two of silence, Sue Beezon said, "You're taking a personal day?"

"Yeah," said Cody, "a personal day."

"Then why didn't you just say so?" said Sue Beezon. "You haven't missed a day all summer."

"Hey, thanks."

"See you Tuesday—bright and early."

●○●

Clea called a few minutes later.

"I thought you'd be sleeping in," he said. "Jet lag."

"I'm up," she said. "When are you coming over?"

Cody showered and drove to Clea's. She opened the door the moment he knocked. "I love them," she said.

"What?" said Cody.

Clea turned her head, pointed out the earrings. She also wore a long T-shirt, and maybe not much else. "It was so smart of you," she said.

"Yeah?" said Cody. "In what way?"

She laughed. "Because they match my eyes."

"Oh, right," Cody said. "Sure, yeah." Hadn't even occurred to him, of course. Had Tonya thought it out that far?

"Come on in," she said. "No one's home."

"You said that the last time."

She laughed again, pulled him inside. "Everyone's gone for the day."

"You said that, too."

Clea pushed the door shut with her bare foot. "Expecting lightning to strike twice?" she said.

"Always," said Cody.

Her expression changed. She tilted up her head and kissed him. It turned into a longer kiss. Clea made a little sound that meant open your eyes. He'd forgotten: She'd been gone for a long time. He opened his eyes. Other things about her had changed, but those eyes were still the same. That didn't mean he knew what she was thinking; he just knew what he was thinking: Vermont.

Soon they were upstairs, back in that bedroom with the silk comforter, and Clea was wearing just the earrings. Hair a lot different, voice a little different, even her body not quite the same—leaner yet somehow more womanly at the same time, if that made sense. But some things were exactly the same, and if not exactly, then even better, for sure.

They lay side by side, under the comforter.

"You've grown," she said.

Cody was about to go over it again, almost an inch, fifteen pounds, when he realized there'd been something in her tone—amused, or maybe teasing. He laughed. She rolled on top of him, kissed the tip of his nose. They stopped laughing. "Thanksgiving's not that far away," she said.

"No?"

● ● ●

Cody took Clea out to a late breakfast at the Big Chief Diner, best breakfast in Little Bend, with a view of the nicest part of

Main Street, with all the old, solid-looking buildings. They had the Big Chief Diner pretty much to themselves. Cody ordered the huevos rancheros with sides of bacon and toast, plus OJ and coffee; Clea had the same, except for the coffee.

"You drink coffee now?" she said.

Cody nodded. Frank Pruitt was a big coffee drinker, always had a thermos in the truck, and he'd gotten into the habit.

When the food came, they demolished it all, ate like starving people, hardly talking. After, Clea burped and said, "That's the best meal I've had all summer."

"No way."

"It's true."

Cody stirred his coffee, stared at the tiny whirlpool he'd made. "Maybe tourists from Hong Kong will start coming here."

Under the table, her foot pressed against his.

"What was the conversation like?" he said.

"What conversation?"

"About this school, Darby or whatever the hell it is?"

"Dover," she said. "And didn't I already tell you?" Clea's eyes went a little vague. "I was so wiped out last night."

"Tell me again."

"My uncle Bill's friends with the headmaster. My dad called my uncle and he called the headmaster. Done deal." Clea shrugged.

"I meant the conversation with you," Cody said. "Convincing you to, you know, go."

"There was more than one conversation," Clea said. "My dad actually flew to Hong Kong just to talk to me."

"And?"

"And what?"

"How much of a fight did you put up?"

Her foot moved away. "I fought."

"How?"

"Argued. Yelled and screamed. What do you think?"

The waitress appeared. "Anything else, kids?"

They shook their heads. The waitress added up the check, handed it to Cody, and went away.

Clea leaned forward. "What would you have done?" she said.

"Me?" said Cody. Deep down, he knew he wasn't sure, couldn't really put himself in her place—Hong Kong, headmasters, investment banking, snorkling with dolphins. But he kept going, sure or not. "Refused," he said. "I'd have refused."

She sat back in her chair. Now her eyes seemed different, too, just like the rest of her. That made him angry, very angry, although he didn't really know why.

"Flat out refused," he said. "Flat out fucking refused."

Clea crossed her arms over her chest. "And then what?"

"What do you mean—and then what?"

43

"Exactly," said Clea. "What do you do when they say the choice is Vermont or Hong Kong?"

"Hong Kong?"

"Private school in Hong Kong, living with Uncle Bill—that's an option. Or them buying a condo in Vermont, me going to Dover as a day student, dad and Fran flying back and forth—another option. The only nonoption was staying here and going back to County. What am I supposed to do? Run away to Mexico?"

Cody started to get it. And what was there to get? Basically it was pretty simple: They were sixteen. "And this is all because of me?" he said. "It's just to get us apart?"

Clea looked at him, and then away. "No," she said. "That was just . . . the catalyst, maybe."

Catalyst? What did the word mean, exactly? Cody remembered some story about an explosion in chem class, a class he'd get to senior year, if at all.

"It's more the whole scene," Clea said.

"What whole scene?"

"This place. Little Bend. He's got this idea in his head about Harvard or Yale or one of those, and a town like this just isn't the right kind of . . ." Her voice trailed off.

"He wants you to go to Harvard?"

"Or another, you know, top school. He's got a list."

"And you can't get into them if you're from Little Bend?"

"It's not that. It's more that I won't really be prepared."

"Prepared? You're the smartest kid in town. You've already done calc."

"And got a B," Clea said. "At a place like Dover there'll be a dozen kids with As in calc every semester. And they go on to multivariables and other things I don't even know about yet."

Cody was a little lost, but for some reason that *yet* stuck in his mind. "I think you want to go."

She reached across the table, laid her hand on his. "I love you," she said.

"But other than that?" he said.

"Other than that? *That* is the most important thing in my life."

Cody withdrew his hand. "But this is a big opportunity, right? That's what you think."

Clea was silent for a few moments. The morning light emphasized the green of her eyes, and Cody saw that the earrings didn't really match. "Harvard and those places take football pretty seriously, in their own way," she said.

"What are you saying?"

"They look for good players. Take Williams, for example. It's out in the country, really beautiful, and they play in a D-3 league. You could be the big star, easy."

Cody had never heard of Williams; and playing D-3? What was even the point? "I don't understand," he said.

Clea's foot moved under the table, found his, pressed against it once more. "I've been thinking."

"Thinking what?"

"These two years," she said. "Junior and senior—they're just going to fly by."

"And then?"

"Then? We could go to college together, you and me, get an apartment off campus, just really . . . live."

"Are you nuts? You think I could get into Harvard?"

"Maybe not Harvard. Some of the others on the list are easier to get into—I've done some checking. And they look for football players, I told you. As long as you do half decent in school, football gets you in."

"And who's going to pay?"

"These colleges are all loaded. They give out grants. You wouldn't have to pay a dime. And till then we have the summers, and all the holidays, and—and maybe you could even come and visit me once or twice."

"In Vermont?"

She nodded.

Did it all sound impossible? Not to Cody, not then.

"Still mad at me?" she said.

"No," Cody said. "And I wasn't mad."

She smiled. "Then let's go somewhere. I have to get back at four."

"Why?"

"That's when they're coming for Bud."

"You're selling him?"

"Sell Bud?" Clea said. "He's going, too."

"Going where?"

"To Dover. They've got an equestrian team. The coach thinks I'll be on varsity right away."

Although it made no sense, that was the moment—hearing the news about Bud—when Cody felt a first little twinge of impossibility.

○ ○ ○

After he dropped Clea off—the horse trailer was already in the driveway at Cottonwood—Cody stopped at the cable office and paid three months in advance, the least they'd allow, for a DSL hookup. One way or another, college was coming; he had to be ready. He had everything installed and working right, was watching a YouTube video of the Willams College team—they didn't look particularly big or fast; in fact, he was sure he'd played against at least some better players already—when his father came in, carrying a case of twenty-four.

"Cody, Cody, Cody," his father said. "What's up?" He was

in one of those good moods; they just seemed to happen some-times.

"Not much."

"Want a bevo?" Bevo was a word his father used for beer, but only at good-mood times. Offering one to Cody? Maybe once or twice before. Cody said what he'd said on those occa-sions.

"I'm good, thanks."

"Suit yourself." His father snapped one open, came over to the computer. "What's this?" he said, maybe not even noticing how fast the computer was running now; his father didn't seem to have any interest in online things.

"College football."

"Yeah?" His father leaned over Cody's shoulder. "Don't rec-ognize the teams."

"Williams versus Amherst," Cody said. "Williams is in purple."

"Never heard of neither of them," his father said. He watched for a minute or so. "Can't play for shit," he said. "What's so interesting?"

Cody had no intention of giving anything like a real answer, but at that moment something happened that hadn't happened in a long, long time. His father touched Cody's shoulder. A light touch, almost shy, if that made any sense, and then gone.

"I want to go to college," Cody said.

"Yeah? That's a long way off. Don't want to get ahead of yourself—see how this season goes first. Junior year's the biggie." His father watched a little more of the YouTube highlight. "And you wouldn't want to end up playin' with a bunch of plumbers like them guys."

"I don't know," Cody said. "There's more to college than football."

"Maybe for some," said his father.

For me, Dad. For me. But Cody didn't say that. Instead, to his own surprise and embarrassment, out came: "Clea's leaving."

"Huh?"

Cody went silent. His father knew he and Clea were going out, had made an astonished kind of face on first learning the news, and Cody had divulged just about nothing since.

"What do you mean—she's leaving?"

Cody shrugged.

"Leaving for where? The Westons are moving?"

Cody shook his head, took a deep breath, blew it out. "Just her. They're sending her to boarding school in Vermont."

"So you broke up?"

Cody turned to his father. "No," he said.

His father's good mood started slipping away; Cody could see it on his face, like clouds moving in. "Gotta be realistic in life," his father said. "Life like ours, verse the Weston types."

Versus, not *verse:* Why did his father, and so many other people Cody knew, always get that wrong? The little detail maddened him almost more than his father's whole statement. "What the hell are you talking about?" he said.

His father didn't like that tone, got a mean look in his eye, but no hitting would happen now: Those days were over, on account of this fairly recent size difference. Instead, his father backed away, toward the counter where the case of beer sat waiting. "Girl like her," he said, reaching for a fresh one, "where she's going you can't follow. Best to make a clean break, best for the both of you." His father went into the bedroom and closed the door.

Cody went online, found the Dover website, looked at pictures of the kind of kid who went there.

○ ● ○

Tuesday Cody went to work. No reason not to: Fran was taking Clea shopping in Denver and they wouldn't be back till after supper. Or dinner, as the Westons called it. What was that expression from science? Fault line? Was there a fault line between supper people and dinner people? Fault lines, Cody remembered, were where earthquakes happened.

"Quiet today," said Frank Pruitt, as they drove up to a mall under construction in the middle of nowhere, a half ton of two-by-fours in back. "Somethin' on your mind?"

"Just, um, a little tired," Cody said.

"Okeydoke," said Frank.

○ ○ ○

It was close to sunset when Clea called. "I'm back," she said. Cody drove over. Clea was waiting in the driveway. Cody parked and got out of the car.

"I have to get up at three thirty," she said.

"Yeah, I know." The sky was blazing in the west, a blaze reflected in Cottonwood's many windows, as though the house were on fire.

Clea leaned forward, nuzzled her head against his shoulder. "Good-byes suck," she said.

Cody could foresee a whole future of good-byes suck, like some scene shrinking in a series of funhouse mirrors. And there he was in the scene, getting smaller and smaller, but still in Clea's life, standing between her and opportunity: the true picture—at that moment, he was sure—and it had come from his father, of all people. He backed away, let her go.

"I think we should break up," he said.

Clea's eyes opened wide, her mouth, too. "What did you say?"

Cody made himself repeat it.

"But—but why?" she said.

51

"I just think we should."

"You don't mean it."

"I do."

"Explain."

"I can't."

"You can't?" Clea said. "Are you saying you don't love me anymore? Because that's the only reason there could be for breaking up."

Cody shivered, couldn't help himself. "Yeah. I'm saying it."

"You don't love me anymore?"

"No."

"Then—" She started to cry. "Then what was yesterday all about?"

"I can't say," said Cody.

"You can't say?" Her tears dried up and anger caught fire. "What the fuck? You can't say what yesterday was all about?"

The only thought that came to him was this: *Screw your courage to the sticking-place.* He shook his head.

"And all the other times? Are you just a liar?"

A jumble of words got stuck in his throat, almost choked him. He shook his head again.

"Say something! Talk! Explain!"

Cody screwed his courage to the sticking-place. "I don't love you anymore."

"I don't believe you," she said.

That left him nothing but the biggest lie of all. It almost made him sick to say it. "And never did."

Clea slapped his face, good and hard. Then she whirled around and ran into her house, stumbling a little on the stairs. Cody kicked his car as strong and viciously as he could, leaving a big dent in the fender. Overhead the sky turned dark purple.

FIVE

COACH HUFF HAD A SIGN over the locker-room door: RUN FASTER, HIT HARDER, BE SMARTER. Right from the first practice, Cody knew he was running faster—the stopwatch told him that. And when they got the pads on and started hitting one-on-one, he knew he was hitting harder from the way some of the kids didn't seem to want to go up against him, shuffling to other places in the line. Not Junior Riggins, of course. Junior loved hitting anyone. He even did sound effects, like it was a video game. *"Bam! Crunch! Kapow!"* Coach Huff loved to watch Junior hit people.

"Tha's the way, campers, tha's the way."

As for being smarter, Cody wasn't sure about that. But running the Rattlers' wing-T offense didn't require much intelligence. They had hardly any plays: counter, draw, dive, sweep, option, plus three passing plays of which two were hardly ever used. The third, blue three, a post to Dickie van Slyke, the wingback, off a play-action fake, was never used, never even practiced, but it was Cody's favorite because it kind of resembled a real NFL play. Once in a while Cody, Dickie, and Jamal Sayers, the tailback, would linger after practice, fool around a bit by themselves with blue three.

"What we do, campers," Coach Huff liked to say, "we run it down their throats." Sometimes he said, "We run it down their fuckin' throats." If a teacher was around, he added, "Pardon my French." Back in freshman year—Cody and Junior had both made the varsity, Junior even starting most of the time—Junior had asked Cody if *fuckin'* really was French. Cody hadn't known. He'd looked it up, found that the derivation was complicated, uncertain. In fact, the whole history of the word, apparently thought of as a bad one from early times, was kind of interesting: He'd never thought about where words came from.

"Not French," he'd reported back to Junior.

Junior had shaken his head. "Coach Huff don't know shit," he'd said.

The week before school started, the two-a-day practices began, so Cody's last day of work was the Saturday. Sue

Beezon handed him his check. "A job's waiting for you any-time, Cody."

"Hey, thanks. Maybe next summer."

"See you then. Good luck on the field."

A heat wave moved in, stayed for the whole week, made Coach Huff very happy. "Just what we need," he said, dripping sweat even though he was doing nothing harder than fanning himself with the playbook: "Toughen you up. Case you haven't noticed, we ain't the County Creampuffs. What are we?"

"Rattlers," they'd all shouted. Coach Huff had cupped his hand to his ear and they'd shouted it again, this time at the top of their lungs, their faces all red, practice uniforms soaked right through, vomit patches fermenting here and there on the turf. Cody was so whipped at the end of each day that his mind was completely blank, which was fine with him. He hardly thought about Clea at all.

● ● ●

The last Saturday before school, they took the bus up into the mountains to play Foothills High, their oldest rival and Thanksgiving Day opponent. Even though the starters were all out by the end of the third quarter, they still won 43–6. Hey! They were good. No one said it, of course: Saying anything like that meant laps, and lots of them. Cody had scored one touch-down on a ten-yard keeper, pitched to Jamal, a senior and star of the team—from Texas, but his father had been posted to the base in Little Bend the year before, maybe the happiest day in Coach Huff's whole life—for three more. College scouts came to watch Jamal play; even at this preseason scrimmage, there were at least three or four. One of them approached Cody at the end of the game, as the players walked off the field.

"Hey, Cody, Tug Brister"—or some name like that—"from Penn State."

"Uh, hi," said Cody. They shook hands.

"Like the way you play football, son."

"Um," said Cody. "Uh."

"Ever been to Pennsylvania?"

"Uh-uh," said Cody. "No. Sir."

"Prettiest state in the whole union."

Cody hadn't known that, knew very little about the state of Pennsylvania. But Penn State—that was different. He knew lots about Penn State football.

"Keep doin' what you're doin," said the scout. "Might be able to arrange a little meet-and-greet in the spring."

"Meet-and-greet?"

"A visit, like," said the scout. "To State College, all expenses paid."

"That would be . . . nice." Nice? Couldn't he have done better than that? A trip to State College, meaning he was being recruited by Penn State, would be awesome, fantastic, incredible. But too late: They were already shaking hands again. That night despite how tired he was, Cody lay awake for hours, thinking about Clea's college plan.

○ ○ ○

Foothills High was their oldest rival, but Bridger was the biggest school in the conference and had fielded the best teams for the past four or five seasons, even going to the state championship the year before. They had huge linemen, an all-state quarterback who could really throw, and a tailback and linebacker named Martinelli, bigger than Jamal and just as fast, who ranked number seventy-one on ESPN's list of the top one hundred high school players in the country.

The game was at Bridger, big crowd, first Friday night of the season, lights on but overwhelmed at the start by a wild western sunset, the sky all red and gold. The Rattlers, in their white road jerseys and blue pants, gathered around Coach Huff. "Team," he said. "Play as a team and you'll win." He held up his hand. The Rattlers all reached for it, coming together. "Run it down their fuckin' throats," said Coach Huff. The Rattlers roared.

Bridger won the toss and the Rattlers kicked off. Bridger marched right down the field, running Martinelli on sweeps, sometimes passing to number 80, a tall tight end, right over the middle. Cody played safety on defense, meaning right over the middle was his responsibility. Number 80 would slant in, taking three big strides, then turn and the ball would be there. All Cody could do was hit him right on the numbers as hard as he could, hoping to jar the ball loose. But the ball never came loose; number 80 didn't fight for extra yardage, was content to go down, both arms wrapped around the ball, reeling off six or seven yards a pop. The opening drive took half the first quarter: Bridger 7, Rattlers 0.

Dickie ran the kickoff back to midfield, and Jamal ran a sweep left, smothered by Martinelli for no gain; followed by an option right with a pitch to Jamal that went for three yards; and then an option right where Cody kept the ball, made what he thought was a nice move, and then got flattened by Martinelli, who'd somehow come all the way over from the other side, all his breath knocked clean out of him. No one had ever hit Cody harder, except for maybe Junior in practice. Cody fumbled the ball—was aware of it bouncing out of bounds, thank God—and then went a bit foggy. He tried to rise, failed, and was trying again when Junior reached down and helped him up. Cody staggered the slightest bit—surely not noticeable—and lined up for the punt, playing deep blocker. Jamal punted the ball away.

Cody remained foggy for most of the rest of the game, little of which stayed in his memory. On the next Bridger series, something happened in a pileup that pissed Junior off, pissed him off big-time. He went a bit crazy and there was no stopping him after that. Bridger double-teamed and triple-teamed him but none of it did any good. Junior mauled them all, doing his video-game sound effects at the same time: *"Bam! Crunch! Kapow!"* He put their center out of the game, and then the tight end, number 80, too, taking away that problem. Bridger's offense ground to a halt.

But Bridger's defense held. When they saw that the Rattlers weren't going to pass, they put everyone in the box and managed to stack up most of Jamal's runs despite Junior's blocking. At halftime, Cody, puking quietly in the toilet, heard Coach Huff from the locker room on the other side of the wall: "Got 'em right where we want 'em." But they were still down seven–zip. On the way back out to the field, Cody said something—he wasn't quite sure what—about maybe trying a pass. Coach Huff's face went all red. "Dint you get the message yet? We're gonna run it down their fuckin' throats."

The Rattlers went back out, resumed trying to run it down Bridger's fuckin' throats. They started moving the ball a bit better, getting some first downs. Junior put another kid on the sidelines. Jamal almost broke off a long run on a dive up the middle, Martinelli making a shoestring tackle. But every drive ended up stalling outside field goal territory, which in the Rattlers' case was about the twenty, although Dickie, their kicker, could easily miss from closer than that. And the whole time, through the third quarter and into the fourth, the fog in Cody's mind just wouldn't lift.

● ● ●

With less than a minute to go in the game, score still seven–zip, Rattlers' ball on their own thirty-two, and no time-outs remaining, Coach Huff called yet another option left. Cody took off, saw that Martinelli was shading toward Jamal, and cut inside, taking off for a fifteen-yard run that ended with another huge hit. Cody didn't have to look to see who it was; by now he knew Martinelli just by feel. But then a funny thing happened: His head cleared, just like that, as though Martinelli had descrambled what he'd originally scrambled.

"Huddle up," Cody yelled. The team huddled around him. Cody was suddenly aware of all kinds of things: the noise of the crowd, the smell of sweat, Jamal bleeding from the nose, Junior growling. The guard came in with the play from Coach Huff.

"Green, eighty-six, left."

Green 86 left? That was the exact same play they'd just run. Cody glanced at the scoreboard clock in the end zone, the end zone they needed to reach, so far away. Thirty-two seconds and ticking.

"Nope," he said.

All eyes widened. Coach Huff sent in every play. He'd never actually said changing the play in the huddle was forbidden. He hadn't had to: It was unthinkable.

"Blue three," Cody said. Blue three, the play action post to Dickie. For a moment, no one moved.

Then Junior said, "Drop the ball, Dickie, and I'll fuckin' kill you."

"On two," said Cody, clapping his hands. They clapped their hands.

The Rattlers trotted up to the line of scrimmage, took their stances. Martinelli, crouched and waiting between the tackles, stared into Cody's eyes, then shaded to his right, instinctively anticipating the play that Coach Huff had called.

"Hut," Cody called. "HUT!"

The ball slapped up into his hands. He turned. Jamal came pounding up and Cody slammed the ball into his belly, then pulled it back out. Jamal, hunched over, hit the line full speed, just as though he were carrying the ball, and got swarmed, Martinelli leading the charge. Cody took three steps back, the ball hidden behind his right leg, and looked downfield. And there was Dickie, all alone at the forty-five, hands up, pleading for the ball. Cody zinged it to him—a rope, spiraling perfectly against the night sky. Dickie caught the ball, pulled it in, and scampered all the way down the field and into the end zone untouched, no one even near him. The Rattlers went racing after him, screaming and jumping. Time on the clock read zero zero, meaning that after the extra point they'd go into overtime.

"Huddle up," Cody shouted. The Rattlers were still celebrating, punching each other and smacking Dickie on the head. "Dickie!" Cody yelled; Dickie had to make this kick. "Huddle up." The ref blew his whistle, starting the play clock.

The Rattlers huddled up. Cody felt energy all around him, enough to fight gravity, lift the team right off the ground. The guard came running in. But instead of saying, "Kick the bastard," which was the way Coach Huff called for the PAT, he said, "Green, eighty-six, left." Coach Huff's favorite play: They were going for the two-point conversion, the outright win, no overtime! "On three," Cody said, and clapped his hands.

The Rattlers took their stance on the two-yard line, Cody lined up under center, no kicker, no holder. Too late, Bridger realized the Rattlers weren't kicking the single-pointer, started looking confused. Martinelli raised his hands to call for a time-out, then remembered that Bridger, too, had none left, and lowered them.

"Hut," said Cody. "Hut, HUT!"

The ball slapped into his hands. He took off to the left, Jamal on the outside. Martinelli came sprinting over. Cody faked a pitch and Martinelli bought it, angling toward Jamal. At the same instant, Junior pancaked the end and Cody cut right. Someone hit him from the side. Cody rammed him with a straight arm, came free, saw the safety cutting across, ran right over him—ran right over him and into the end zone, into the end zone for two points! Two points and the game! They'd beaten Bridger! He was just starting to turn, about to raise the ball high in triumph, when Martinelli hit him helmet first, square on the side of Cody's left knee. Cody heard a horrible popping sound, felt a jolt of pain, the worst in his life, and crumpled to the ground.

SIX

ALL THE HIGH SCHOOLS in the conference had health insurance policies to cover kids hurt on the field, a lucky thing since Cody and his father had no health insurance of their own.

"This is called a pivot shift," said Dr. Pandit, orthopedic surgeon at Western Memorial.

"What do I do?" said Cody, lying on an examining table.

"Just relax," said Dr. Pandit. He placed one hand under Cody's left knee, the other under the top of his calf, pressing sideways a little. Then he slowly pushed up, bending Cody's leg at the knee. "Nice and easy." All at once, Cody felt a strange sliding that seemed to be happening inside his knee—as though it were coming apart—followed by a sudden sharp pain. It made him hiss; he couldn't stop himself. "All right, now, all right," said Dr. Pandit. He released the pressure, gently straightened Cody's leg. "Okay," he said. "All there is to it. You can put those trousers back on now."

Cody put his pants on, slid his feet into his sneakers.

"Well?" said Cody's father, hovering by the examining table.

Dr. Pandit directed his answer to Cody. "Torn ACL," he said.

Cody knew what that meant before Dr. Pandit spoke another word: He was done for the season.

"But junior year's the year that counts," his father said, voice rising. "He doesn't play this year, he falls right off the radar."

"Radar?" said Dr. Pandit.

"Fuckin' hell," said Cody's father.

"Dad!" Cody said.

"Scouts, college, getting out of this goddamn town, his whole future—and you're saying that's all up in smoke?"

"The boy," said Dr. Pandit, "is sixteen years old. Surely his whole future—"

"Time for a second opinion," Cody's father said.

"That's your ri—"

"Come on, Cody. We're out of here." His father grabbed

Cody's hand, pulled him forward. Cody missed his step, and his knee came out on the spot. He cried out in pain, so sudden and surprising it caught him completely unprepared.

"Jesus Christ," said his father, still sounding pissed off, but a kind of realization was dawning in his eyes.

○ ○ ○

The swelling went down. Dr. Pandit took some MRI pictures, found no other damage, operated on Cody. The operation went fine. Not too long after, Cody was back in the gym, first just on the stationary bike, soon lifting light weights, his left leg so weak it shocked him. Cody dealt with that by working out harder and harder, hitting the gym before and after school, icing down his knee in the evenings. Some days the school part didn't happen at all.

On one of those days, he was asleep on the couch, in between workouts, when someone knocked on the door. His mind a little foggy—he'd taken one of Dr. Pandit's Percocets—Cody rose and opened up.

"Hi," said Tonya Redding. "Hey, did I wake you?"

"No," said Cody.

"Bullshit," said Tonya. She handed him a sheaf of papers. "Mr. Lorrie was looking for someone to bring you the home-work assignments. I volunteered—my mom's working downstairs anyway."

"Uh, thanks."

"Say it like you mean it."

Cody didn't say anything.

Tonya looked down at his knee; he had his sweats rolled up because he'd been icing. "Yuck," she said.

"It's not as bad as it looks."

"Coulda fooled me," Tonya said. She looked over his shoulder. "Cool place," she said. "First time I've been here. Anybody home?"

"No," said Cody.

Tonya laughed that loud laugh of hers. "What about you? Aren't you here? Or is this a ghost I see before me? Got to read act one of *Hamlet*, by the way."

"How long is it?"

"Not too long—we could go over it together. Like now, if you want."

Cody tried to think up some lie, could not. "Maybe some other time."

Tonya's voice changed. "Sure."

"Thanks. Uh, thanks for the homework."

"You bet," said Tonya.

"No, really," Cody said.

"No problem," Tonya said. She bit her lip. He saw, maybe for the first time, that she had nice lips, full and well shaped.

"How's Clea doing?" she said.

"Don't know."

"You haven't heard from her?"

Cody shook his head.

Tonya brightened. "Coming to school tomorrow?"

"Yeah."

"See you."

○ ● ○

Cody went over the *Hamlet* assignment: Read Act One and answer three of the following five questions. He sat at the kitchen table, opened his copy of *Hamlet,* and started reading. It made no sense to him. The next day he went to the gym three times, but not to school.

SEVEN

THE NEXT AFTERNOON, or the one after that—or maybe the next one—Cody was asleep on the couch, ice pack on his knee, when the phone rang. The phone didn't actually ring; he had it on vibrate, in his chest pocket. Cody snapped it open.

"Cody?" It was Clea.

"Hi."

"I heard you hurt your knee."

"Yeah."

"I'm sorry."

"It's not too bad." He sat up. "Are you here? In town?"

"No. I'm at school."

"Darby?"

"Dover," Clea said. "It sounds like I woke you. Didn't you just get out of class?"

Had to be Monday. "You didn't wake me," Cody said. "How are . . . things?"

"No complaints."

"What's it like?"

"Different," Clea said.

"Like how?"

"Hard to describe. Kind of amazing, really—the buildings, the landscape, the teachers. Bud loves it here." Clea laughed.

That laugh: one of the best sounds he'd ever heard. "He's so funny," she said, and started in on a story about some adventure of Bud's, a story that Cody lost track of, maybe because of the Percocet, or because he wasn't quite awake yet, but he got caught up in the sound of her voice and that was enough. After a while came a silence; had he missed something? "Cody?" she said.

"Yeah?"

"I asked you if it hurts."

"If what hurts?"

"Your knee, of course."

"Nah," said Cody.

"But I heard you're out for the season."

"Who told you that?"

"A few kids." She named them, all from the highest academic classes at County, none well known to Cody.

"Yeah, well, no big deal," said Cody.

"But you're still . . . keeping your grades up, and everything?" Clea said.

"As always."

She laughed; he laughed, too—long and unrestrained, and felt better than he had for days—since that first visit to Dr. Pandit. Then, in the background, he heard a voice, a guy's voice: "Hey, Clea, all set?"

"Cody?" she said. "Got to go. I just . . . hope you're all right, that's all."

"Christ," said Cody, his mood changing fast. "I'm fine." He clicked off.

● ● ●

Cody had a follow-up appointment with Dr. Pandit. "Fine range of motion for this stage of recovery," Dr. Pandit said in the examining room. "Impressive strength."

"So I'm ahead of schedule?" Cody said.

"Absolutely," said Dr. Pandit, writing on a pad.

"If I keep on being ahead of schedule, do you think, um, well . . ."

"Think what, Cody?"

"That I can maybe get back on the field? This season, I mean."

Dr. Pandit smiled and shook his head. "Afraid not," he said. "But keep up the good work. In moderation, of course. Healing takes time."

The Rattlers were in a tailspin. Coach Huff tried almost everyone at quarterback, without success. At first Cody watched from the sidelines, then from the stands, finally not at all. He tried to catch up with his schoolwork, but his mind refused to concentrate. *Hamlet*, quadratic equations, the Dred Scott case, cellular division: They all mystified him. He stopped doing his homework, fell further and further behind. Mr. Lorrie, his English teacher and faculty adviser, spoke to him after school.

"Sit down, Cody." Cody sat. Mr. Lorrie, a nice old guy with a droopy face, gazed at him from across the desk. "How's the leg?"

"Good."

Mr. Lorrie nodded. "Glad to hear it," he said. "Although Coach Huff told me the unhappy news that you're done for the season."

"That's what they say."

"The thing is, Cody, there's more to high school than just sports."

Cody said nothing. He wanted to be out of there.

"Have you ever thought about what you'll be doing," Mr. Lorrie said, "say, three years from now?"

Cody nodded.

"I'm all ears," said Mr. Lorrie.

"College," Cody said. "I'll be going to college."

"And studying what?"

Cody shrugged.

"How about after college—what about then?"

"That's a long time away," Cody said.

"You're wrong," said Mr. Lorrie. He snapped his fingers, a surprisingly loud sound in his cluttered little office. "It's that soon," he said.

Cody didn't believe that. He was starting to find Mr. Lorrie not so likable.

"Tell me this," Mr. Lorrie said: "What are you passionate about?"

"Passionate?"

"What do you like to do, most of all? For example, my passion is teaching."

That was easy: Football was Cody's passion. Was it possible that someone could care about teaching a roomful of kids, many of whom didn't even want to be there, as much as he cared about football? But Cody sensed that football was the wrong answer and stayed mum.

"Let me guess," said Mr. Lorrie. "Your passion is playing football."

Cody nodded.

"Football," Mr. Lorrie said. "We're getting somewhere. Too bad about your knee, but I assume you want to play next season."

Of course he wanted to play next season. The problem, as his father had pointed out, was the importance of junior year when it came to attracting college attention. Cody didn't get into all that with Mr. Lorrie, just said, "Yeah."

"In order to do that," Mr. Lorrie said, "you've got to be academically eligible. Which means" —he opened a folder, glanced at a sheet of paper—"you're going to have to get with the program in terms of your classwork." He leaned forward. "If grades were submitted today, you'd be failing every subject, Cody. Every single one, including mine. You got a zero on the first *Hamlet* quiz. You're a bright kid—how did that happen?"

Cody stared back at Mr. Lorrie, said nothing.

"There's after-school academic help, Tuesdays and Thursdays," Mr. Lorrie said. "Room four-one-nine for juniors. Plus I'm just about always here for half an hour or so after the last bell."

Hanging around the school for longer than he had to, maybe hearing the thump of a punted football coming from the practice field while he labored over some assignment? No way. And Mr. Lorrie had it wrong about him being a bright kid. That was so ridiculous, it must have been some strategy, maybe to pump him up.

"So, Cody, what do you say?"

"I'll do better," Cody said. "But on my own."

Mr. Lorrie frowned and closed the folder.

○ ○ ○

Cody tried to do better. Was there any choice? Not if he wanted to keep playing football. Was there a chance he could still be recruited? Had to be. Hadn't he read somewhere—maybe on ESPN.com—about some big NFL star who'd missed his whole junior year of high school, possibly more? Cody spent some time online searching for the story, but never found it.

Trying to do better meant flushing the remaining Percocet pills down the toilet. It meant not merely arriving at school on time and staying all day, but really paying attention in class. That was the hard part: His mind would not cooperate, insisted on tuning out after ten minutes, or five, or three, so that whatever the teacher was saying didn't even sound like English, and whatever was written on the page twisted into an uncrackable code.

After school, Cody hit the gym, then went right to the apartment, where he'd open his school books and fall asleep over them. That was another problem. He was sleepy, very sleepy, almost all the time. On nights his father didn't come home,

Cody often slept all the way from homework time till the ringing of that five-thirty alarm, especially if he'd tried doing his homework on the couch. On nights his father did come home, he would wake Cody and say, "Hittin' the books pretty hard this year, huh?" And Cody would pull out the pull-out part of the couch and crawl under the covers.

Cody dropped out of school after Columbus Day weekend. He didn't make a formal announcement or discuss it with anyone—although he did write Clea an email about it, never sent because of how rambling and stupid it seemed when he read it over—but simply stopped going.

● ● ●

Junior came over. "What the hell are you doin', man?"

"I'm sixteen. You can drop out when you're sixteen."

"They changed it to seventeen."

"So? That's two months away. They going to arrest me? School sucks."

"I know. Christ, believe me, I know, but what else is there?"

"Real life."

"Real life?" said Junior. He gazed out the window of the apartment. Rain was falling hard, slanting down at a sharp angle. Junior pounded his fist into his other hand. "If I ever see that fuckin' Martinelli . . . "

"Nah," said Cody, even though he'd had the same thought, more than once.

○ ○ ○

Cody's father figured it out a few days later. He didn't argue, didn't try to change Cody's mind. All he said, after gazing at Cody lying on the couch, was: "Means you'll be getting a job, right? And soon."

Cody called Sue Beezon at Beezon Lumber. "Ms. Beezon? It's me. Cody."

"Hi, Cody. I hear you hurt your leg."

"It's not too bad. I, uh . . . "

"The team sure needs you. That's what everyone's saying."

"Thanks," Cody said. "Uh, Ms. Beezon? Remember when you mentioned about a job next summer and everything?"

"Sure," she said. "And I meant it."

"I was wondering if maybe I could start sooner."

"Sooner?"

"Like this week, if possible."

"We really don't hire any part-time help, Cody. With the paperwork and all it's just not worth it."

Cody cleared his throat, suddenly all blocked up. "The thing is," he said, "that's what I'm kind of talking about."

"What is, Cody?"

"Full-time," Cody said.

Sue Beezon was silent for a moment or two. Cody thought of his mother, something that didn't happen much anymore. "How's Monday to start?" she said, her voice a little softer than it had been.

"Thanks, Ms. Beezon," he said. "Seven sharp."

○ ○ ○

Cody spent most of the time till Monday at the gym. His range of motion kept improving. His strength rose up above pitiful. His knee swelled up at night. He iced. He slept.

He reported to the yard Monday at 6:55. Right from the beginning, things weren't the same as they'd been in the summer. For example, Frank Pruitt no longer worked for Beezon Lumber. He'd quit or been fired; Cody never did find out which. The new driver was called Dax. Dax was a poor driver, a horn honker who went much too fast, didn't see things he should have, rolled through every stop sign. He chewed tobacco all day long—spitting out the window when they were in the truck, spitting just about anywhere when they were on a work site—and also smelled bad. Worst of all, he was a bigot, and every time he opened his mouth, out came a nasty comment about anyone different from him. What made him think that a potbellied, bad-smelling white guy who never did any of the heavy lifting was somehow at the top of the heap? Cody thought of asking him, but he didn't know what would happen

79

next and he needed this job. Mostly he stayed silent all day long.

But the pay was good—still $10.75 an hour—although overtime didn't seem to happen when the weather cooled. Probably a good thing: At first, Cody's knee swelled up terribly and he often limped while making the deliveries at the end of the day. If Dax noticed, he made no comment. After work Cody usually bought a sandwich at the Main Street Deli and stopped by the gym. His range of motion returned to normal; his strength improved, but oh, so slowly. From the gym Cody went home, iced, slept. He got into a routine. Sometimes he heard news from school—Tonya had started going out with Dickie van Slyke, Jamal had signed a letter of intent with Boise State—but it all seemed distant. He began to hang out with older kids, nineteen- and twenty-year-olds, not really kids, in fact, who had jobs in construction, or at the mine, or at Home Depot; or no jobs at all. He found himself at parties with lots of booze, went home one night with a waitress who had a baby sleeping in the next room. The weekend after that he stayed home.

At the end of the season the Little Bend *Guardian*, the local weekly, always published a special issue with pictures of all the players. Cody was at the Main Street Deli, picking up his after-work sandwich, when he saw the football issue in the rack. He moved toward the rack, wondering whether there'd be anything about him, going back and forth in his mind about whether to buy the paper or not.

Cody never got to the football article, because of something on the front page; something that got his heart beating fast, something, in fact, that woke him up and made him feel alive, as though he'd been in hibernation. Alive, but not in a good way: What Cody saw on the front page of the *Guardian* was a photograph of Clea. Over it, a big black headline read: "Local Girl Missing."

EIGHT

Local Girl Missing

Authorities in the town of North Dover, Vermont, have reported the disappearance of sixteen-year-old Clea Weston of Little Bend. Ms. Weston, a boarding student at Dover Academy, was last seen on Wednesday, horseback riding on trails in a wooded area near the campus. Within hours of the horse returning alone to the stable, local police assisted by volunteers began a search of the area. The search continued yesterday, supplemented by the presence of Vermont State Police Search and Rescue and tracking dogs, but as of today at 2 A.M. MST no trace of Ms. Weston has been found. Her father, well-known Little Bend investor Winthrop C. "Win" Weston, could not be reached for comment.

CODY, STANDING BY THE NEWSPAPER RACK at Main Street Deli, read the article three times, forcing himself to go slow, to try to make sense of it, to absorb all the facts. It made no sense, no matter how slowly he went, and he couldn't believe they *were* facts, any of them. When the paper started shaking in his hands, he dug out his cell phone and called Clea's number.

"Hi, this is Clea. I'm not here right now, but please leave a message and I'll get back to you."

"It's me," Cody said. "I—are you all right? You're in the paper but I just can't believe . . . Call if you—when you get this. I hope everything's . . ." He clicked off.

"Next," said the cashier.

Cody paid for his sandwich and the paper, went outside. For a moment or two he couldn't breathe. A cold west wind was blowing down Main Street; dark clouds, almost charcoal colored, swept across the sky. Cody turned his face to the wind, took a deep breath. He had air in his lungs, plenty of it, but still felt like he couldn't breathe. His cell phone rang. He snapped it open. Clea?

Not Clea. "Hey," said Junior, "heard this news about Clea?"

"I just—yeah, it's in the *Guardian*. But is it true?"

"Everyone's talking about it. You know Matty Karlinsky?"

Cody had a vague memory of a skinny kid with glasses. "His old man works for Mr. Weston, and he says they think she must of fallen off her horse and gotten lost in the woods. Mr. Weston flew out there yesterday. It's gonna be on the news."

"She's a good rider," Cody said.

"Anyone can fall off a horse," Junior said. "Horses suck, you know that."

"Was she riding Bud?"

"Who's Bud?"

"Her horse."

"From here? She took her horse with her?"

"Why not?" Cody said, annoyed by the question—as though Junior had made some criticism of Clea.

"Hell, I don't know," Junior said. There was a silence. "How's the knee?"

"Gettin' better."

"Nice," said Junior. "Everything's so fucked up, you know?"

"Yeah."

"They say there's a party tonight, up by the lookout. You wanna swing by?"

"I don't know."

"Come on."

"I'll think about it," Cody said.

"You broke up, right? You and her?"

"Right."

"Okay, man. Later."

"Later."

Cody clicked off. He didn't feel like a party, getting drunk on a cold night, fifty-fifty chance of the cops busting it at any moment. Where he wanted to be was in those Vermont woods, searching for Clea. He went back to the apartment over the Red Pony, switched on the TV in time to catch a still photograph of her.

Clea was sitting in a lawn chair, one wing of Cottonwood in the background, a big smile on her face. Then a reporter with a microphone came on-screen, a tag at the bottom reading NORTH DOVER, VT. The reporter stood beside a big red barn in bright daylight, meaning they'd taped the coverage earlier. Speaking at first with the camera on him, then over video footage, the reporter said what Cody already knew from the *Guardian* article. Cody concentrated on the video footage: views of the most beautiful school he'd ever seen, huge buildings of brick and stone facing each other across broad green quadrangles; twenty or thirty people, some in uniform, working their way up a wooded hillside, yellow leaves clinging to a few branches, but most of the trees bare; a horse—Bud, as Cody could tell from that diamond-shaped blaze—munching hay in a stall. Then the reporter was back on the screen, with two people beside him, one a cop in uniform, the other a blond-haired kid a little older than Cody.

"On my right is Sergeant Ted Orton of the Dover police. Sergeant, what can you tell us about the progress of the search?"

"At this point," said the sergeant, a burly guy with a red nose and a bushy white mustache, "we're still working on the assumption that the girl got thrown from her horse, maybe losing consciousness for a while, and then became disoriented and wandered off in the wrong direction. It's easy to get lost in these woods even for a local, and the young lady in question was new to the area. If the weather holds, we should have a state police helicopter on scene in an hour or so."

"You mention weather, sergeant. What role does weather play in the search?"

"Weather's been warm for the time of year, low forties at night," the sergeant said. "Could be a lot worse."

"Sergeant Ted Orton of the Dover police, speaking of the chances of survival in the night woods," said the reporter. "And on my left, a senior at Dover Academy and fellow member of the equestrian team, Townes DeWitt. I understand, Townes, that you were one of the last people to see Clea Weston."

Townes DeWitt nodded. He was tall and strong looking, his

blond hair very straight and kind of long, drooping down over one eye.

"What can you tell us about that, Townes?"

"We were coming back from practice a little early," Townes said. "Clea wanted to try one of the trails in the woods. No one thought much about it—she's done it before, and she's an excellent rider."

The reporter nodded and said, "That's the latest from North Dover, Vermont. Now back to the studio." There was a pause with the three of them standing in front of the big red barn, the reporter and the sergeant gazing into the camera, Townes DeWitt glancing at something off to one side—maybe something amusing, from the slight change in his expression.

○ ○ ○

Cody couldn't sleep that night. He finally got up, went online, looked for breaking news about Clea. All he ended up finding was that same TV report he'd already seen, posted on YouTube. He watched it over and over—gazing so deeply for meaning into the faces of the reporter, Sergeant Orton, and Townes DeWitt that they disconnected into a blur of incoherent pixels. Only the face of Bud kept its shape, somehow calming him. Cody kept searching—a virtual search, he realized, parallel to the real one going on in Vermont at the moment, where it was probably daytime already—until it was time to go to work.

87

The first job was a delivery of masonry forms to an outlet mall going up near Fort Collins. Dax had one of his hangovers, the grim, heavy kind that made his driving even worse but kept him from chewing his dip; an acceptable trade-off, in Cody's opinion. On the way back, after a handful of pills swallowed with black coffee, Dax finally felt well enough to talk.

"See about that girl from the high school?" he said. "Missing in Maine somewheres?"

"Vermont," Cody said.

"Whatever," said Dax. He took out his dip, plucked out a wad, shoved it in his cheek, chewing quietly for three or four exits. Then he said, "Some babe, that one."

"What are you talking about?" Cody said.

"That chick," said Dax. "From the high school, what I was just tellin' you about. Her picture was on the news. I been around. Know a babe when I see one."

"Shut up," Cody said.

Dax turned to him, mouth open in shock, tarry strands hanging down from the roof of his mouth. "What did you say?"

"You heard me," Cody said. He got ready to fight, the knowledge that a fistfight in the cab of a truck going seventy-five could not end well temporarily absent from his mind. But there was no fighting. Dax's face went bright red.

He turned, spat out his open window, didn't say another word.

They got off work early, which sometimes happened on Saturdays. Dax went into the office; Cody went to the gym. He rode the bike for an hour, did leg curls and leg extensions, first with his left leg, then the right. They could have been the legs of two separate people, didn't even look the same. On the extensions, his right leg zipped through three sets, ten reps each, at one hundred pounds. The left leg faltered halfway through the third set, and that was at thirty pounds. Cody rested for a minute or two, worked that bad leg again and again and again, until it was throbbing from the tip of his toes all the way up to the top.

He drove home and iced, at the same time checking online and on TV for news of Clea. There was none. His phone rang.

"This is Sue Beezon."

"Hi."

"I understand there was some trouble between you and Dax today."

"Um, I wouldn't say—"

"You'd better take a week off and think about it. Without pay, need I add."

"But I—"

"Dax has worked here for seventeen years. He also happens

to be Mr. Beezon's second cousin once removed. Mr. Beezon wanted you fired, Cody. Take the week off. Come back with a better attitude." *Click.*

"Christ." Cody raised his cell phone, got ready to hurl it against the wall. But could he afford a new one? Could he afford to lose this job? Cody grabbed his jacket. He had to get out.

Downstairs in the entrance hall, he met the mailman coming in. "Two A?" said the mailman.

"Yeah."

The mailman handed Cody a letter, a letter addressed to him. Cody couldn't remember the last time anyone had sent him a letter; who wrote letters anymore? But he knew who'd written this one, just from the handwriting. He tore it open.

Dear Cody,

There's something about a letter, at least for me—as opposed to email or texting or anything else, even talking sometimes. Blah blah blah. The point is, I've been thinking about you a lot, can't help it. You pop up in my mind so often. I'm not sure I even understand how everything ended, and what I want to say is that if you ever (well, maybe not ever, but in the reasonable future) change your mind—about you and me—then let me know.

Things here are pretty good. The classes are

better—but not all of them!—and the facilities are amazing of course, and the place is gorgeous, especially when the leaves were changing. Bud loves it and is doing great in competition. Some of the kids are cool, some are snobby, make me feel kind of hickish. One or two I don't like at all. It's hard to know who to trust sometimes. Like rolling the dice—a cliché that turns out to have real meaning. But that's true everywhere—right?

Well, I'm off to rhetoric class, actually my favorite. You have to give a speech and explain the importance of it. Everyone does stuff like the Gettysburg Address or Winston Churchill, but I'm doing Lady Di's brother's eulogy at her funeral. That'll shake them up a little.

Hope your knee's all better.

Lots of love,
Clea

There was no date on the letter. Cody checked the postmark, went to the wall calendar, figured out that it had been mailed on Wednesday, the day Clea had disappeared. He found he was shaking; the letter was like a message from the . . .

But no: He pushed that thought away, refused to allow his mind to even think it, not once. He reread the letter, kept coming back to those two lines: *One or two I don't like at all. It's hard to know who to trust sometimes.* Could they now be considered some kind of . . . evidence? Evidence of what? Cody didn't know. All he knew was that those two lines bothered him. And if there was any chance they were evidence, how could he keep the knowledge to himself? For a few moments he thought about trying to contact that cop, Sergeant Orton. But Cody doubted his ability, even if he reached the guy, to get his point across on the phone. Instead he went out to the alley behind the Red Pony, climbed into his car, and drove to the Heights.

Cody had parked in the driveway at Cottonwood and was walking toward the front door, letter in hand, when he realized Mr. Weston probably wouldn't be inside, had to be in Vermont searching for his daughter. Cody knocked anyway. The door opened and there stood Mr. Weston.

Mr. Weston looked terrible. All those past times Cody had seen him, he'd been perfectly groomed, almost like an actor playing a rich guy, but now he needed a shave, his thinning reddish hair was reduced to sprouts here and there, and blemishes spotted his nose and cheeks. He blinked in the light, although it was a dark day with low-flying clouds, and didn't seem to recognize Cody at all. Cody had prepared a little speech about the letter, but instead he blurted the first thing that came to mind: "Is there any news, Mr. Weston?"

Mr. Weston started to shake his head; the motion sent a little invisible booze cloud wafting Cody's way. Then his expression changed, recognition dawning. "What are you doing here?" he said.

"Or you?" said Cody; more blurting, but he just couldn't help it: If there was no news, meaning Clea hadn't been found, then what the hell was Mr. Weston doing back in Little Bend?

Pink patches rose to the surface of Mr. Weston's face. "How dare you—" At that moment, Fran came up behind him, a very good-looking woman who'd once been a model, but now for the first time Cody saw how old she really was.

"Win?" she said. "What's going on?" She became aware of Cody and frowned.

"Mrs. Weston?" said Cody, taking the letter from his pocket, "I got this letter from Clea. It just came but must have been written the same day she—"

Mr. Weston snatched the letter, started reading, his eyes desperate, those pink patches spreading on his face.

"Skip the first bit," Cody said. He stepped around, pointed at the middle section of the letter. "There's this part I don't—"

Mr. Weston backed away, out of Cody's reach. "'Thinking about you a lot'—goddamn it," he said. He glared at Cody. "None of this would have happened if it hadn't been for you."

"You're blaming me?" Cody said.

"Now, Win," said Fran, touching his shoulder. At that moment a limo rolled into the driveway. "Come," Fran said. "We've got to catch the flight back."

Mr. Weston didn't notice the limo, seemed to be aware of nothing but Cody. He shook off Fran's hand. "Yes, you sneaky bastard," he said, his voice rising and rising. "I do blame you. If you hadn't come barging into her life, derailing everything I've worked so—" All at once, although Mr. Weston's mouth was still moving, no sounds were coming out, no sounds except for little gasps. Mr. Weston's hand went to his throat—the letter floating from his grasp—and he started pushing at his windpipe as though something had slipped out of alignment.

"Win?"

And then Mr. Weston spun around in a kind of limp sinking pirouette and fell on the marble floor of Cottonwood's entrance hall.

○ ○ ○

The limo driver knew CPR. Maybe because of him, Mr. Weston was still breathing and his heart was still beating when the ambulance came a few minutes later. A few minutes after that, Cody was standing all by himself in front of Cottonwood. He picked up the letter, pulled the door closed, checking carefully to make sure it was locked before he drove away, like that would make all the difference.

NINE

CHANCES OF SURVIVAL IN THE NIGHT WOODS: Cody couldn't get that phrase out of his mind. Back at the apartment, he looked without success for news of Clea and then checked the weather in North Dover, Vermont. Rainy and windy, high 45, low 33. Thirty-three was cold, could easily turn that rain to snow. Cody was already pretty sure about his plans, but the weather report moved him closer to certainty. He took out his cell phone and tried her number again.

"Hi, this is Clea. I'm not here right now, but please leave a message and I'll get back to you."

That was it, end of story. "Clea," he said. "I'm on my way." Cody was aware how stupid that might have sounded, say to some all-knowing observer, but he didn't feel stupid, not the least bit. He went to MapQuest, entered Little Bend in one box and North Dover, Vermont, in the other, and printed the results.

Cody didn't have any real luggage, just a big duffel he used for sports equipment. He started packing: jeans, extra sneakers, a few T-shirts, sweats, underwear, socks. What else? He couldn't think of anything. With what he was already wearing—his other pair of jeans, flannel shirt, fleece—he had all he needed.

He thought of calling his father but couldn't imagine a way for the conversation to go right. Instead he wrote a note and stuck it on the fridge.

Dad,
    I'll be gone for a few days. Looking into this job out of town. I'll call.

                                    Cody

Looking into this job out of town: vague enough to be almost true. Cody had reached the point of knowing that lying was a necessary life skill, and even that some of those who went furthest in life lied the best, but he hadn't reached the point of getting comfortable with it.

Duffel in one hand, car keys in the other, he glanced around the apartment, suddenly saw it for the first time not as just simply home, but as the dingy dump it was. A scary idea hit him: He wouldn't be back. But that was crazy. He started for the door, realized he'd forgotten his toilet kit—toothbrush, razor, all that. And what about taking along a sandwich or two, and water?

Five minutes later, and now fully packed, he left the apartment and went down the stairs. At the bottom he realized he hadn't thought of his bad leg, hadn't favored it at all, not the whole way down; meaning the knee wasn't so bad anymore and he was getting better. His heart lifted inside his chest; relief turned out to be a real physical feeling. He popped the trunk of his car, threw in the duffel, and thought: *Low 33—winter jacket.* Cody climbed back up the stairs, found the apartment door locked, reached into his pocket, and: no keys. Locked out. He'd left them inside. Step one on the journey: kind of funny.

Cody drove out of the alley and turned onto the street, where he paused behind a car letting someone off at the Red Pony. He'd just had time to see that the someone was Mrs. Redding when the driver's door opened and Tonya came running out. Cody rolled down his window.

"Hey, Cody."

"Hey."

"This is so weird. Clea and everything. Plus have you heard the latest?"

"About Clea?"

"Nothing new about her, not that I've heard. I'm talking about her father. He came back from the search for business or something and now he had a heart attack. They had to do one of those bypasses."

"How do you know?"

"Friend of my mom's is a nurse at Western Memorial—she thinks he'll make it." Tonya glanced into the car. He caught her smell; a very nice one. "Where you headed?" she said.

"No place special."

"Sounds good."

"Huh?"

"No place special, Cody. Got room for me?"

He almost said Huh? again. Instead, for once, he did a little better. "How's Dickie?"

"Dickie," she said, "is a dick."

Cody laughed. All his impressions of Dickie—someone he'd been dealing with since the earliest days of Pop Warner—came snapping together into an accurate picture.

"So what's the answer?" Tonya said. "Got room for me?"

Their eyes met. Maybe hers weren't quite symmetrical, maybe her hair, cut in a lopsided way, with purple at the ends, was a little silly, but there was something about Tonya. "You're going places, Tonya." That just popped out; he was blurting all sorts of things in the past little while.

Tonya's mouth opened in surprise.

"Later," said Cody, and he drove away. He glanced back in the rearview mirror. She was giving him the finger, a smile on her face.

○ ○ ○

Cody stopped at an ATM and took four hundred dollars from his account, the most it would give him in one day. Then he got on the interstate and headed east, away from the mountains. He'd been west, into the mountains—and even across and all the way to San Diego once, a long time ago, blue waves just at the edge of memory—but he hadn't been more than twenty miles the other way, east of Little Bend. He thought of the scene in the *Lord of the Rings* movie where the hobbits stop at the edge of a cornfield marking the border of the Shire. His own border was an exit in the middle of a flat nowhere: INDIAN VALLEY, 6 MILES. Cody hadn't been planning to do this, hadn't had the slightest notion, but he took the Indian Valley exit.

Cody had been to Indian Valley twice before. The first time, with his mother, to see the farmhouse where she'd grown up, he barely remembered. The second time, to her funeral, he didn't remember much better, although by then he'd been almost eleven. He had clear memories from that year—returning the opening kickoff for a touchdown in his very first Pop Warner game—so why was his mother's funeral reduced to just a few shadows? Cody drove into Indian Valley—a crossroads with endless fields all around, now bare until spring—and parked behind the little church.

There was no one around. Cody made his way through the cemetery. He couldn't remember the exact location of his mother's grave, but the Indian Valley cemetery wasn't very big, and soon he was standing before it: a small dark stone, rounded at the top and glinting with mica or some other mineral. It had her name, Gina Laredo, and her dates, much too close together for bracketing a human life.

You were supposed to bring flowers: Cody knew that from the movies. He looked around for something pretty, but nothing qualified. He bent down, swept away a few scraps of paper and some dead leaves. His mom had kept the reality of things hidden from him. All that—what was the word? Trauma. All that trauma: the discovery, very late, of an aggressive form of breast cancer; mastectomy; chemo or radiation or maybe both—Cody still wasn't sure. What the hell difference does it make now? his father had said the one time he'd asked. But whatever the treatment, she'd lost her hair, and that couldn't be hidden, although she'd tried. He'd lain beside her on her bed—this was before the apartment, in their house, a nice little house with a park across the street—and she'd told him she'd been sick but was all better now, and her hair would soon grow back. And her hair did grow back—but different, with gray in it—and she'd returned to her job in a lawyer's office. Then one day, carrying groceries up the front steps, she'd tripped and fallen. Cody, beside her, heard a cracking sound, and his mother had cried out in pain. "Mom! Mom! Are you okay?" He'd helped her up and she'd limped into the house, partly supported by Cody's shoulder. The cracking sound had come from her leg breaking, not one of the two smaller bones below the knee, but the big one from the knee to the hip, which doesn't break often. His mother's bones had turned out to be full of cancer. It hadn't been long after that. That bone crack: Cody remembered it more clearly than her face.

Light faded. Her name and dates grew invisible. Cody had an idea. He went back to the car, opened the trunk, took out an old practice football he kept in there just in case an opportunity for throwing it around came up. In the glove box he found a Sharpie. He wrote on the ball: RIP MOM. LOVE CODY, 11. Football players always followed their name with their uniform number. He went back to the gravestone and laid the ball in front of it.

Cody drove out of Indian Valley, got back on the interstate. The way his father was now: How much came from his mother dying, both the fact of it and the how of it? Some, for sure, but hadn't there always been too much drinking? Cody thought so. And what about the meanness? Cody wasn't so sure about that. Who'd first taught him football, shown him how to throw and catch? His father, of course. He owed him for that. Maybe his father had knocked him around some in those sessions, but hadn't that been to toughen him up? You had to be tough, and not just in football.

The stars came out, so many and so beautiful in the black sky, but not much company. Cody tried to find something on the radio. He drove through the night. The road went on and on, lit-up sights flashing by but mostly just the darkness. For the first time in his life he felt American. He'd been American the whole time, of course, just had never translated it into a feeling. Did all Americans share the feeling, have it the same? Cody didn't know. At some point during the night, he realized he'd forgotten his boots.

○ ○ ○

And maybe he was going to need them. Snow was falling the next day when he reached Chicago. He hadn't slept and his eyes were getting heavy, but Chicago didn't look like a good place for sleeping. He kept a lookout for Soldier Field but didn't spot it.

Halfway across Indiana, or maybe a little more than that,

traffic, so heavy since Chicago, finally thinned out. A sign rising high over the flat land read: MOTEL. Cody took the next exit. He'd stayed at motels before—with his parents on the San Diego trip, and several times on the road for Pop Warner tournaments—but he'd never handled the signing in before. It turned out to be easy, especially when you paid with cash in advance. Ten minutes after getting the key, Cody was fast asleep in room twenty-three of the Hoosier Grand Motel.

○○○

It was dark when Cody woke up, and for a few moments he didn't know where he was. He got up, felt his way around the room, parted curtains, looked out at the unfamiliar. On the other side of the wall, a woman was saying, "I've had it up to here with the bastard." Cody thought of turning around, going home, a thought he overcame after a minute or so. He took a shower, changed clothes, went to a diner across the street, where he was the youngest person in the place by far. Cody ate two cheeseburgers with sides of fries and cole slaw, drank a Coke, felt better. He paid the check, calculating the tip by doubling the sales tax, the way experienced restaurant-goers did it, according to Frank Pruitt. Taking his change, Cody realized he was still hungry and bought himself a KitKat, the biggest size they had.

By dawn—a gray, colorless dawn and the New York State

Thruway cutting endlessly through brown scenery—he was hungry again. Just past Syracuse, he took a pit stop. He gassed up, bought coffee and muffins, found an ATM and withdrew another $400, leaving a balance of $946—not bad. A school bus parked beside his car just as he was getting back in. Some kids who looked about his own age gazed down. A window slid open and a girl called out, "Hey, Colorado!" And behind her another girl said, "Take me with you." Balancing the tray with coffee and muffins, Cody glanced up at them, couldn't think of anything to say. "Are they all as cute as you in Colorado?" the first girl said.

"I'm the cutest," Cody said. "They threw me out." Hey, all of a sudden thinking of something to say.

The girl looked surprised, then started laughing. "What did he say?" said the other girl.

Cody got in his car, rolled back onto the Thruway. The kids on the bus seemed a lot like the kids at County High. He felt good to be out on his own, crossing all these states. Just another driver on a long, long road: If he didn't screw up, no one would care about his age or anything else. It was a free country.

Cody left the Thruway in Albany, continued east on a smaller road that slowly rose into greenish-brown hills. Just as he crossed into Vermont, the sun came out, and the hills grew prettier, if not quite so nice as the mountains back home. But as he turned north, the hills got taller and nicer, took on all sorts of interesting, rounded shapes; and he realized he'd never seen anything like this; every size was just right, if that made sense. Cody went through a beautiful little town with a village green and a white church, and then a few more, even more beautiful. At 1:07—Cody noted the exact time—he drove into North Dover, the most beautiful of all.

He went down a road lined with tall old trees and big old houses, came to a main street, parked by a café called the Rev, a cool place, you could just tell. Cody got out of the car, intending to ask directions to Dover Academy. He paused; he'd been out of touch: Was it possible Clea had turned up, that everything was all right? He reached for his cell phone, about to try her number, but as he did, heard a drone from the sky. Cody looked up and there, over high wooded hills to the north, saw a helicopter flying low. That answered both his questions. He got back in the car.

TEN

CODY FOLLOWED THE MAIN STREET—Spring Street, according to the signs—for two blocks, then turned up Mountain Road. The helicopter's drone grew louder, and once or twice he spotted it, dipping low over the wooded hills to the north. After a few hundred yards, he reached two tall stone gateposts: Dover Academy, 1886. There were no actual gates. Neither was there a wall: The school was separated from the rest of the town not by an obvious barrier but by something invisible, like a force field. Cody could feel it.

He drove through the gateposts, followed a long drive, began to see grand buildings he recognized from the TV report. Kids of about his own age walked across those big grassy quadrangles; the boys all wore khakis, the girls wore khakis or skirts. That was one difference from home, where just about everyone wore jeans. Another difference was that while most of the kids wore fleeces, as at home, these fleeces were better quality; somehow, even at a distance, he could tell. A few of the Dover kids, boys and girls, also wore scarves; you might see a girl or two at County in a scarf, but a boy? No way.

Cody passed a tall bronze statue of a man in a long coat holding a book and began seeing signs: Admissions; Baxter Hall; Goodrich Field; Griffin Dance and Performance Theater; Carnegie Gymnasium; Kravis Observatory; Mellon Memorial Museum of Art; Dover Equestrian Center. He took that road, a road that curved around a covered hockey rink with walls that seemed to be made mostly of glass, went by a series of tennis courts—an arrow pointed to Golf—and up a tree-lined hill, nice houses spaced far apart on either side. He saw a few little kids out playing. Were these houses for the teachers? Cody thought so, but mainly he was thinking: *This is a high school?*

A huge red barn—also familiar from the TV report— appeared on his right, at the end of a white-gravel lane. He let out his breath, as though he'd just accomplished something. But—apart from the journey, making it all this way to something glimpsed on TV—exactly what? Where was he at?

Maybe square two. Cody turned onto the lane, followed it to a parking lot beside the barn, and found a space between a horse trailer and a North Dover Police cruiser.

Cody got out of the car, his knee stiff, and felt the wind, a cold wind and rawer than the kind of cold wind he knew, maybe because there was more moisture in the air. He zipped his fleece to the top, shoved his hands into his pockets, and walked toward the barn, limping for a few steps and then not. There was no more time for any of that. In the distance the helicopter hovered over the hilltops.

A notice tacked on the shingles by the open barn door read: SEARCH HQ. Cody went in. Stalls lined both sides of the barn, horses in most of them; in the broad hallway between the stalls, people stood around a desk. But what Cody noticed first—before the stalls, horses, or people—was the photograph displayed on the desktop: Clea. Cody recognized that photograph, even knew when it had been taken: at the sophomore class picnic up at Custer's Point; and by whom: a *Guardian* photographer; the *Guardian* had included it on the monthly What's Up at County High page. The picture showed Clea sitting on a park bench, a smile on her face and a soda in her hand. In the original, Cody had been sitting beside her, also with a soda and a smile. In this print, here at the Dover Equestrian Center, Cody had been cropped out.

Cody approached the desk. A white-haired woman behind it was passing out flyers. People took them, turned, walked past Cody on their way out: a middle-aged couple, a few men a little older than that, and a bunch of Dover Academy kids. They had a look that Cody could spot already. In a few moments Cody and the white-haired woman were alone.

"Hi," she said, glancing up at him. She had a soft, friendly face, like someone's friendly grandmother. Not Cody's: His mother's mother had died young, also of breast cancer; his father's mother, who lived up in Casper, did not have a friendly face.

"Hi," Cody said. "What, uh—"

"First time here?" she said.

He nodded.

"Thanks for helping out," she said. "I'm Mrs. McTeague, volunteer coordinator. Help yourself to a doughnut."

"Uh, no thanks."

Mrs. McTeague helped herself to a doughnut, chocolate with sprinkles. With her free hand she shuffled through some papers, produced a map overlaid by a grid. "Familiar with the woods around here?" she said, not quite finished with her doughnut.

Cody shook his head.

"You're not at the academy?"

"No."

"We've had a number of volunteers from the high school," Mrs. McTeague said, and Cody offered no correction. "And we appreciate it very much. So nice to put some of those old town-gown quarrels to rest." She turned the map so he could see, pointed with a pen. "We are here—at the red X. This is the Dover campus, the village green, and Route Seven would be over there, just off the edge of the map, meaning north is like so. The main riding trail enters the woods here." She pointed to the beginning of a blue line on a green background. "It's a three-mile loop, with many trails, marked in blue, branching off as you can see, and even though some aren't suitable for riding, the search has expanded to include them all."

"But the horse came back," Cody said. "Doesn't that mean—"

Mrs. McTeague shook her head, cutting him off. "Because we're working on the assumption that she was thrown from the horse and got confused, we have to check all the trails, and the woods in between, of course. Naturally, we've canvassed residents for miles around, all the backwoods people." She pointed again. "These boxes have been searched—A-one through B-three. Today we're working on C-two." She handed him the map. C-2 was about a thumb's width east of the loop. A single blue line labeled Upper Mountain Crossover cut across it from

110

the loop all the way to the right-hand edge of the map.

"So I just go up there?" Cody said.

The woman nodded. "It's a bit of a hike. You'll find a police officer where the loop meets the crossover. He'll assign you a sector." She gave Cody a flyer with the word *Missing* at the top, followed by a smaller version of Clea's photo and her name in big black letters. "Keep an eye out for any clothing items on this list."

"Okay," Cody said, and headed for the door. He heard a sound from the loft, looked up, and saw a man descending a ladder, a rake in one hand. He reached the ground a few steps ahead of Cody, a tall, thin red-eyed man, with a wild graying beard and a long graying ponytail.

"Hey, Ike," said the woman. "Say hello to the new volunteer."

"Too many cooks," Ike said.

"Come on, Ike," the woman said. "Be nice."

Ike glanced at Cody. "Nice guys finish last," he said. Coach Huff liked that one too.

Cody moved around Ike, walked past the stalls. All the horses stood quietly, some watching him, the others gazing at nothing. All the horses but one: The last horse on his left was restless, shifting around in the stall, tossing his mane, rolling his eyes. Cody recognized him right away, from the diamond-shaped blaze. "Hey, Bud," he said.

Behind him, the woman called, "That's Clea's horse—how did you know his name?"

Cody made an instant decision, based on no facts, just a feeling. "Yeah?" he said, not turning, "I was just like 'hi, bud, buddy,' you know? A coincidence."

"Oh," said the woman. "The poor thing's been so anxious."

Cody went closer. Bud noticed him, grew still. Cody extended his hand, patted Bud's face. He looked into Bud's big brown eyes, thinking: *You know. Whatever happened, you know.* Bud pressed his head against Cody's hand, but those eyes revealed nothing. Bud's like an open book, Clea had once said. But not to him.

"Get a load of this, Ike," said the woman. "Our new volunteer has a way with horses." Ike grunted. "Ike's just jealous," Mrs. McTeague said. "Bud hasn't been letting anyone near him."

Cody stopped patting Bud and turned. Ike stood in a stall, raking out dirty straw, his ponytail bobbing; the woman was watching Cody. "How come he didn't stay with her?" Cody said.

"Good question," the woman said. "We wondered about that. Sergeant Orton—he's in charge—let Bud out the very next morning, hoping he'd lead us back to the scene, but he wouldn't leave the yard."

"Horses ain't dogs," said Ike. The woman looked ready to argue with him, but her cell phone rang. She answered it. Cody lingered, hoping for news, until she said, "I'll pick it up on the way home."

He went outside, checked the flyer. It described Clea—sixteen, dark hair and fair skin, five feet five, 130 pounds, no distinguishing marks or tattoos. *When last seen, she was wearing black riding boots and black riding helmet, black sweatpants bearing the Dover Academy logo, a short red jacket, red leather gloves, and possibly a light-colored scarf. Clea is an excellent rider and is in good physical condition.*

Cody crossed the yard, went by a riding ring with jumps set up inside, and came to the loop trail entrance. The woods—and hills rising beyond them—were different shades of brown and gray with dark evergreens mixed in; wouldn't a red jacket—Cody knew the one—be very visible? He couldn't be sure. Cody had hardly even been in woods before, just a few times on mountain outings; there was nothing you could call woods in Little Bend.

Cody started up the trail. Right away, the wind died down to almost nothing and it got very quiet; he no longer heard the helicopter. The trail was broad and hard packed, with little mounds of horse shit here and there, and sometimes a horseshoe print. The trail curved around a tall spruce tree and began to rise. Going uphill was actually easier on his knee.

He picked up the pace, but always glancing to one side or the other, looking for a flash of red. From the map, he knew he was in A-1, a square already searched and probably heavily trafficked, being so close to the search headquarters, but he couldn't help it. Once or twice he almost called her name; and inside his head he was calling it, many times. He could easily picture her coming around the next bend, sitting straight up and still in the saddle, the way she did. Cody got a funny feeling at the back of his neck, like she was close by. He even turned to look, and saw nothing but the empty trail and the tall trees, with no red showing between their trunks or bare branches.

● ● ●

Cody passed several trails entering the loop and soon heard sounds in the distance: a man's laugh, a dog's bark. He went around a big mossy rock, almost the size of a house, with a big crack down the middle, and saw two men up ahead, one in uniform. The uniformed man sat on an ATV, a German shepherd at his feet; the other man stood to the side, a walkie-talkie in his hand and binoculars around his neck.

The dog must have heard Cody coming—its head turned suddenly in Cody's direction, and it started barking. The men turned, too. "Easy, girl," said the uniformed man. The dog fell silent.

Cody went up to the men, spotted an intersecting trail and

a sign nailed to a tree: UPPER MOUNTAIN CROSSOVER—4.5 MILES TO ROUTE 7. "Hi," he said, recognizing the uniformed man from the TV report: Sergeant Orton. "Mrs. McTeague said, um—"

"New volunteer?" said Sergeant Orton; his shoulder patch read NORTH DOVER POLICE: TO SERVE AND PROTECT. The dog sniffed at Cody's leg.

Cody nodded, giving her a little scratch between the ears. Sergeant Orton saw him do it; his eyes—not very noticeable at first, kind of overwhelmed by his big red nose and bushy white mustache—shifted slightly, and changed expression; and for a moment somehow became his dominant feature.

"I'm Ted Orton," said the sergeant. "This is Mr. Stein from the school." They shook hands, the men with their gloves on, Cody barehanded because he hadn't thought of bringing gloves. "And you're?" Sergeant Orton said.

"Cody," said Cody.

"Thanks for coming out, Cody," said Mr. Stein. He turned to the sergeant. "Want to put him over with those kids on the east ridge?"

The sergeant nodded. "Just follow the crossover about a mile. You'll come to a little bridge. There's a party sweeping the woods off to the right. Tell them I sent you."

"I can walk you over," said Mr. Stein.

"That's all right," said Cody. "I've got the map." He started up the trail.

"No hiking boots?" Mr. Stein called after him. "It's a bit steep."

"I'm okay," Cody called back. He felt their eyes on him until the first bend in the trail, maybe fifty feet away. No gloves, no boots, no jacket: He knew he stood out, also knew he wanted to avoid a whole lot of questions, although he couldn't say why.

The Upper Mountain Crossover, much narrower and rougher than the loop, began rising in a series of long switch-backs. His knee hurt, but at least it seemed stable, and stronger than even a week ago, a good thing because of all the rocks and tree roots on the trail. Maybe too tricky for horses—there were no signs of them now. Cody kept scanning the woods. Nothing red appeared. And if he did spot Clea's jacket, either she would be wearing it or not. Not wearing it was the better option; his mind shrank away from the other one.

The trail grew steeper. Sometimes Cody had to grab a branch to pull himself along. Once or twice he almost went down on all fours. He began to sweat a little, not good in the cold—"stay dry or die" was another favorite saying of Coach Huff's. Although there was nothing about outdoor survival in the health class textbook, he spent weeks on it, telling and retelling hair-raising tales of the Old West, the one about the Donner Party being his favorite.

A while later Cody heard flowing water, soon saw a narrow

stream, a stride's width across or less, blinking through the trees. It came closer, running fast and clear on a rocky bed, sometimes frothing over a fallen branch. The trail curved up around a huge oak and then flattened out for ten or twenty yards, and in that flat part the stream cut across, spanned by a little wooden bridge. Three kids, all warmly dressed, were sitting on it, legs dangling—a boy and two girls, one big, one small.

Cody approached. The kids looked up. "Hey," Cody said. "They sent me up here to help out."

The kids gazed at him. The big girl had braces on her teeth; the other looked partly Chinese; and the boy wore the expensive kind of glasses Cody had seen on models in magazine ads. They were all smart—somehow he knew that at once—much smarter than him.

"'They' meaning Stein?" said the boy.

"Yeah," said Cody. "Mr. Stein."

"He's insufferable," said the Chinese girl.

Cody wasn't sure what that meant. "I'm Cody," he said.

"That's a first," said the Chinese girl.

Cody didn't get that either.

"Meaning you're her first Cody," said the girl with the braces. "I'm Alex. This is Larissa. And he's Simon."

"You from the high school, Cody?" Larissa said.

"No," said Cody, wondering about the best way to reveal who he was. "Where are we supposed to be searching?"

Simon waved vaguely at the hill rising upstream. "Right now, we're on a break." He took the top off a thermos. "Coffee?" he said.

"No, thanks," said Cody. "I'd like to get started."

"As you wish," Simon said. He poured coffee in the thermos cup and, as steam rose, took a bottle from his pocket—Armagnac, Cody saw from the label, a drink he'd never heard of—and added some of that. Simon passed the cup to Larissa and said, "Hang a right after that rock—"

"The one that looks like a giant boob," said Larissa.

"And somewhere up there you'll hear Townes thrashing around," Simon said.

"Townes?" Cody said, remembering the big blond kid from the TV report.

"Clea's boyfriend," said Larissa.

"The missing girl," Alex explained.

"He never takes a break," Simon said, sipping from the cup.

Cody heard sounds from above. The idea of explaining who he was lost any appeal it might have had.

ELEVEN

CODY MOVED OFF THE BRIDGE. His face felt hot. Clea had a boy-friend, that Townes kid from the TV report? She'd said nothing about that in her letter. But maybe there'd been a hint, something between the lines. Cody wasn't sure; all he remembered by heart from the letter were those two sentences: *One or two I don't like at all. It's hard to know who to trust sometimes.* The letter was in the glove box of the car; Cody made a mental note to go over it the moment he got back, although written material—reading between the lines or just the lines themselves—was not his strength. That first act from *Hamlet*, for example: impenetrable.

The slope rose steeply to Cody's left: no trace of a path,

just rocks, moss, patches of dirt, acorns, dead branches, dead leaves—mostly yellow or brown, with a few dull red ones mixed in, not the kind of red he was looking for. He climbed for a few minutes, reached a tall, slanting rock, and leaned against it, resting his knee.

"Hang on," Alex called from below. "I'll come with you."

Cody watched her climb. She followed the same route up from the bridge that he'd taken, climbed it pretty easily. Alex was strong, with broad shoulders—broad for a girl, at least. She reached the tall rock, straightened, gazed up at his face.

"Play any sports?" she said.

"Some," said Cody.

"Like?"

"Football."

"Lucky you."

"How come?"

"Football rocks," Alex said. "I'd love to have played."

"Yeah?" said Cody. He'd met very few girls who even liked watching football, if they were honest about it. "What position?"

"Safety."

"Good choice," Cody said.

"Because you see the whole field?"

He nodded.

"Cool." Alex peered up the slope. "Onward," she said, and then after a pause, "Although it really doesn't make much sense."

"Why not?"

"Think about it," Alex said. "The working hypothesis is she fell off her horse, got knocked a little silly, and wandered around in confusion."

"What doesn't make sense about that?" Cody said. He remembered getting knocked silly by Martinelli in the first quarter of the Bridger game: Wandering around in confusion made perfect sense to him.

"I suppose it's possible," Alex said. "But confused wandering in an uphill direction? That does not compute."

She was right. "So we should be working downhill," Cody said, "on the other side of the bridge."

"Except they swept that sector yesterday," Alex said. "With the dogs. Finding zip." She bit her lip, her braces glinting in the light. "All this looking and not one single clue," she said.

Meaning they had to keep looking: Was there another choice? "So we go up?" Cody said.

"Nowhere else to go," Alex said. "These woods have been pretty much searched now—hundreds of people, ATVs, dogs, choppers, you name it—all the way to Route Seven."

"What if she crossed Route Seven?" Cody said.

"You know how busy it is—hard to imagine that no one would have spotted her, or that she wouldn't have asked for help." Their eyes met. Alex's eyes were dark, intelligent, worried. "I really like her," Alex said. "Clea, I mean. No offense, but all this is different when she's a real flesh-and-blood person in your life."

Cody felt a thickness in his throat, could not have uttered a word at that moment.

"She lived—lives—next door to me, in Baxter," Alex was saying. "Clea's new—came as a junior from out west. Not easy, but she handled it so well. Naturally, it helps when you're someone like her."

Cody cleared his throat. "Someone like her?"

Alex took a deep breath. "Better get moving," she said. "Night comes so early." She turned and started up the slope, Cody following. Her quickness surprised him; even with two good knees, he might have had trouble keeping up.

"Someone like her?" he said again.

Alex, still climbing, her back to him, said, "Heard you the first time. I just don't want to sound all snotty."

"I can take it," Cody said.

Alex laughed, a surprised kind of laugh. "I forgot—did you say you went to the high school?"

"No."

"Do you know much about Dover Academy?"

"No."

"Well, this is the snotty part—there's lots of very accomplished kids here. They come from all over the country—all over the world, really—to Dover and a few places like it. Sounds unfair, maybe, but it's a fact."

"Unfair because you're all rich?" Cody said. They reached a narrow ridge, worked their way along it, the wind picking up as a stony summit came in view off to the right.

"Not all of us," Alex said. "I'm not rich."

"You're not?" Cody would have bet anything she was.

"I'm on full scholarship," Alex said, gripping an overhanging branch to pull herself along.

"Yeah?"

"Single mom situation," Alex said. "Renting out the top of a Dorchester triple-decker."

Cody didn't know where Dorchester was—or the exact nature of a triple-decker—but he got the point. Maybe like living over the Red Pony: not terrible—he had no complaints—and there was much worse, and also much better. "So you must be super accomplished at something," he said. First time he'd used the word *accomplished* in a conversation, for sure.

123

"I wouldn't say super accomplished," Alex said. "But the answer is it's crew."

"Crew?" Cody was at a loss.

"Sculling," she said. She looked back, maybe saw he still didn't understand. "Rowing," she explained.

Rowing was a competitive sport? Cody kept that thought to himself.

"I got involved with a Harvard program, crew for inner-city kids," Alex said. "I was one of the inner-city kids. With Clea it's riding. Of course, she *is* rich, although not rich for here. Plus she's just so good at everything. Larissa—she's the lit mag editor—said Clea submitted a poem that blew her away. On top of that, she's a wizard at math, and—"

"I'd like to see it," Cody said.

"See what?"

"The poem."

"You're interested in poetry?" Alex said.

"Not really."

"Then why do you want to see the poem?"

"No reason," Cody said.

They came to a rocky cliff, maybe ten feet high, with a trickle of water running down its face. Here and there at the edges of the trickle, the water was starting to freeze. Alex glanced up at the sky. It seemed smaller here than back home in Little Bend, although Cody knew that had to be impossible. Cody also remembered it being blue when he'd entered the woods; now it was gray, the clouds dark and sagging. Alex and Cody moved along the base of the cliff, came to a strange-looking bowl-shaped hollow full of stunted evergreens, not much taller than a person.

"It was called 'Bending,' I think," Alex said.

"The poem?" said Cody.

Alex opened her mouth to reply, but at that moment they both saw a man seated on a tree stump at the far side of the hollow, smoking a cigarette. He was dressed in black, except for a bright red headband, the only red Cody had seen in the woods; in fact, that red flash was the first thing he noticed. The man looked up, saw them; no, not a man, but a kid, like them.

"Townes?" Alex called to him. "What's up?"

Yes, the TV report kid, the one with long blond hair falling over one eye. Townes took one last drag from the cigarette, rose, and ground the butt under his heel, then moved toward them, smoke curling up from his nostrils. He carried a long stick, used it to raise a branch of one of those dwarfish trees, hack at another. Was this part of looking for Clea? Alex stepped down into the bowl, and Cody followed.

They met halfway across. At first Cody thought he was much shorter than Townes, then realized it was mostly an illusion from the way Townes carried himself, head tilted slightly back. In fact, he was only an inch or so taller than Cody, and not quite as broad. "Townes, Cody," said Alex. "Cody, Townes. Cody's a volunteer from the town."

Townes glanced at Cody for maybe a split second—his name not ringing the slightest bell, as far as Cody could see—and turned to Alex. "Where the fuck is she?" he said. His eyes were red. Had he been crying? There was no sign of tears. Cody glanced down, saw that his hands were balled up in fists, like they were doing things on their own; he jammed them in his pockets.

"We've got to keep looking, that's all," Alex said.

"You don't think I know that?" Townes waved his stick—a hardwood branch trimmed except for a big knob at the end—at the stony summit. "You think I'm going to stop looking?"

"I didn't say that," Alex said. She took out one of Mrs. McTeague's maps. "Aren't we supposed to be checking down there?" She gestured toward the woods at the other side of the bowl, where Townes had been smoking his cigarette.

"Apparently," said Townes.

"Then let's do it," Alex said.

Cracking sounds came from the other direction, back by the cliff. A few seconds later Larissa and Simon walked down from the ridge, breath clouds rising over their heads, and joined the others in the bowl.

"Is anyone else freezing?" Simon said.

"This way," said Alex.

They all followed her into the far woods, Simon last. "I hate nature," he said. "Despise, detest, loathe."

They stepped into the trees, the ground sloping up again, but not steeply. "Spread out," Alex said. Everyone spread out, Alex on the far left, Cody on the far right, with Townes closest to him, whacking at the undergrowth with his stick. Cody moved around a big rock, kept his eye out for anything moving, anything red. But all that moved were the darkening clouds and themselves, five kids that Cody could only think of as four and one; and the only red to be seen was Townes's headband.

"There's no God," Simon called out. "Brambles are the proof."

They crested the top of the hill, found themselves on a narrow ledge. Beyond the ledge, the trees thinned out and the ground sloped toward a distant paved road. A semi went by, lights on, and then a car with skis on the roof.

"Route Seven?" Larissa said.

Alex checked her map and nodded. "If we head north off the ledge, we should find a trail to the bottom."

"Perfect," said Simon. "We can take a taxi back."

"Calling a taxi how, precisely?" Townes said. "This is a dead zone."

But just as he said that, Cody's cell phone rang. They all

looked at him in surprise. "What service do you have?" Simon said.

Cody took the phone from his pocket. "Hello?"

"Where the hell are you?" It was his father. His voice was loud; he might have been standing right there.

Cody moved away, although there really wasn't anywhere to go on the ledge. He lowered his voice. "I left a note," he said.

"I saw your fucking note," his father said. "You think that's good enough?"

Cody, aware of the Dover Academy kids watching him, took a few steps off the ledge onto the steep slope, and slipped on some dead leaves. He felt a sudden twinge in his bad knee, for an instant thought it was coming apart again, but his knee held, and somehow he stayed on his feet. "Can't talk right now," he said. "I'll call soon."

"Call soon? Who do you think you're talking to?"

"I'm sorry," Cody said.

"Ain't that the truth," his father said. "Now answer my question—where are you? What are you doing?"

Cody's knee started to throb. He glanced back, saw the Dover Academy kids gazing down from the ridge. "Read the note."

"What did you say to me?" His father was shouting now, shouting and drunk.

"You heard."

"Think you can talk to me like that, boy? I'm your goddamn father."

"Why?" Cody said. The word just popped out, totally unplanned, not even making any sense that Cody could see. He clicked off.

The Dover Academy kids were still watching him. "What service do you have, again?" Simon said. Cody noticed they all had their cell phones out, maybe hadn't overheard the conversation, maybe had no interest in it, not the slightest. He named the service. They stared at the tiny screens, shook their heads, put their cell phones away.

"At least we'll be able to call the cab," Simon said. A fat snowflake wafted by, followed by a few more. "Let's take it all the way back to Manhattan," he added.

"Really," said Larissa. A snowflake landed in her hair. For some reason the sight—snowflake so white, hair so black and glossy—had a calming influence on Cody, just at a time when that was what he most needed. The snowflake melted and disappeared.

TWELVE

THEY MOVED NORTH OF the ridge, soon found the trail. Snow—"A trifle early, no?" Simon said—fell lightly, sifting down through the bare branches like salt from a giant shaker.

"You limping, Cody?" Alex said.

"No." They were walking in single file. Cody drifted to the back.

"The helicopter has been conspicuous by its absence," Simon said.

"Mr. Negative," said Townes.

"I'm merely noting the fact," Simon said.

"Shut up," Townes said.

"Hey, come on," said Alex. "It's probably just refueling, anyway."

They continued in silence, Alex, Simon, Larissa, Townes, Cody. Snow coated the trail now, a fraction of an inch, but enough to record their footprints. Something about the snow bothered Cody, maybe just the thought that it had in fact come too late. Wouldn't snow last Wednesday have captured Clea's footprints, led the rescuers right to her?

"Hear the latest?" Larissa said. "Clea's dad had a heart attack. He's in the hospital."

"How do you know?" Townes said.

"The cops were talking about it in the barn," she said.

"How bad?" Townes said.

"How bad what?" said Larissa.

"The heart attack, for Christ sake."

Larissa gave him a look; despite the fact she was half his size, the look said she wouldn't be pushed around. "No idea," she told him.

"He struck me as the heart-attack type," Simon said.

"Shut up," said Townes.

"Hey, come on, guys," Alex said.

"Speaking of the barn," Simon said, "what's the story with this Ike character?"

"No story," Townes said. "He mucks out the stables."

"I refer to his whole *Deliverance* aspect," said Simon.

"He's harmless," Townes said.

"Maybe," said Simon, "but he really should do something

about his—" Simon cut himself off. Up ahead, and not too far off the trail, a small cabin appeared.

"Just one of those warming huts," Alex said.

"They've all been searched," said Townes.

A minute or two later they were even with the warming hut: square and squat, with walls made from rough-hewn logs, a lopsided roof, a slanting chimney. "I'd like to take a look," Cody said.

"I just told you," Townes said. "They've all been searched."

"You guys go ahead," Cody said. "I'll catch up."

"But how will we call the cab without your phone?" Simon said.

Cody didn't want to lend them his phone, partly out of fear that his father might call again, partly because, apart from Alex, these kids seemed so strange to him. "I'll just be a minute or two," Cody said, and turned off the trail.

"But no more, if it's all the same to you," said Simon. "Hypothermia is setting in, and my funeral would be so awkward for my parents, having to stand together in the reception line and all."

Larissa laughed. The Dover Academy kids kept going down the trail.

Cody stepped over a fallen branch, got tangled in some brambles, freed himself, reached the hut. He felt better away from

132

those kids. They—or maybe just Simon—took up all the air.

Cody walked around the hut, looked through the grimy little windows, didn't see much: a potbelly woodstove, a table, shadows. He returned to the front, tried the door: unlocked. Cody went in.

It was colder in the hut than outside, kind of strange—cold enough to make Cody shiver. He examined the interior of the hut: a single room, woodstove in the center, the table against one wall, a bench against another, two wooden chairs and a stool, a pile of split wood in one corner. Easy to imagine a confused person stumbling into a hut like this, maybe resting on the bench: but he saw nothing red, no sign of Clea, or anyone else. Cody read a notice tacked to the wall.

Welcome to this warming hut, maintained for the
comfort and safety of hikers, skiers, and snowshoers
by the Vermont Trailblazers Society. If unfamiliar with
the operation of the woodstove, please do not use.
Please leave the hut the way you found it.
Pack out what you pack in! Safety first!
Enjoy our beautiful mountains!

Cody moved over to the bench, got down on his hands and knees—one knee, anyway, the good one—and peered underneath. Why bother, if, as Townes said, the hut had already been searched? Cody didn't know. He saw a big circular spiderweb hanging from the underside of the bench. Two flies, a moth, and another insect Cody had no name for were caught in the web; he couldn't find the spider. He remembered how Junior was afraid of spiders, just about the only thing in the whole world that scared him. Kind of weird, what with Junior being such a warrior. *Wish you were here.*

Cody rose, walked to the woodstove. He knew woodstoves: Junior's mom had one, heated their whole house with it in winter. Cody raised the cook lid; the little cooking bowl beneath it was empty. He opened the feed door at the side, bent down, saw a pile of white ashes; and what was this? Cody reached in, took out a beer bottle, the top broken off, the end jagged. He examined the bottle. It hadn't been inside while the stove was hot: The paper label was intact. Bud Light. *Bud,* he thought; completely meaningless, of course, unconnected to Bud the horse.

Cody sniffed at the bottle. He detected no beer smell at all, just ashes. Completely unconnected but—from behind came a voice, so sudden and unexpected it made him jump.

"What are you doing?"

Cody turned. Townes stood in the doorway.

"Looking for Clea," Cody said.

"Hard of hearing?" Townes said. "They've searched all the huts." His eyes went to the bottle. He pointed at it with his stick. "What's that?"

Cody knew the huts had been searched, didn't need reminding. Also, he didn't like the stick or that particular way of pointing it. But most of all—what was that expression Alex had used? About things not computing? How did you compute that bit from Clea's letter—*I've been thinking about you a lot, can't help it*—with this new boyfriend, Townes DeWitt, or whatever the hell his stupid name was? Cody didn't think about all those things; they were just there, egging him on. "Here," he said, and tossed the broken bottle to Townes.

A soft toss, neither spinning nor rotating, unbroken bottom end first: in other words, catchable. But Townes made no attempt to catch it. He leaned slightly out of the way—a bit like a matador Cody had seen on TV—and the bottle arced past him and smashed on the floor.

"What's your problem?" Townes said.

"No problem."

Townes looked down at the broken glass, toed some of it aside, then gazed at Cody, maybe actually seeing him for the first time. "You from the high school?" he said.

"I dropped out," said Cody.

"Yeah?" Townes said. "How ballsy."

Cody shrugged.

Townes glanced around the hut. "Seen enough?" he said.

Cody didn't know about that. He wished he hadn't broken the bottle, although it couldn't have anything to do with Clea: She didn't even like the taste of beer.

"Isn't it obvious she's not here?" Townes said.

"Maybe she was," Cody said; not because he thought so—he'd just proved the opposite to himself—but more because he didn't want to agree with Townes about anything. He realized he was jealous and felt ashamed. It took him a moment or two to even understand the feeling, put a name to it. Cody had never felt a whisper of jealousy in his life. It was a bad feeling, tumultuous, dark, powerful. And indulging in it now, with Clea missing, in trouble, maybe even something worse? That was low.

"What do you mean, *maybe she was*?" Townes said.

"What I said. Maybe she was here."

"Is there evidence of that?" Townes looked around the cabin again, slower and with more care this time. "I don't see anything."

"Maybe she likes Bud Light," Cody said. He realized he was toying with Townes, a sneaky little game cooked up by this new jealousy demon inside him.

Townes glanced down again at the remains of the bottle. "Are you suggesting that she wandered in here with a concussion and funneled down a quick one?"

"You'd know," Cody said. He was out of control now, the jealousy demon in full command.

Townes's face changed; hard to describe how, exactly: It was almost as though he suddenly felt unwell. "What the hell is that supposed to mean?" he said.

Cody shrugged. "Alex says you're going out with her."

"Alex has a big mouth."

"Meaning you are going out with her."

"What's it to you?"

"Nothing," Cody said.

Townes gazed at him, at the same time easing more of the shattered glass against the wall with his foot. His face—a good-looking face, the kind that might turn up in some clothing catalog, no way Cody could avoid noticing that—returned to normal, as though the sudden illness had passed. "I can tell you that Clea is not the funneling type," he said.

"But does she like beer?" Cody said.

"Margaritas are more her speed," Townes said. Cody nodded.

A composed sort of nod, perhaps, but inside he was very mixed up, as mixed up as he'd ever been. Margaritas? That wasn't Clea, not at all. How well did this guy, this rich asshole, the new boyfriend, even know her? The wind rose, blowing a little twister of snow through the open doorway.

"How about we get going?" Townes said.

Cody didn't want to leave the warming hut, although for no reason he could express. He moved toward the door. Townes stepped aside. They didn't look at each other. Cody stepped out of the hut, Townes following and closing the door.

They walked out to the trail, Cody still leading the way, trying not to limp. The wind blew harder now, and the snowfall thickened. Cody pictured his winter boots—sturdy, waterproof, lug soles for traction—in the closet back home. His feet were cold, his ears, too; just about all of him. He should have made a list before packing; making lists was something he never did. That was one thing he should change about his life, and soon. Clea made lists all the time.

They reached the trail, turned right; the footprints of Alex, Simon, and Larissa were quickly filling up with snow, getting smoothed away. The trail soon widened, and Cody and Townes were side by side.

"What's she like?" Cody said.

"Who?"

"Clea."

Townes glanced over at him. Cody kept looking straight ahead. "Anyone ever mention you ask a lot of questions?" Townes said.

"No."

"Well, you do."

They continued without talking, rounded a bend, passed through a dense stand of evergreens that for a few moments blocked the wind and snow, muffled all sound.

"It, uh," Cody began. What was he trying to say? These Dover kids were all so articulate; somehow he had to step it up. "It makes sense," he said.

"What does?" said Townes.

"Asking questions," Cody said. "In a situation where someone's lost." The truth of that hit him as he spoke.

Cody felt Townes's gaze on him again. "Fair enough," he said. "Clea's cool."

"Cool?"

"You asked what she's like. Cool is the answer, although I don't see how that's going to help find her."

Cool? Clea was cool? True, in a way, Cody supposed, but if asked to describe her, that wasn't where he would have started.

"What else?" he said.

"What else?"

"About her. Something that might help."

"Like what?"

"I don't know," Cody said. "She's new here, right?"

"How do you know that?" said Townes.

"Alex."

"Of course," Townes said. "Yeah, she transferred in as a junior—comes from some hick town out west."

Cody had a thought; a genuine, possibly useful kind of thought, having nothing to do with the jealousy demon. "Maybe she didn't like it here," he said. He had to study that letter of hers, first thing.

"Huh?"

"And wanted to get away."

"That doesn't happen. People kill to come here."

But Clea hadn't. Her father made a few calls, end of story. Without really knowing why, Cody decided he had to find out for sure whether Townes knew anything about him. "Why did she come here?" he said.

"For the opportunity, like anyone else."

"But why junior year?"

"Why not? It happens all the time."

So Townes didn't know. They walked out of the muffled space between the evergreens—more like a high-ceilinged interior space, a chapel, say, than the outdoors—and back into the snow and wind. The trail led them to a lookout with a picnic bench, all covered in snow. Down below they could see the highway, three figures standing beside it, gazing back up in their direction.

"How come she went off riding all by herself?" Cody said.

Townes shrugged. "She likes riding, can never get enough." That was just about the only positive thing he'd found about Townes so far: Unlike some of the others, he never referred to Clea—or started to refer to her and then caught himself—in the past tense.

And the answer was believable, totally. Clea loved riding. There was just one little thing. "You're on the team too," Cody said.

"I'm captain."

Cody turned to him. "Why didn't you go with her?"

A tiny muscle in Townes's face twitched. "Midnight overheated during the workout. I wanted to get him back in the barn."

"Midnight is your horse?"

"Correct."

A big lump of snow fell off a branch, thumped down right beside Cody, a quiet white explosion. The jealousy demon retreated into Cody's internal shadows.

◦ ◦ ◦

They walked down to Route 7. Cody produced his cell phone. Simon knew the number by heart. A few minutes later a battered-looking taxi arrived and they all squeezed in. The

141

driver dropped them on the Dover Academy campus in front of Baxter Hall, a big brick building with yellow trim and yellow columns by the door. Cody gazed up at the windows, wondering which one was Clea's.

The fare came to twenty-six dollars. The Dover Academy kids scrounged around for money. Alex had three dollars and fifty cents, Larissa two dollars and some euros, Simon a crumpled-up $5000 birthday check from his grandfather, Townes nothing. Cody ended up paying the driver.

THIRTEEN

DARKNESS WAS FALLING FAST as Cody walked past the Mellon Memorial Museum of Art—a neon sculpture resembling a rocket ship glowed outside—and the temperature was falling, too, as well as the snow: everything falling. He took the road by the hockey rink, and through the glass walls saw a game in progress. Cody didn't know much about hockey—his athletic life, meaning much of his whole life, had always been football in the fall, baseball in the spring, basketball in between, mostly to stay in shape—but he lingered outside the rink, long enough to see Dover Academy, in red and gold, score a goal against a team in green and white. The Dover players all raised their sticks as the puck went in the net. It looked like fun.

The road, recently plowed, took him past the tennis courts,

a flat whiteness with dark net posts poking up in regular patterns, and up the tree-lined street with nice houses, everyone inside except for one man trying to shovel his walk while his dog raced around undoing all his work. The lane leading to the barn soon appeared on Cody's right. No plow had reached it yet, but there were tire tracks going down the middle, and Cody walked in those, sneakers wet, feet moving beyond cold toward numb. He'd gone about halfway to the barn—mostly dark, just one or two lights showing through the windows—when a car came his way, snowflakes black in its headlights. Cody stepped aside, up to his mid calves in snow, to let it go by, but the car didn't go by, instead rolled to a stop beside him.

A cop car. The window slid down and Sergeant Orton peered out. "That you, Cody?" Snowflakes blew into the car, got caught in his mustache.

"Yeah."

"Must be freezing your ass off."

"I'm okay."

"Find those kids all right?"

"Yeah."

"Anything to report?"

Cody shook his head. "Did anyone else, uh . . ."

"Nope," said Sergeant Orton. "Can I give you a lift someplace?"

"I'm okay."

"I forgot, been so busy—you go to Ethan Allen?"

"Ethan Allen?"

"The high school."

"I dropped out of high school," Cody said.

"How old are you?"

"Going on seventeen."

"Old enough to make your own decisions," said Sergeant Orton. Cody nodded. That cop episode at Black Rocks made him wary, but Sergeant Orton didn't seem so bad. Then the sergeant added, "Right or wrong." And the wariness returned.

Plus Cody didn't see his decision ending up wrong. Couldn't he always go back for his GED? Besides, he had other things to think about right now. "This snow," he said, "how's it going to, uh . . . affect the search?"

"We'll see in the morning," said Sergeant Orton. "How come you dropped out, if you don't mind telling me?"

"I'm not good at school," Cody said.

"Academics, you mean?"

"Yeah."

"There's more to school than academics," Sergeant Orton said. "Sports, for example. You look like someone who might be useful at sports."

Useful? Cody didn't know how to interpret that. "I like sports," he said.

"What's your favorite?"

"Football."

"Shoulda known," said Sergeant Orton. "Let me guess—you're either a wide receiver or a quarterback."

"Quarterback."

"Ah," the sergeant said. He seemed to have all kinds of time for this casual conversation, taking place with himself comfortably in the car, heater blasting, and Cody out in the cold. "Couldn't help but notice you're limping a bit—that from football?"

"I'm not limping," Cody said. The wind rose, made high-pitched sounds in the trees, and he shivered, nothing he could do about it. "I'm worr—" Cody stopped himself, tried again. "What's the temperature going to be tonight?"

"They're predicting a low of nineteen, twenty, some-where around that." Sergeant Orton's small eyes, normally dominated by that mustache, by that nose, were suddenly dominating again: Cody felt their gaze, almost painful, like some kind of probe trying to get at his mind. "Any special reason for asking?"

"Not special," Cody said. "Just, you know, survival in cold weather. At night."

Sergeant Orton nodded. "Been thinking the same," he said. "Tell me something."

"What?"

"Say it was you out there, lost in the woods—what would you do?"

Cody thought about that. An idea, kind of obvious, probably suggested by recent experience, came to him pretty quickly. "I'd try calling on my cell phone," he said. "Some friend, or maybe 911."

"Good thinking," said Sergeant Orton. "We searched her room at the dorm, of course, plus her lockers at the gym and at the barn. No phone, meaning she probably had it on her, like most people these days. But the phone company shows no calls originating from her number from about an hour before riding practice till now."

"Maybe her phone wouldn't work," Cody said, "out in the woods."

"Some services don't," said the sergeant. "Hers does."

That was bad. Cody tried to bend the cell phone facts into something not quite so bad, and failed. "But—but you haven't found any . . . thing, any evidence."

"Not a speck," Sergeant Orton said. "So let's keep thinking—what else would you do in her place, supposing, say, you were not only lost, but hurt, too, maybe not capable of moving around too much."

Cody's mind squirmed away from picturing Clea like that. All of a sudden, out of nowhere, he felt tears on the way, such an unusual sensation—he'd never been a crier, had cried for the last time at his mother's funeral—he almost didn't recognize what was happening. But he got hold of himself in time—you had to be tough, and not just in football, had to screw your courage to the goddamn sticking-place—and no tears came. *Screw your courage to the sticking-place / And we'll not fail:* Maybe the best piece of advice he'd ever gotten, coming from Ms. Brennan the English teacher, of all people, along with the D minus.

He felt more of Sergeant Orton's silent probing, backed a half step or so from the cruiser, trying to get out of his range. "Maybe hole up in a cave or something," he said, "if I really couldn't move."

"Not too many caves hereabouts," the sergeant said. "But some, plus little crannies by and by, in the rocks, under an uprooted stump, that kind of thing. Believe it or not, these old mountains haven't been completely mapped out yet."

Cody hadn't looked for any of that—caves, crannies, hollows in the ground. "So that's what we'll concentrate on tomorrow?" he said. "Caves and stuff?"

Sergeant Orton gave him one last long probing scan, then nodded. "Meantime, how about a drive somewhere?"

"That's okay."

"Live nearby, Cody? You look cold."

"Not far," said Cody. "And I'm not cold." Sergeant Orton's window slid up. He started to drive away, then backed up, and the window slid down again.

"You into drugs, Cody?" said the sergeant.

"No." And that was the truth. Cody knew kids who were, but he'd never been interested. Drinking: a different story—deep down he knew that about himself already.

"Just asking," Sergeant Orton said. He drove away. Cody stepped into the cruiser's ruts and followed them toward the barn.

◦ ◦ ◦

Cody's car, covered in snow, was the only one left in the parking lot. He pulled the sleeve of his fleece down over his hand, began sweeping the snow off the windshield; halfway done, he stopped, approached the nearest window of the barn and peered in.

Low lights shone over the doors at both ends. The only other light came from a candle burning on Mrs. McTeague's desk. Mrs. McTeague was no longer there. In her place sat Ike, gazing into space, a knife in his hand. Then his lips moved, as though he were talking to himself, and he turned to a block of wood sitting on the table. He began—what was the word?—whittling; he began whittling with the knife. Ike was very good, very fast. In no time at all, a tiny horse started to take shape, head thrown back, mouth wide open. Cold, wet, tired, hungry—despite all that, Cody was transfixed. He stayed by the window until Ike, without warning, stopped work and went back to gazing into space.

Cody returned to his car, finished sweeping snow off the windows. He got in, turned the key, switched on the overhead light, took Clea's letter from the glove box. His fingers were so numb that it slipped, drifted to the floor. He picked it up with both hands, blew off a few grains of dirt, read the whole thing again, found that some of the phrases were now embedded in his memory. Phrases like: *You pop up in my mind so often; well, maybe not ever; some are snobby; One or two I don't like at all.* And that bit that had puzzled him the first time and still did: *Like rolling the dice—a cliché that turns out to have real meaning.* In fact, Clea's whole letter, from beginning to end, was a puzzle, the most puzzling question of all being: How could Clea have written it if she was going out with Townes DeWitt?

Cody looked up, saw that the dashboard temperature needle had risen above C. He turned up the heat full blast and headed into town, first carefully following in Sergeant Orton's tracks to keep from getting stuck, then faster as he reached plowed roads. He came to Spring Street, spotted warm-looking light glowing through the big front window of that café, the Rev.

Cody parked across the street but didn't switch off the

engine. Instead he took off his shoes and socks and held his feet—the skin kind of bluish, but that might have been a trick of the light—up to the blower. Cody started to feel better right away. He rolled up his left pant leg, checked his knee. Not too bad, he told himself. He reached around to the backseat, fumbled through his duffel, found fresh socks, his other sneakers, a T-shirt, and a sweatshirt, all blessedly dry.

Cody crossed the street, entered the Rev. The Rev had a wide-plank pine floor, little chairs and tables, a high ceiling that seemed to be made of metal, maybe tin, and a big stone fireplace with a roaring fire. Cody took a seat at the table nearest the fireplace, felt the heat right away. He glanced at the other customers—a few middle-aged couples, three kids, almost certainly from Dover Academy, sitting in one corner, all of them busy on their laptops, and a man in a tweed jacket, alone at the bar, his back to Cody.

The waitress came over. "Sure you want to be so close to the fire?" She had an eyebrow piercing and a pleasant accent, maybe Irish; Cody wasn't sure, had never met an Irish person before.

"Yeah," he said.

She handed him a menu. Whoa. The prices were kind of high, like $10.95 for a burger, but all at once that was what he really wanted. Cody ordered the burger, plus onion rings and a Coke.

"The burger comes with fries," the waitress said.

"Great," said Cody, only realizing after she'd gone that maybe she'd been hinting at some overlap between onion rings and fries. But he was hungry.

The food came pretty quickly, and for a moment or two Cody was unaware of anything but getting lots of it inside him. Then he relaxed a bit, sat back, found a good position for his left leg. This was the best burger he'd ever had, also the best fries and the best rings. Cody felt good, at least physically. He was about to take out Clea's letter, go over it again, when he noticed the man in the tweed jacket glancing at him. Cody was almost sure he recognized the man—Mr. Stein, from out on the trail. The man himself showed no sign of recognition, turned away, and was soon talking on his cell phone. Cody polished off every morsel, including the pickle slice, and he hated pickles. *Despise, detest, loathe.* What would it be like to have so much money you could forget about a $5,000 check? Cody remembered once, a few years before, when he'd thrown a pair of jeans with a forgotten five-dollar bill in one of the pockets into the laundry basket, and his father, taking clothes out of the dryer, had found it. "Don't care much about money?" he'd said, and ripped it into little pieces right in front of him.

"Dessert?" said the waitress.

Cody checked the menu, saw they had pecan pie. He loved

pecan pie, but a slice cost $5.95—$6.95 à la mode—and he'd already spent too much money. "No, thanks." She wrote up the check. Cody paid.

He shifted his chair, moving closer to the fire, and was taking Clea's letter from his pocket when the man in the tweed jacket left the bar and came over, a cup of coffee in his hand.

"Cody?" he said. Cody put the letter away. "Jonah Stein. We met on the trail."

"Yeah," said Cody.

"A frustrating day," Mr. Stein said. "Mind if I join you for a moment?"

"Uh, no," said Cody, sitting up straight.

Mr. Stein pulled up a chair, sat down. He'd been wearing a big fur hat out in the woods; now Cody got his first good look at him, a small, wiry man with hollow cheeks and dark circles under his eyes. "We appreciate your effort," Mr. Stein said.

"This'll be the sixth night," Cody said.

"I'm sorry?"

What had he said? And why then, so out of the blue? "Just, uh, how long she's been missing."

Mr. Stein nodded. "It's very worrisome." He stirred his coffee, stared at the tiny whirlpool he'd made.

"What do you think happened?" Cody said.

Mr. Stein looked up, took a deep breath. "The theory is she

was thrown from the horse, perhaps suffering a concussion, and then got lost in the woods."

"But you've searched all those sectors."

"It's rough country," Mr. Stein said. "Impossible to cover ever, square inch." He sipped his coffee, watching Cody over the rim of the cup. "Have any theories of your own?" he said.

"Me?" said Cody.

"You seem like a bright kid." Cody said nothing. "She's bright too. Clea, I mean. And resourceful. I have her in rhetoric class—one of the most promising students I've come across in some time." A quick smile crossed his face. "Among other things, we study famous speeches. Clea did Earl Spencer's eulogy at Princess Di's funeral." A fact that Cody already knew, from Clea's cheerful little mention in the letter; now, for some reason, it gave him a chill. "At Wednesday's class, in fact," Mr. Stein went on, the smile now gone. "Only a few hours before she . . ." He stopped, cleared his throat. "Recited the whole speech from memory, but the best part was her analysis of the politics of it."

Cody didn't know anything about that; mostly, at that moment, he just knew he didn't want to talk about eulogies. "What if she lost her memory?" he said. "Maybe forgot who she was."

"We thought about that," said Mr. Stein. "Checked the

hospitals, of course. And she's been all over the news. Anyone who found her would have called in." Mr. Stein drained the rest of his coffee. "Any other theories?"

Cody shook his head.

Mr. Stein put his hands on the table as though to get up. "I forgot—did you say you were at Ethan Allen?"

"No."

"St. Joe's?"

"I'm not in school anymore."

"What do you do?"

Cody came close to telling Mr. Stein the truth. But he couldn't get beyond how stupid it looked, how lame—the old boyfriend turning up when the new one was on the scene, chopping his way through the woods; plus all these people were so strange to him—could he trust any of them? Silence was best—the boys from Little Bend learned that young—but he had to say something. "I'm looking for work," Cody said.

"How old are you?"

"Eighteen."

Mr. Stein gazed at him for a moment, then rose. "I hear you're good with animals," he said.

FOURTEEN

MR. STEIN LEFT THE REV. The waitress returned with Cody's change. He calculated the tip according to Frank Pruitt's formula, handed her the money. She took it with a smile; Frank Pruitt knew what he was doing.

"Know of any motels?" Cody said. "Something . . ." What was the word people used when they meant cheap? Cody found it, kind of unusual for him. "Reasonable," he said.

"The Green Mountain Inn," she said. "That's about as reasonable as it gets in North Dover. Take Spring south, left on Governor, and it's just past Big Len's Sports Bar. Can't miss it."

Cody went outside. It was much colder now, and windier,

too, with the snow falling at a sharp angle. He glanced up at the dark mountains rising over the town, then swept the snow off his car again, drove south on Spring, found Governor—blowing snow stuck on the street sign making it almost unreadable—and turned left.

Governor Street wasn't like the rest of North Dover. Cody passed a boarded-up gas station, a few run-down houses, a vacant lot. Then, on the other side of the street, came Big Len's Sports Bar, dark and windowless, a picture of a longhaired guy with one of those bandit-style handlebar mustaches painted on the sign, and below it the words: "Happy Hour Noon to Six." As Cody went by, the door opened and he glimpsed a football game on a big-screen TV—college football, Cody could tell even at that distance—but what caught his attention was the person coming out. This person, no longer dressed for an outing in the woods, now wore a long black coat and a scarf, but: Townes, beyond doubt. Townes was a senior, seventeen—eighteen at the most—and Cody was pretty sure about the drinking age being twenty-one in every state. But maybe Big Len's Sports Bar had a separate alcohol-free area, or things were somehow different in Vermont, or—Cody couldn't think of anything else. He pulled over to the curb and cut the lights.

Townes leaned against the front of the bar, under an overhang, partly protected from the snow. He lit a cigarette—the end burned bright; he blew out a smoke cloud. At that moment a big black pickup drove out of an alley beside the bar. Townes ran to it, held up his hand, and the pickup stopped. The window slid down and Cody caught a glimpse of the driver—a long-haired man with a bandit-style handlebar mustache. Then Townes stepped in front of the driver's-side door, his back blocking Cody's view. Townes made arm gestures, frustrated gestures, possibly angry. He was still making them when the pickup sped off, window sliding up. Townes stood in the street for a few seconds, then moved onto the sidewalk and started walking in the direction that would take him back to campus. Cody made a quick decision, based on nothing coherent, pulled a quick U-turn, and followed the pickup.

He kept what he thought was the right kind of inconspicuous distance, maybe ten car lengths. After a block or two the pickup turned left onto a side street; no signal. Cody took the same turn. The side street was poorly lit and rutted, the houses small with snow-covered junk in some of the front yards: It reminded him of the worst parts of Little Bend. The plow had been by, but had cleared only a single narrow lane right down the middle, and the snow was filling it in fast. Despite that, and the poor visibility, too, the pickup barreled ahead and Cody could hardly keep up. He leaned forward, concentrating so hard on keeping the car in that yellow-lit tunnel through the storm that he was only subconsciously aware of leaving North Dover, of dense forest on either side, of going up and up.

The road wound into the mountains. Sometimes the pickup's taillights would blink out, but Cody soon realized it just meant the pickup had rounded a bend. When he rounded the same bend, the double red glow would appear again, always having gained a little more distance on him. That sequence happened maybe six or seven times. Then the next time, it did not. Cody went around a bend, a ruined farmhouse standing close to the road, and saw, beyond the reach of his headlights, only blackness, no red at all.

"Damn it."

He stepped on the gas—too hard, too sudden—and right away felt the rear end slide, fishtailing to the left. Cody knew to take his foot off the gas and steer into the direction of the skid—had even done it successfully once before, goofing around in a snowstorm, not this bad, the very first day he'd had his car, back in Little Bend—but this time it didn't work. The rear end kept sliding, right around, completely out of control. Cody shouted something, he didn't know what, and hit the brake even though that was the very worst thing to do. The car spun three or four times, sliding and sliding, back in the direction of the last bend, careening toward a big tree in front of the ruined farmhouse. Cody squeezed the wheel with all his strength. Then from down below came a shriek, the shriek of rubber on a bare road. The car stopped, just like that, shuddering a few feet from the tree. Cody sat there, still squeezing the wheel, still pressing on the brake. He was shuddering too.

Had he hit a patch of bare pavement? Cody shifted to drive, engaged the emergency brake, turned off the engine, got out of the car. Yes, a bare patch, maybe caused by the big tree; the wind was blowing from that direction. He circled the car. It looked okay. He was okay. Blind luck. Cody looked around, saw no lights, red or any other color, heard nothing but the storm. He surrendered to the obvious: The pickup was gone. Cody got in the car and drove back to town.

● ○ ●

The Green Mountain Inn turned out to be an ordinary motel of the L-shaped kind, with parking spaces in front of every room, all empty. They had a special midweek rate, $49.95 a night. Cody paid cash for one night, was given the key to Room 11. That lifted his spirits a little—eleven was his number. How dumb could he be?

Cody carried his stuff into Room 11; an ordinary room of the painted-cement-block-walls kind, not warm, and no thermostat he could find. A hot shower sounded nice. Cody kicked off his sneakers, sat for a moment on the bed, just for a breather. His feet were cold. He pulled them up, tucked them under the bedspread, lay down, only for a second or two.

Cody had a dreaming thought: *I'm going to be late for school.* His eyes snapped open and he woke in the cold cement-block room, dim gray light wedging through venetian-blind slats, browned with age; woke and remembered where he was and why. He rose, walked toward the bathroom, couldn't do that without remembering his knee. Then came other memories, none good, not the recent ones.

But in the shower he saw his knee wasn't too bad, just a little swollen, the surrounding muscles less feeble-looking. *What doesn't kill you makes you stronger.* Another Coach Huff favorite, especially during the hottest, most bug-infested two-a-days, except that he always mangled it, saying, *What kills you makes you stronger.* Or, more accurately, *What kills you makes you stronger, ladies.* Standing in the shower, the water not hot, just barely warm enough, Cody pretended to take a snap from center, turned, quick and precise, and handed off the imaginary ball to a phantom Jamal.

He dried himself with a towel so thin it didn't absorb water, more or less just brushed it off. The face in the mirror could go one more day without a shave, maybe two. Cody got dressed, at the same time switching on the TV, a tiny one. There was something wrong with the picture. He fiddled with the controls for a minute or so before realizing that this was a black-and-white TV, the first he'd ever seen. Cody found a news show from a station in Burlington: not a word about Clea.

Cody packed up and turned in his key, thinking he'd try to find someplace cheaper—wasn't there such a thing as rooms by the week? That thought, the implications of it, made him pause as he swept the snow off his car. Bad implications, for sure: He forced them from his mind and drove toward the center of town.

Snow no longer fell, but the sky was gray, the wind strong. Cody headed back down Governor, toward the nice part of North Dover. Big Len's Sports Bar appeared on his right, and he took a good daylit look: a brick—what was the word? facade?—painted black; a grated window, the glass so dirty he couldn't see through; and that bandit picture, the colors bright and gaudy. Without much thought, Cody turned into the alley that the black pickup had driven out of the night before.

It led him around to the back of the bar: Dumpster, a few aluminum kegs, the black pickup, and a skinny dog sniffing at a McDonald's carton lying in the snow. Cody stopped behind the pickup, read the bumper sticker: THIS TRUCK PROTECTED BY SMITH & WESSON. His father had a small-frame Smith & Wesson .38, kept it in a shoe box under his bed. Cody got out of the car, walked over to the pickup, peered into the back, saw not much: tire chains, an ax, a six-pack of Bud Light empties. He felt something against his leg, looked down; and there was the skinny dog, wagging its frayed little tail. "Hey, boy." Cody gave the dog a pat. It wagged harder. Dogs were not permitted in the apartments over the Red Pony.

As Cody got back in the car—the dog following him all the way—something made him glance up. There were three windows at the top story of the building. The man with the handlebar mustache was watching from the middle one. The painting on the sign out front made him look kind of amusing, like a cartoon character. He was different in real life.

Cody found a frozen french fry on the car floor, tossed it to the dog, drove off. North Dover, all covered in snow, almost seemed like a different town from the one he'd first seen yesterday; even more beautiful, maybe, but the change disturbed him in some way he couldn't put into words. He stopped at a convenience store at the corner of Governor and Spring, bought a premade egg salad sandwich and a large coffee, had breakfast in his car; radio on, no news of Clea. When he was done, he went back in, bought another egg salad sandwich, ate that, too, standing by the car. He had a good view of the mountains, all white now, except for that stony summit he'd seen yesterday from the hollow with the dwarfish trees. From here, down in the town, the stony summit seemed very far away.

○ ○ ○

Cody drove through the Dover Academy gates, followed the road to the equestrian center. Ike, wearing a plaid hat with earmuffs sticking straight out to the sides, was at the wheel of a

Bobcat, plowing the parking lot. He glanced at Cody, showed no sign of recognition. A few cars sat in the freshly plowed part, none of them official. Cody parked near them and went into the barn.

Except for the horses, standing quietly—although somehow their presence filled the barn, a physical sensation Cody felt—Mrs. McTeague was all alone. She sat at the desk between the two rows of stalls, packing papers in a cardboard box.

"Cody, wasn't it?" she said, looking up.

"Yeah." He noticed there were no doughnuts today; he'd been planning on taking a couple out on the trail.

"Morning, Cody."

"Morning."

Mrs. McTeague smiled at him, her friendly face looking even friendlier. "Word is you're looking for work," she said. Cody was still trying to remember who he'd said that to when she went on: "You seem to be good with animals. Ever worked in a stable before?"

"No," Cody said.

"Not to worry," said Mrs. McTeague. "Experience isn't essential—attitude always ends up being a hundred times more important. So what do you say?"

Cody was confused. "About what?"

Mrs. McTeague laughed. "Getting a little ahead of myself.

We're looking for someone to help out with the feeding, the walking, the mucking out. There's really too much for one man, and Ike could use a break now and then. Good physical work, Cody, and not always clean, plus it only pays nine fifty an hour to start, but it comes with all the usual Dover Academy benefits, room included."

"Um, I, uh," Cody began, then just blurted out the first thought that came to mind, completely irrelevant. "I thought you were in charge of the search."

"Only the volunteer coordinator," said Mrs. McTeague. "I'm also assistant HR director for the school."

Cody took that in, felt no wiser. A job at Dover Academy? He hadn't come here for a job. But supposing the search took a few more days, even a week, wouldn't he need money, a place to stay? "Thanks, ma'am," he said. "Very, uh, nice of you. If it's okay, I'll think it over while I'm out there."

"Out where?" said Mrs. McTeague.

Cody gestured toward the woods outside. "With the search," he said. "Where am I supposed to go today?"

Mrs. McTeague gazed at him. Light, streaming down from a loft window, glared off the lenses of her glasses, obscuring her eyes. "You haven't heard?" she said. "They've called it off."

FIFTEEN

CODY'S FIRST RESPONSE wasn't very logical. "You found her?" he said.

The light still glared on Mrs. McTeague's glasses, a pearly sheen that hid her eyes. "Oh dear me, no," she said. "What with all this snow, it's apparently not realistic to think of finding anything."

Cody didn't get that at all. What difference did snow make if Clea was holed up in a cave, or some cranny in the rocks, as Sergeant Orton believed? Wasn't that Sergeant Orton's true belief? He tried to go over their last conversation, Cody standing in the cold beside the cruiser, the sergeant talking to him through the open window. All Cody remembered clearly was

Sergeant Orton's probing gaze. At that moment a realization struck him, abrupt and hard: Sergeant Orton didn't believe Clea was holed up in some natural shelter—that wasn't his true belief at all. They were no longer looking for a living person. That was why searching after the snowfall made no sense.

Cody felt his face growing hot. They were wrong, pure and simple. "Does Mr. Stein know about this?" he said.

"Mr. Stein?" Mrs. McTeague said, looking confused. "Yes, certainly—a school-wide email went out first thing this morning. Why do you ask?"

Why did he ask? Because, goddamn it, Mr. Stein had said that Clea was resourceful; bright and resourceful, to quote. And not just that, but she was tough, too, strong and physical, unfazed by things that fazed other girls—and some boys—like taking that long leap at the Black Rocks quarry. Cody kept all that to himself—too complicated to explain, at least for him— and just shrugged.

Mrs. McTeague reached for the mounted photo of Clea, the one with him missing from the right-hand side, and laid it face-down in the cardboard box. "So," she said, "about that job?"

Cody thought: I'm missing from the picture, and now Clea's missing, period. "Yeah," he said. "I'm interested."

"Wonderful," said Mrs. McTeague. "Welcome aboard." They shook hands; Mrs. McTeague's hand was soft and warm, her grip not strong at all. "If you'll help me load these boxes in my car, I'll show you the ropes."

○ ○ ○

Mrs. McTeague showed Cody the ropes. "Mostly," she said, "you'll just be assisting Ike."

"Means muckin' out," said Ike, following along behind them, a three-pronged rake his hand. Cody wasn't afraid of mucking out; he'd done it before, helping Clea in Bud's paddock at Cottonwood.

Mrs. McTeague went over the chores: feeding and watering the horses, walking them, answering the phone, fire prevention, a few others he didn't catch the first time around. "This is the tack room," said Mrs. McTeague. "The competitive season is over now, but the riders still come to the barn three or four times a week to exercise the horses. They're responsible for saddling their own mounts, so you don't have to worry about that. Here's a list of important numbers, starting with 911 of course, and the vet." Cody scanned the list. Number three read Chef d'Equipe. Perhaps Mrs. McTeague saw him pause there, guessed his confusion. "That's the coach," she said. "But he won't be around—he's working with the Argentine Olympic team right now. Ike—why don't you show Cody the living quarters?"

"The little room up top?" said Ike.

"That's the one," said Mrs. McTeague.

"Le's go," Ike said.

Cody followed him toward the door.

"One more thing," said Mrs. McTeague. "I'll need your social security number."

Cody knew it by heart, rattled it off. This job, plus the place to stay, had come along at the exact right moment. He had no idea what he'd have done with the search called off. But no matter what—even without this stroke of luck, if that was the right term—how could he have called off his own personal search?

"Never say it out loud," Ike muttered as they went outside, maybe to himself. "Numbers kill."

Cody said nothing. Ike slowed down to let him draw even, but then when he did, sped up again. He spoke over his shoulder. "Know how to shoe 'em?"

"Horses?" said Cody.

"They don't shoe pigs, do they?"

"No," said Cody. "I don't know how."

Ike made a little sucking noise between his teeth. He led Cody past the corral, around the back of the barn, toward a narrow plowed path Cody hadn't noticed before. It cut through the woods, opened into a clearing, and there stood a small cabin, smoke rising from the chimney, straight up in the still air.

"They like it," Ike said.

Cody took a guess. "Getting shod?" he said.

"Course not," said Ike. "How would you like it, gettin' shoes nailed into your feet? What they like is wearin' 'em, the shoes." How did Ike know that? Cody kept the question inside, but Ike seemed to answer it anyway. "Just like us," he said. "We're wearin' shoes. We're animals." Ike pointed to the front door. "That's my door." He walked around the side of the cabin, past a woodpile, stopped at a second door, much smaller. "This is your'n." He took out a key and opened the door. "Don't be forgettin'."

"I won't."

Ike turned to him. Cody noticed he was missing a few teeth. "I'm talking about us bein' animals, what not to forget," he said. Ike stepped inside, entering a tiny, closet-size entrance hall with a steep staircase rising to the right. Cody followed him up. Ike opened another door at the top, this one unlocked, and gestured for Cody to go in. "Know how to use a woodstove?"

"Yes."

"Easy on the wood. Room heats up quick."

Cody looked around. Not hard to see why: The place was tiny, with a narrow bed along one wall, a counter bearing a small square fridge and hot plate against the opposite wall, sink and toilet in one corner, woodstove in the other; hardly enough space left over for both of them to be inside at the same time. Frost coated the windows, and Cody could see his breath. A little wave of happiness took him by surprise: This was the first place he could call his own.

"Don't lose this," Ike said, handing him a key.

"I won't. Thanks."

"Easy on the wood."

○ ○ ○

Cody fired up the woodstove, went back to the car for his things. The room heated up fast, the frost melting off the windows. Cody gazed out at the woods and saw something red almost at once: a cardinal. It stood on a branch near the window, seemed to be staring right back at him; then, without any sign of preparation, the cardinal took off and flew over the forest, losing first its redness, then its shape, and finally vanishing altogether. Cody went downstairs, locked the door, returned to the barn.

Mrs. McTeague, all her things, including maps, flyers and phone, even the desk: gone. Cody didn't understand. Was the search over forever? What if the snow melted? Didn't there have to be some backup plan? He saw Ike moving through the shadows at the back of the barn, on the way to the tack room with a saddle over his shoulder.

Cody went into the tack room. Ike was setting the saddle on the floor of one of the lockers. Open, stall-type lockers lined one wall, a locker with a name plaque for each member of the team. Clea's locker stood next to Townes's.

"Hey, Ike."

Ike dropped the saddle, whirled around. "Don't you be scarin' me like that."

"Sorry. I was wondering what the chances were of the snow melting."

Ike blinked a few times, seemed to compose himself. "Always does."

"Soon?"

"By May," said Ike, "at the latest." Was that meant to be a joke? Cody couldn't tell. A wall phone rang. Ike answered it, listened for a moment, said, "Yup," and hung up. He turned to Cody. "Know how to polish a bridle?"

Cody nodded. He'd seen Clea do it once or twice.

"Polish them ones up," he said, pointing with his chin to a couple of bridles lying on a workbench. "I'll be back."

Ike left, putting on his plaid hat with the ear flaps sticking out to the side. Cody went over to the workbench, picked up one of the bridles. From the doorway behind him came Ike's voice, startling him the same way he'd startled Ike. "Wash those bits," he said. "And get the dirt out of the leather first— no point oilin' otherwise. 'Cause why? 'Cause you're just oilin' in the dirt, is why."

Ike went away. Cody soaked the bits, washed the leather

with saddle soap, patted it dry with a towel, applied neat's-foot oil from a bottle on the shelf. Not bad work; in fact, he kind of enjoyed it.

Ike hadn't returned by the time he was done. Cody examined Clea's locker. What he saw: saddle, bridle, reins, halter. What he didn't see: boots, helmet, anything personal. She'd been wearing the boots and helmet, of course, a good thing, the helmet especially. He carried Clea's tack to the workbench, cleaned and polished it all. Still no Ike. Cody left the tack room, walked through the barn, stopped at Bud's stall. He had two or three sugar cubes in his pocket—but also the halter in his hand, so a certain plan must have been forming in his mind all on its own.

Bud snorted, rolled his eyes.

"Hey, Bud," Cody said, "it's me." He stroked Bud's face. Bud calmed down. His big brown eyes looked unhappy, but Cody knew it was more likely he himself was just—what was the word? projecting?—yeah: He was projecting his own mental state into Bud's eyes. Except that Bud really did look sad. "What happened, Bud? Where is she?" Bud stood very still. At the other end of the barn a horse neighed, a high-pitched sound that sent a funny feeling down Cody's spine.

He looked around, saw no one; only the horses, a calming sight, for some reason. They were all watching him in a trusting kind of way; or at least that was how Cody interpreted their expressions. He went to the window. His car was the only one in the lot; nearby stood the Bobcat, untended; beyond, the empty lane leading back to campus, snowbanks lining both sides. No one in sight.

A minute or two later he was leading Bud out of the barn. The halter looked a little lopsided on Bud's head—Cody had never put one on before—but he didn't seem to mind, following along without protest, applying no pressure at all on the reins.

Cody walked Bud across the yard, by the riding ring and onto the loop trail. Snowmobiles had already passed through, packing down the snow. Cody glanced back, saw that Bud wasn't having any trouble, certainly less than he was, with snow already invading his sneakers. "I know you remember," he said. Bud snorted, tossed his head a bit; Cody felt Bud's tremendous strength through the reins. He held out a sugar cube. Bud grasped it with those big, loose lips of his. They walked on.

The woods had changed, were quieter now, snow muffling all their sounds, also coating the evergreens and toning down their greenness, leaving a simple world of brown and white. All that whiteness covered the horseshoe prints Cody had seen before. Was it possible there was something distinctive about Bud's hoofprints, some mark that could have left a trail right back to where things went wrong? A question too late in coming, but had the searchers thought of it, back on day one when it might have done some good?

"Whoa," Cody said.

Bud halted, gazed straight ahead. Cody dropped the reins, went back to examine Bud's hoofprints. Loose snow had obliterated most of them, but he found a few sharp-edged impressions, nothing distinctive about them. Bud twitched his tail, stamped his right front foot. Was he impatient to get going? Cody picked up the reins, stroked Bud's face. "What happened?" he said. Bud's eyes didn't look sad anymore, were just big brown liquid pools, revealing nothing.

They kept going, past two or three trails entering the loop, smooth unmarked snow covering all of them, and came to the house-size mossy rock with the big crack down the middle. Snow had somehow filled in the crack, leaving a jagged white mark on the rock face, a sight that for some reason made Cody uneasy. He gazed at it for a while; then came an idea. Maybe, around the back, this rock concealed one of those crannies Sergeant Orton had mentioned. Had anyone looked?

Cody dropped the reins. "Don't go anywhere," he told Bud. Bud stood still. Cody circled the rock, up to his knees in snow right away, saw no cranny, no hole, no hollowed-out depression. He bent down, dug through the snow with his bare hands, and found underneath nothing but dead leaves, stiff and frozen.

He took the reins, led Bud along the loop, got used to the warm feeling of Bud's breath in the small of his back. A few minutes later, he spotted the sign nailed to a tree up ahead: UPPER MOUNTAIN CROSSOVER—4.5 MILES TO ROUTE 7. At the same time, Bud's nose nudged his shoulder, as though urging him to pick up the pace. Cody picked up the pace, but there'd been less snowmobile traffic here, and once or twice he sank down in the snow. His knee began to hurt. Bud nudged him again.

"What is it?"

Bud made a whinnying sound. Cody glanced back, saw he was doing that eye-rolling thing.

"What's on your mind?" Cody held out another sugar cube. Bud took it, relaxed a little. They went on, reached the crossover trail, marked with snowmobile tracks. Cody halted and turned to Bud. "Which way?" he said. "Straight ahead, or do we—" With no warning, Bud neighed—a piercing, wild sound, terrified and terrifying—and rose up on his hind legs, front hooves flailing the air, just missing Cody's head. Cody dropped the reins, leaped back.

"Hey," he said. "What's going on?"

Sergeant Orton stepped out from behind a tree, not ten feet away. "I'll ask you the same question," he said, right hand on the butt of his gun.

SIXTEEN

BUD STAMPED HIS FOOT and tossed his mane, backed away a step or two and then went still. Without taking his eyes off Cody—or his hand off the gun—Sergeant Orton bent down and grabbed the reins. Three breath clouds rose in the air—Cody's and Sergeant Orton's, plus Bud's, much bigger—and drifted off in their separate ways. "I asked you a question," the sergeant said.

"I'm, uh, working here now," Cody said. "A job. At the barn."

"That's not what I asked."

"Um, I thought, maybe that Bud would lead me to wherever . . ."

"That was one of the first things we tried," said Sergeant Orton. "You aware of that?"

Cody hesitated, trying to see down the two diverging roads leading away from yes and no. He got nowhere.

"Any weapons on you, Cody?" said the sergeant.

"Me?"

"Little popgun, maybe? Knife of some sort?"

"No," said Cody.

"Just keep your hands where I can see them."

Cody kept his hands by his side, exactly where they'd been, but now he was hyperconscious of them.

"Ever been arrested?" the sergeant said.

"Never."

"A snap for me to check," Sergeant Orton said. "That part of the job gets easier every day."

Cody said nothing. He'd had a run-in or two like the one with the cop out at the quarry—pretty common kind of thing for boys in Little Bend—but none had led to arrest, and Sergeant Orton could check all he wanted.

"A bit of a tough guy, huh?" said the sergeant.

Cody did not reply.

"I'm dressed warm and you're not," Sergeant Orton said. "Many many layers."

Cody shrugged.

"Meaning I can wait out here all day."

"For what?" said Cody.

"The answer to my question—were you aware we'd already tried this horse idea?"

Cody gave up trying to see the future. He chose the truth, maybe because it seemed easier, or maybe—he got a sudden glimpse inside himself—because that was his default setting. "I knew," he said. "Mrs. McTeague told me."

Sergeant Orton nodded, a tiny movement, but something about it told Cody that the sergeant had known this bit of information about Mrs. McTeague from the get-go. His hand came off the gun butt. "And she told you the idea came to nothing?"

Cody nodded.

"Raises the obvious question," the sergeant said. Then came a pause, and in that pause Cody tried and failed to figure out any obvious question. "Which is," Sergeant Orton said, "how come you thought you'd do any better?"

"It's just that Bud—the horse—trusts me, and so . . ."

"Any special reason for Bud trusting you?"

Cody felt those probing eyes. Was this another question Sergeant Orton already knew the answer to? Cody took a deep breath, made a decision; right or wrong, he didn't know—all he knew was he started to feel better at that moment. "The thing is," he said, "I'm from Colorado, the same town as Clea."

"Hell, I know that," said the sergeant. "Ran your plates the same hour you first showed up. Or let's maybe delete that *first* for the moment, stick to you just showing up at the barn. The big question is where you were last Wednesday." The feeling-better thing vanished at once. In its place came dizziness, as though Cody had suddenly grown much too tall, his head way too high off the ground, total collapse coming next. "What . . . what are you saying?"

"A simple matter of fact," said the sergeant. "Account for your whereabouts last Wednesday."

"But that's the day she disappeared."

"Go on."

"I was at work."

"Where?"

"Delivering lumber."

"Where?"

"Back home," Cody said. "In Little Bend."

"Can you prove it?"

"But I don't understand," Cody said. "Are you saying something's—"

Sergeant Orton's voice rose over his. "Want me to cuff you? Answer the goddamn question." Bud got nervous, started shifting away. Sergeant Orton gave the reins a sharp tug, strong enough to pull Bud's head down.

Cody didn't like that; it made him combative. "I haven't done anything wrong," he said.

Sergeant Orton's free hand shifted back to the gun. "Five seconds," he said.

For four of them, Cody considered the idea of bolting away through the woods. On the fifth, he said, "I can prove it."

"How?"

"Ms. Beezon. She can tell you."

"That's your boss?"

"Kind of. At Beezon Lumber."

"You don't go to school?"

"I don't have to," Cody said. "I'm almost seventeen."

"I know how old you are." Sergeant Orton reached into an inside pocket, took out a cell phone. "Call her."

"Don't know the number," Cody said.

"That meant to be funny?" said the sergeant. "Don't know the number of your employer?"

"It's not meant to be funny," Cody said.

Sergeant Orton punched some numbers on his phone, then paused, index finger curled over the keypad. "This Ms. Beezon know you're here?" he said.

"No."

"Who does?"

"From Little Bend? I guess nobody."

"What about your parents?"

"There's just my d—my father. He thinks I'm looking for work, but not this far away."

Sergeant Orton gave him a long look. Then his finger pressed the last number. "Beezon Lumber, Little Bend, Colorado." He waited, the phone to his ear, his eyes on Cody. Cody tried to remember some previous time he'd told Sergeant Orton his age and couldn't. "Ms. Beezon, please," said the sergeant. "Ms. Beezon, I'm with statistics, Department of Education. Just checking to see if you can confirm an employee, recent dropout name of Laredo, first name Cody." Sergeant Orton listened, nodded, then said, "Did he work last week?" More listening. "Monday to Friday?" The sergeant nodded again. "And what were the hours?" He listened some more, said, "Much obliged," clicked off. Then his eyes were back on Cody.

Cody thought: *No way to trust a guy like this, not ever.* Up above, the wind was stirring, rattling the upper branches.

"Ever been in North Dover before?" said Sergeant Orton.

"No."

"Have any relatives here, any friends?"

"No," said Cody, then added, "except for Clea."

"I hear she was your girlfriend."

"Who told you that?"

"The way this works," said the sergeant, "is I ask and you

182

answer. Was Clea Weston your girlfriend?"

Cody nodded.

"I also hear you broke up before she came to the academy. What can you tell me about the circumstances?"

"We broke up."

"And how did you feel about that?"

Cody shrugged.

"Losing such a bright, beautiful girl, my guess is it got inside you, twisted around, riled you up."

"Riled me up?"

"Made you a bit crazy—a possible plea down the line, if you play your cards right, meaning tell the truth."

"I don't understand a word you're saying," Cody said, but all at once he felt the cold, through and through.

"It's actually kind of common," said Sergeant Orton. "A syndrome, you might say. Some guys get this idea in their heads and can't shake it. All they hear in their minds is this same one thing, over and over—if I can't have her, then no one can."

Cody didn't think. He just hit Sergeant Orton in the mouth as hard as he could.

Maybe not quite in the mouth. Sergeant Orton turned out to be pretty quick for an overweight, middle-aged guy. He shifted his head, just enough to change the angle of the blow, diminish it a little. At almost the same time he drew his gun, started to raise it. But Bud, maybe scared, was moving too. He reared up again, and again flailed the air with his front hooves. One of them came down on Sergeant Orton's hand, knocking the gun loose. Cody wheeled around and took off down the crossover trail.

"Halt!" Sergeant Orton shouted.

Cody didn't halt. He kept running, but so slow, like an underwater runner, his feet sinking a few inches into the snow with every stride.

"Halt or I'll shoot."

Cody didn't believe that, not for a second. He kept running, a vague plan forming in his mind, a plan based on getting to Route 7, flagging down a—

Crack! Crack of a gunshot, sharp and clear in the woods. At just about the same instant came a second cracking sound, and something invisible splintered the bark of a tree a few feet ahead of him. A tiny cloud of sawdust spurted from the trunk. Cody stopped running.

"Hands up high."

Cody raised his hands.

"Turn around real slow."

Cody turned.

Sergeant Orton came trudging up the trail, gun raised. Bud stood quietly behind him, as if he, too, had been ordered to halt. The sergeant spat; a red glob landed in the snow. "The type that makes everything harder than it has to be, aren't you?" he said.

Cody didn't know what to say about that. He was going to be arrested. He had rights, didn't he? On *Cops*—Junior's favorite show—no one ever seemed to know about their rights, blabbed everything. Cody knew he had the right to remain silent. On the other hand, he hadn't done anything wrong—except for that one punch. And what was there to say about that? The punch was undeniable—hit someone in the mouth and both of you remember it forever—but also not wrong, not in this case, and Cody didn't regret it.

Sergeant Orton came right up to Cody, the gun still up, pointed at Cody's chest. The sergeant's bushy gray mustache was tinged with red. He spat again, spattering more red on the snow at Cody's feet. "Assaulting a police officer," he said. "Any idea of the future, you get charged with something like that?"

Cody remained silent.

"Charged as an adult, I'm talking about, which I'll make goddamn sure is what happens? State pen, three-year mini-mum, record or no record."

Cody came close to hitting him again, stopped only by that gun, unwavering in the sergeant's hand.

"That how you want this to play out, boy?"

At that moment, Cody remembered his last conversation with Mr. Lorrie, his English teacher and faculty adviser. *Have you ever thought about what you'll be doing, say three years from now?* Although he couldn't see much similarity between the two men, Cody realized that conversation with Mr. Lorrie resembled this one, almost a practice version, like running through the plays with no pads on; or maybe like touch football compared to the real thing. That time, with Mr. Lorrie, he'd ended up quitting school. *Three years.* Cody shook his head, a tiny movement, barely made at all.

But Sergeant Orton caught it. He lowered the gun. "That's smart," he said. "You wouldn't do so good behind bars. No one does, actually. Even the ones that are already ruined get ruined more." He dabbed at his mouth with the back of his sleeve. The temperature was falling. Cody could feel it in his feet, hands, ears; and could see it in Sergeant Orton's mustache, where the ends of the hairs had frozen, looked like tiny sprinkles of red glass. "What you're going to do now—you want any chance of coming out of this undamaged for life—is come clean. No lies, no halfway lies, no bullshit." Sergeant Orton's face was close to Cody's now. Cody could smell his breath, not good.

"Come clean about what?" Cody said.

"And no stalling."

"I'm not stalling. I don't—"

186

Sergeant Orton cut him off. "Start with how come you hid who you really were, let folks go on thinking you were local?"

Cody just stood there. The real reason was quite simple, simple and stupid at the same time: Clea had a new boyfriend, making him, the ex-boyfriend, look like a pathetic loser, no better than a gawker at some wreck on the highway. Maybe not quite so simple: How did breaking up with Clea, pretending he didn't care anymore—supposedly a noble gesture, supposedly for her own good—how did that factor in, especially given how quickly she'd moved on to someone else? For one thing, it made him a fool, a fool as well as a loser.

"Haven't got all day," said the sergeant. "Haven't got more than a minute."

Cody just couldn't bring himself to confess the truth. Sergeant Orton reached around his belt. Cody heard a cold, metallic clink, handcuffs for sure; even then, he couldn't do it. But at the last moment, he found words that at least had some truth in them. "These people," he said. "They're all very different from me."

"So?"

"I couldn't . . . if they'd known where I really, you know, came from, then . . ."

"Spit it out," said Sergeant Orton.

"There'd have been a lot of questions," Cody said.

187

"About you?"

"Yeah. But none of that would have helped find Clea." The sergeant gave Cody one of those deep, probing looks. "You obsessed with her, is that it?"

Obsessed? Obsession had sickness in it, and there was nothing sick about Clea's place in his mind. "No."

"Then how would you put it?"

"I love her," Cody said, without hesitation—it just came right out, very natural—and also without the slightest feeling of being a loser or a fool.

The expression in Sergeant Orton's eyes grew distant, as though he'd been struck by a thought. "This business of holding back who you really were, avoiding questions—anything else to it?"

"I told you—it wouldn't help finding her."

"Yeah," said the sergeant. "I can remember back that far. Any more to it than that?"

"Like what?" Cody said.

Sergeant Orton laughed. A big surprise for Cody, almost as unsettling as the moment when he'd stepped out from behind the tree. "You tell me," the sergeant said.

Any more to it than that? Sergeant Orton had an answer waiting in his mind, and somehow Cody knew it had nothing to do with all that fool and loser stuff. Something else; not

188

just something else, but something *more*. How could hiding his true self be about *more* than the fact that revealing it would only be a distraction, wouldn't help find her? Deep in the silent woods, Bud motionless, temperature falling, wind rising, this cop right in front of him, gun in hand, and his own lips going numb, Cody took a guess. "Maybe nobody knowing about me would actually help find her." The thinking seemed logical; the words sounded right; the implications completely escaped him.

"Yup," said Sergeant Orton. "What took you so long? I'm freezing my ass off."

Cody was a little lost. They looked at each other. Cody couldn't read the sergeant's mind at all. "Am I under arrest?"

For a second or two the sergeant seemed about to laugh again, but no laugh came. "Stay away from questions like that," he said. "Some people might miss your charm." He smiled and gave Cody three taps on the cheek with his open hand, friendly taps except for the last, which was more like a slap. Yes, a slap. Cody felt the sting. Sergeant Orton's smile got bigger. Something had amused him, but Cody had no idea what it was.

SEVENTEEN

SO WAS HE UNDER ARREST or not? How could he not be? He'd punched a cop in the mouth. But the cuffs had never come out, and now the gun was back in its holster.

"Let's get moving," Sergeant Orton said. He handed Bud's reins to Cody.

Where? Cody followed the advice Sergeant Orton had just given him and kept the question inside. They headed back up the crossover trail. When they came to the loop, the sergeant walked around a thick spruce, the Christmas-tree kind. Cody followed and saw a snowmobile parked behind the tree.

"You knew I was coming," Cody said.

Sergeant Orton smiled. Cody decided he didn't like the

sergeant's smile, preferred his face in its usual unsmiling and watchful mode. "Meet you back at the barn," Sergeant Orton said. "And no dillydallying," he added, "not when you're working for me."

"I'm working for you?"

Cody hadn't gotten all those words out before the sergeant cranked the engine, drowning him out with its roar. He zoomed off.

Cody stood at the loop-crossover junction, the reins in his hand. He wasn't under arrest; in fact, might even be free to go. "What do you think?" he said to Bud. He stroked that long face with the diamond-shaped blaze and actually thought he glimpsed what was going on in Bud's mind at that moment: It was all right with Bud if he wanted to climb up and ride him back to the barn. Cody had never ridden bareback, had little riding skill of any kind, but he got one hand on Bud's mane and climbed up. Without any signal from him, Bud started walking down the loop trail. Cody held the reins loosely, made no attempt to guide Bud's movement, just sat there, feeling the horse's great warmth.

"We'll find her," he said. There was nowhere to go, not with Clea missing.

○●○

Sergeant Orton was waiting inside the barn, no one else there. Cody got Bud in his stall, removed the halter, hung it in Clea's locker in the tack room; and felt Sergeant Orton's gaze on his back.

"Did you arrange this job for me?" Cody said. He turned. The sergeant was smiling again. Cody noticed he'd washed the blood off his face; the smile no longer seemed so scary.

"Got a brain locked away in there someplace, huh?" the sergeant said.

"Why did you do it?" Cody said.

"Need to keep an eye on you."

"Why?"

"You're the anomaly."

"What's that?"

"The thing that stands out. Like an eagle in a flock of geese. Only got one card, you play it."

"I don't understand."

"There's a whole syndrome of perps joining search parties like this."

"Perp? You think I'm a perp?"

"Not anymore," the sergeant said, and in a lower voice, maybe to himself, added, "in all likelihood."

"I'm not a perp."

The sergeant gazed at Cody for a moment, then filled two Styrofoam cups from a coffeepot by the workbench. He handed one to Cody. "Take a seat." They sat on stools, a few feet apart, sipped coffee. Weak coffee, and maybe a bit stale, but it felt good. "When people disappear," the sergeant said, "there's only a few possible explanations." He set his cup on the workbench, ticked them off on fingers. "Runaways. Kidnappings. Homicide. Getting lost. Death in some unwitnessed accident where no corpse shows up, like in a drowning. Amnesia victims, forget who they are, wander off. That one's much rarer, but it happens." He looked up. "Any others?"

Cody couldn't think of any others.

"In this case, we started off thinking accident, all the way. An accident mixed with the getting-lost variant, or even the amnesia possibility, which is why we checked all the hospitals. But we're a week out now, and what do we have? Zip. You can get lost in these woods, true, but for how long? They're really not that big, with plenty of trails, all eventually leading back to people."

"But what if she's injured—holed up somewhere, like you said before?"

"We looked. Found squat."

"So you're just giving up?"

"Didn't say that." Sergeant Orton picked up his cup, took a sip. "And not finding anything—at this stage, that's a good result."

"Meaning . . ." This was hard to say out loud. Cody tried

again. "Meaning there's a better chance she's still alive?"

Sergeant Orton nodded, a very slight nod; Cody hoped there was no significance in that slightness. "Also meaning we've got to open up the investigation, look into those other possibilities, starting with the most likely, namely runaway."

"What about kidnapping?" Cody said. "Clea's not a runaway."

"What makes you so sure?"

"She . . ." Cody paused, thought about it. "She has a life."

"What do you mean by that?"

Cody shrugged. "A good life. There's nothing to run away from."

"She into drugs?"

"No."

"What about sex?"

"What about it?"

"People sometimes go off the rails in that area."

"Clea's not off the rails in any area."

Sergeant Orton had his head tilted to one side, perhaps waiting for Cody to say more. Cody kept his mouth shut—Clea's sex life was none of the sergeant's business.

"A young woman sometimes runs off with an older man."

"Not Clea."

"How do you know?"

194

It was unimaginable. But Cody knew unimaginable wouldn't do for Sergeant Orton. He surprised himself by coming up with something else. "She'd never do it like that—leaving Bud by himself out in the woods."

Sergeant Orton sat back a little, as though struck by the force of his argument. But then he shook his head. "People can make bad decisions."

"She loves Bud," Cody said. "So that leaves kidnapping." He took another sip of coffee, found that his hand was suddenly unsteady.

"Want to talk kidnapping?" said the sergeant. "Okay. Basically three kinds—political, ransom, weirdo. Pretty safe to rule out political in this case, bringing us to ransom. Problem here is—no ransom demand. Who ever heard of a ransom kidnapping with no demand?"

"How do you know there's no demand?" Cody said, surprising himself again.

"What do you mean?"

"Ransom demands are for money, right? So the kidnapper would get in touch with Mr. Weston."

"And the very next minute he—or his wife, what with this hospitalization—is on the phone to me. I explained the importance of a quiet police presence in a ransom situation while Mr. Weston was here, and he agreed."

"Maybe he was lying."

"Any special reason for saying that?"

Cody shook his head.

Sergeant Orton watched him for a second or two, then went on. "If he was lying, he's a tricky customer, seeing as how he let us tap his phone."

"You tapped his phone?"

"Standard procedure—gives us a chance to trace the ransom call in real time."

That left weirdo. Sergeant Orton didn't speak the word. He drained his cup and said, "We've got a couple level-three sex offenders in the area—I visited with them on day one. Doesn't rule the idea out completely, of course. Last, there's homicide. Homicide can result from some of these others—kidnapping, for example. Also from an enemy. She have any enemies you know of?"

"Clea?" No way. But then Cody remembered the letter, still in his glove box. The word enemy didn't appear in it, but there was that part near the end. He went out to the car and got the letter.

Sergeant Orton put on a pair of glasses, suddenly didn't look like a cop, more just like any tired middle-aged guy. He read the letter—in silence until he came to that part near the end. "'One or two I don't like at all. It's hard to know who to trust sometimes. Like rolling the dice—a cliché that turns out to have real meaning.'" He glanced at Cody over the rims of his glasses. "What's that about?"

Cody had no idea.

The sergeant took off his glasses, gave him one of those visual probes, looking like a cop again. "Is she into gambling?"

"Gambling? Kids don't gamble. Not like that, where you'd get in trouble."

"No?" said the sergeant. His little eyes shifted, gazed at the steam rising from his coffee.

Cody remembered that Dickie van Slyke's older brother had gotten beaten up pretty bad after some kind of poker game. "It's just not her."

"People are full of surprises," Sergeant Orton said. "Can I keep this?" Cody hesitated. "You'll get it back."

"Okay."

"Or at least a copy," Sergeant Orton said. He pocketed the letter. "Know what a mole is?"

"An animal."

"What kind?"

"Burrowing."

"Exactly," said the sergeant. "Mole also means a spy, the burrowing kind. You're going to be my mole."

"Your mole?"

"Means you're going to work this job, get to know your way around here, keep your eyes and ears open."

"For what?"

"Information." Sergeant Orton tapped the side of his nose. "I've got a real strong feeling that whatever went bad started here."

"What kind of information?"

"You'll know. Anything comes up, you call me at this number." He handed Cody a card. "Other than that, no contact with me from this point on." Cody hesitated, trying to absorb everything he'd just heard, a hesitation the sergeant must have misinterpreted. "Course you can always say no," Sergeant Orton said. "In which case, I'll slap you with that assaulting-an-officer charge."

Cody's face heated up, right where the sergeant had slapped it. What was the word? Blackmail. The sergeant was blackmailing him. That pissed Cody off. Even worse was the fact that it was unnecessary. "You didn't have to say that," he said.

"Meaning you're a willing volunteer?" the sergeant said. "Hoped you might take that approach." He reached into his jacket, handed Cody a manila envelope. Cody looked inside, found his license plates. "Don't want to invite any annoying questions," the sergeant said. "I put Vermont plates on your car—the special Building Bright Futures ones, my personal

198

favorites." Sergeant Orton rose, gently touching his upper lip, swollen and turning blue. "Any questions?"

Cody had nothing but; the problem was they all got tangled together in his mind, ended up in a confused snarl. Clea was right: *Hard to know who to trust sometimes*.

"Almost forgot," the sergeant said, and gave Cody fifty bucks.

"What's this?"

"Got a fund for this kind of caper."

"A mole fund?" said Cody.

"You can call it that. And one other thing—no more of those expeditions into the woods, you and the horse."

But why not? Wasn't it still worth a try? Sergeant Orton seemed to be waiting for an answer. Cody made a slight movement of his head, perhaps readable as *okay*.

The sergeant left. Cody went out to his car, opened the trunk, tossed his Colorado plates inside. Then he knelt and examined the Building Bright Futures plates, saw, over to the left, a stick-figure illustration of a boy and a girl jumping for joy.

○ ○ ○

Ike walked into the tack room, a toothpick sticking from the side of his mouth. He came to the workbench, checked Cody's work, grunted. Cody could smell him: stale sweat, wood smoke, onions. Ike turned his bloodshot eyes on Cody. "I seen that cop, Orton, comin' the other way. Was he here?"

"Not that I saw," Cody said.

"One sneaky bastard," said Ike.

"Yeah?" said Cody. "Like how?"

Ike's forehead got all pinched. "How? Two-faced is how." Ike waved his finger, the nail blackened, at Cody. "He comes round here again, you keep your trap shut, want my advice."

"Keep my trap shut about what?" Cody said.

Ike's eyes narrowed. "You bein' a smartass?"

"No."

"Can't work with a smartass—tol' Mrs. McTeague once, tol' her a thousand times." He glanced at his watch. "Twelve thirty," he said. "Your lunchtime."

"It is?"

"No one said? Whole country's in the toilet."

"How long is lunchtime?"

"Today? Take an hour. Ain't nothin' goin' on, not with this snow and the search bein' deep-sixed."

Something about that strange expression, the search being deep-sixed, made him ask, "Are there any lakes in the woods?"

"Lakes? Nothin' you'd call a lake. Ponds, maybe."

"Did they get searched?"

"Makes no difference."

"What do you mean?"

"She ain't out there."

"I don't understand."

"I know these woods," Ike said. "World's leading expert. She ain't there, no way, nohow."

"Then where?"

"Why you askin' me?" Ike said. He checked his watch again. "Down to fifty-seven minutes on lunch. And counting."

"Blast off," he added a few seconds later, as Cody went out the door. Cody, in the car, passing the snowed-over tennis courts with the pattern of dark net posts, thought: *Weirdo.* A weirdo who knew the woods; more than that, knew she wasn't there. The mole was starting to burrow.

○ ○ ○

Fifty unexpected bucks in his pocket: Cody remembered the taste of that $10.95 burger and drove to the Rev. It was crowded inside—businesspeople, a big group of guys in snowmobile suits, a few Dover Academy students—all tables and barstools taken. Cody, standing just inside the door, spotted Larissa alone at a small round table by a potted plant. She was bent toward her laptop, her glossy hair sloping down in two wings over her face, but suddenly looked up, right at Cody, and waved him over.

"They called off the search?" she said as he sat down.

"Yeah," said Cody. "The snow."

"Called it off forever?"

"I don't know."

"Oh, God. This is so awful. And now her father's in a coma, back in Wyoming or wherever it is."

"Colorado," said Cody. "And how do you know about her father?"

"Someone said, I forget."

The Irish waitress came over, served Larissa coffee and a muffin. She smiled at Cody, recommended the special, broccoli quiche and a cup of chili. Cody had tasted broccoli once—never again—and hadn't heard of quiche. He ordered the burger again, with a Coke, but skipped the side of onion rings this time for fear of appearing uncouth in some way.

Larissa cut her muffin in quarters, picked at one of them. "I was just writing about you."

"About me?"

"I keep a diary," Larissa said. "It's part of working for the lit mag." She turned to the laptop, scrolled down. "'We sat on a bridge over a stream, drinking some kind of brandy Simon had brought from home. All that did was add a buzz to this helpless feeling. Then a kid from the town appeared, a big kid, lightly dressed as though he didn't feel the cold. He said his name was

202

Cody. It was one of those cases, unlike my own, where a name fits.'" Larissa stopped reading, looked up.

"My name fits and yours doesn't?" Cody said.

Larissa nodded.

Cody didn't get it. Hers didn't fit because Larissa wasn't a Chinese name? Could it be that simple? And his did fit because . . . ? Cody saw no way of asking for an explanation without appearing stupid, but found himself, for some reason, making a stupid joke. "I remind you of Buffalo Bill?"

Larissa laughed. "Exactly! A young Buffalo Bill, fresh out of the wild, wild West." Uh-oh. Did she know something? Cody was trying to think of some subtle way to reinforce his cover story when Larissa went on. "Oh, I know you're a townie— excuse me, a local—but at the lit mag trope trumps all. Hey! *Pas mal.*" She typed something on the laptop, so quickly her fingers were a blur.

Cody, a little lost, headed for more solid ground. "Alex said Clea sent in a poem."

"'Bending,'" Larissa said. "It's great."

He had a sudden thought. "Did she keep a diary too?"

"Not that I know of. The diary thing only applies to staff, not contributors." Her eyes opened wide. "Are you thinking there might be some . . . clue there?"

"Clue about what?"

"Whatever happened. Isn't it time we started coming up with new ideas? That's what Townes was saying last night. Maybe she didn't get lost in the woods at all, maybe she just took off for New York or someplace."

"Townes said that?"

Larissa nodded. "Look at the time." She closed her laptop.

"You think she's that kind of girl?" Cody said.

"She's new—no one really knew her that well."

"What about Townes? Weren't they going out?"

"Sort of."

"Sort of?"

"I don't know the details." She rose. "Have to get to class. Nice seeing you."

"Wait," said Cody. "I'd like to read the poem."

"You're interested in poetry?"

"Yeah," he said, praying there'd be no follow-up.

But follow-up came immediately. "Like what kind of poetry?"

"'Screw your courage to the sticking-place / And we'll not fail,'" Cody said. "For one example."

Larissa smiled, a huge glowing smile. "*Macbeth*," she said. "Numero uno, playwise." She regarded him in a whole new way. "Know where Baxter is? Come by at eight, ring for room thirty-one. I'll get you a copy."

The line was from *Macbeth*? Had he ever studied the play? Cody did have a few vague memories of *Romeo and Juliet*, like a long-ago dream.

○○○

Cody ate his lunch. The Rev emptied out, leaving only Cody, dipping the last few fries in a pool of ketchup, a round-faced man writing on a pad at a corner table, and the waitress, polishing the bar. The front door opened and a big guy in a long leather coat, almost floor length, walked in: a big guy Cody had seen before, with long lank hair and a bandito mustache. He scanned the room, his gaze passing over Cody and settling on the waitress, who had her back to him.

"Hey, Deirdre," he said.

The waitress turned, an abrupt movement that knocked a glass off the bar; it shattered on the floor. "Len," she said. "You startled me."

Len smiled. "Wouldn't want to do that, not in a million years," he said. "That boyfriend of yours around?"

Deirdre had very fair skin; Cody could see her face flush from all the way across the room. "It's Mick's day off," she said. "He went to Boston."

Len's smile vanished, just like that. "Any chance he's avoiding my company?"

"Oh, no," Deirdre said.

"Whew," said Len. "I consider him a pal, when all is said and done. My Irish buddy." Len laughed, loud and sudden, almost a bark. "Tell him the pipes, the pipes are calling." He looked very pleased with himself.

Deirdre's mouth opened, a round black O. Len turned, his gaze again passing over Cody—this time with the slightest pause—and walked out of the Rev. Over at the corner table the round-faced man watched him go.

Deirdre swept up the glass and disappeared through the kitchen door. Someone else came out and handed Cody his check.

EIGHTEEN

CODY WALKED ACROSS the Dover Academy campus. He could have been just another student, but he wasn't a student here or anywhere. A thin crescent moon, edges sharply defined, hung in the black sky. Looked at in a certain way, it could have been a rip in the darkness, an opening to somewhere else. Cody felt a sudden longing for home. He slowed down, stopped, leaned against a tree. She was no runaway; but then came the thought that he, looked at in a certain way, was a runaway himself. The notion to call his father, try to explain, patch things up, just touch base, passed through his mind. But how could that end well? He had to focus, do what he'd come here to do and nothing but. Was it remotely possible she was a runaway after all?

Cody took out his cell phone, pressed 11: Clea.

"Hi, this is Clea. I'm not here right now, but please leave a message and I'll get back to you."

Cody held tight to the phone. The message beep sounded. He didn't speak, just clicked off. *I'm not here right now.* But where? He had to focus, had to deal in facts. Here was an obvious one: Her cell phone still worked. What did that mean? He called again, left a message this time: "I'm here," he said. "Let me help."

Cody crossed the quad, stood in front of Baxter Hall, the big brick building with the yellow trim and yellow columns by the door. He heard a girl's voice on the other side. "I think the pizza guy's here." The door opened and a girl with some kind of green paste all over her face peered out. Her gaze went to his empty hands.

"Is Larissa around?" Cody said.

The girl looked him up and down, very quick. "One sec." She motioned him inside, turned, and climbed a broad carpeted staircase of a type Cody had seen in movies, and vanished around a corner at the top.

Cody found himself in a big entrance hall with a vase of flowers on a glass table, and on the table some newspapers— *The New York Times*, the *Wall Street Journal*, the *Boston Globe*. Against one wall stood rows of small wooden boxes, cubbyholes, each with a name tag. He found Clea Weston, middle of the third row, the box empty. Cody was feeling around in it, just to be sure, when he heard footsteps at the top of the stairs. He turned. Larissa was coming down the stairs, a sheet of paper in her hand. "Hi, Cody. Playing detective?"

"No, uh, I—" He moved away from the cubbyholes.

"Too late, anyway," Larissa said. "The police cleared out all her personal stuff a few days ago, computer and everything."

"And?"

"And what?"

"Did they find anything?"

"Evidently not," Larissa said. "Doesn't mean there was nothing to find, though—I don't have much confidence in their ability."

"How come?"

"I had a brief conversation with that sergeant the other day, down at the barn. Maybe he was just having an off day, IQ-wise." She took Cody's arm. "Let's go in the lounge."

Larissa led Cody through double doors and into a huge room with plushly furnished sitting areas and stone fireplaces at each end, fires burning in both. But only one other person in the whole place: Simon, sprawled on a distant couch, a scarf around his neck and a book propped on his chest.

"Guys and girls live in the same dorm?" Cody said.

Larissa shook her head. "They have to be out by nine on weekdays. Most of the junior and senior guys live in DeWitt."

"DeWitt?"

"Named after Townes's grandfather or great-grandfather or some even moldier old fart." She motioned him toward two leather easy chairs angled toward each other in a corner of the room, a footstool between them. Cody took one of the chairs; Larissa sat cross-legged on the footstool. She was barefoot, her toenails gleaming with some kind of pearly polish. "I just love this poem," she said, handing it to Cody. A typed poem, the lines somehow dense looking and hard to penetrate, the kind of thing that gave him trouble.

Bending
by Clea Weston

Water above, heavy and dead,
Black Rocks all around
and I down here holding my breath,
trophy kid come to this.
He swims to me in smiling bubbles
twisting between my legs and up my back and around
my neck.
"A little bending, nothing to fear my dear."
Oh, temptation!
Far above—is there air still, still air?—
I lose sight of your face through the wet burial layer
heavy and dead. Don't go.

"Well?" said Larissa. "What do you think?"

Cody didn't know what to think. It wasn't ignorance of any of the specific words that stood in his way—he knew every one, not usually the case in his experience with written material—but he couldn't have explained the poem at that moment, wouldn't have known where to begin. All he knew was that the sheet of paper was trembling slightly in his hands. He laid it on the footstool.

"'Trophy kid come to this,'" Larissa said. She shivered in an exaggerated way. "And that snake imagery, simply nailed by the Edenic allusion." Now she'd lost him completely. "My sister's on the lit mag at Princeton," Larissa said. "She showed it to the adviser, who just happens to be some famous poet. He—the famous poet—wants Clea to apply there."

"Where?" Cody said.

"Princeton. Are you even listening?"

Cody felt blood flowing into his face, embarrassed by the brainpower gulf between them. He remembered how Clea's dad was pushing for Harvard and blurted out, "What about Harvard?"

Larissa put a finger to her chin, looked thoughtful. "I would have said Clea's more Princeton than Harvard."

Cody realized he had nothing to say on this subject. They were just names to him, like Shangri-la. "Anyway," he said, "that's not the problem right now." Had he raised his voice on that last part? Larissa looked a little taken aback. "Can I keep this?" he said.

"Be my guest," Larissa said. Cody folded Clea's poem and stuck it in his pocket. Larissa was watching him. He met her gaze. "You think I'm unfeeling?"

"No."

"Because I'm not. I'm very upset about this. And you didn't even know—you don't even know her."

Cody came close to blowing his cover right there, blowing it with some hotheaded reply. Instead he took a deep breath and lowered his head. "Sorry," he said. He had to focus, be smart, keep things inside.

"It's all right," Larissa said. She flexed her bare feet; small beautiful feet, high arched and finely shaped. Cody tried to picture Clea's feet and found he couldn't; he felt sick in the pit of his stomach. "Did you notice she capitalized Black Rocks?" Larissa said. "That caught my attention, for some reason. Not for some reason—the English department here has a fetish for close textual analysis. Anyway, I Googled Black Rocks, and guess what?"

"What?"

She leaned forward. "There's a quarry by that name in the town Clea's from. Little Bend, by the way. What do you think of that?"

He was actually a bit ahead of Larissa on this. What he wanted to do now was get out of there, go somewhere quiet and really study the poem. *Be smart.* "Uh, maybe we shouldn't"—what was the expression?—"read too much into it."

Larissa nodded. "Let what's between the four corners of the page speak for itself?" she said.

"Something like that," Cody said.

"Two schools of thought," Larissa said, then raised her voice and called, "Right, Simon?"

He looked up from his distant spot. "What's that?"

"It's rude to shout from room to room," Larissa shouted, almost a bellow.

"We're in the same room," Simon called back, but he unfolded himself and came over, book under his arm. "As contiguous as it gets," he added. "Hi, Cody." He flopped in the vacant chair. "How's life on planet Earth?"

"I took a job," Cody said. "Working in the barn."

"The barn?" Simon said. "You don't mean the barn inhabited by Ike?"

"Yeah."

"Why would you do a thing like that?" Simon said, reaching into his pocket. "*Chocolat,* anyone?" He passed around small gilt-wrapped bars with foreign writing on the wrappers.

"I needed a job," Cody said.

"Ah," said Simon. "May I ask you something? Why don't you go to school?"

"I was wasting my time," Cody said, and felt the truth of the answer—with the exception of the football part—as he spoke. In fact, that little sentence tolled like a bell in his mind, sending some message about a whole different way for him to look at things, even to live.

"Touché," said Larissa.

Simon clutched his shoulder, as though wounded. Larissa laughed. Then they sat in silence for a few moments, eating Simon's chocolate. Cody had never tasted anything like it. Great chocolate, no question. He kept himself from asking the cost. *Focus.* "What do you know about Ike?" he said.

"He creeps me out," Larissa said.

"Townes likes him," said Simon.

"He does?" said Larissa.

"Thinks he's funny," Simon said.

"Yeah?" said Cody. "How?"

Simon shrugged. "The humorous resists construing like nothing else, as we well know here at Dover. It either is or is not."

"How about an example?" Cody said, only partly sure of Simon's point. "Of Ike being funny."

"Yes," said Larissa. "Because he looks like an ax murderer to me."

Silence fell again, but not like the chocolate-eating silence.

This was the stunned kind of silence that follows a sudden explosion.

"My oh my," said Simon. He rose. "Catullus awaits."

"Who's he?" said Larissa.

"Merely the poet responsible for *nam inista preualet nihil tacere*," Simon said. "Freely translated as 'It's pointless to hide your debauchery.' See what you miss by not taking Latin?"

"Nothing," said Larissa. "My debauchery's right out there."

Simon laughed, an awkward, high-pitched laugh accompanied by blushing. "Why don't you come with me, Cody?" he said. "We'll ask Townes for an example of Ike's hilarity."

"I'll have another one of those chocolates before you go," said Larissa.

Cody and Simon walked across the quad, headed toward a dorm that looked bigger than Baxter, stone instead of brick. That sliver moon still hung in the sky, still spreading unease, at least in Cody's mind.

"That's DeWitt?" he said.

"My home away from home," said Simon, and then, after a pause, "In fact, my home."

"It's named after Townes's family?"

"So goes the tale. Dates back to 1902, I believe."

"They've been rich for a long time."

"They certainly were rich," Simon said. "Rich beyond all reason. As for the present, that's another story."

"What do you mean?"

"No telling tales out of school. Or in school, as the case may be. But a quick Internet search of Pegasus Partners might be revealing."

"What's Pegasus Partners?"

"Not just another hedge fund."

Hedge fund: Cody was vaguely aware of the expression, had no idea what it meant. A question—a strange one for him— formed in his mind. "And what about your family—are you rich within reasonable limits?"

Simon burst out laughing, looked for a moment as though about to pat Cody on the arm. "Afraid not," he said. "My father has this unreasonable gift."

"What gift?"

"For making money—his only real ability. He says wealth never stops circulating, and all you have to do is tap into the flow, like a maple sugar farmer."

"But what does he do?" Cody said.

"I just told you," said Simon. He took out a magnetic card, swiped it through a slot by the heavy wooden doors of DeWitt Hall. "Sorry," he said, "if that sounded rude."

"No problem," Cody said, and asked another question, a question that had been bothering him in a shapeless sort of way and now suddenly took form. "How did they get started together, Clea and Townes?"

Simon paused, the door half open. "That's an odd question," he said. "You're the second person to ask me."

"Who was the first?"

"That cop—Morton or Orton or whatever."

"And what's the answer?"

"What I told him is that I had no idea."

"And me?"

"What I'll tell you," said Simon, his voice softening and deepening a little on *you*, "is that intergender romance is not the specialty of the house."

"Oh," said Cody.

"Enter," Simon said.

Cody hung back, let Simon go in first.

○ ○ ○

Townes's room was on the first floor, at the end of a long corridor. The doors all bore small whiteboards for leaving messages, and sometimes a picture as well, photos of sports stars or musicians. Townes had a photo of himself on a big black horse Cody had seen in one of the stalls; a note on his message board read: *dropped by—c u @ barn.* Must have been an old message: Cody recognized Clea's writing. It knocked him a little off-balance.

Simon rapped on the door.

"Who is it?" came Townes's voice from inside.

"Me," said Simon.

"Unlocked."

Simon opened the door. Townes was at his desk; the computer screen displayed some sort of card game. Townes looked up, saw Cody, raised his eyebrows. The screen went blank.

"Cody here's taken a job at the barn," Simon said.

"The barn?"

"He's got a question for you."

Townes rose. "What kind of question?"

Cody said nothing. Simon answered for him; Cody liked having him for a spokesman. "It's about Ike and his alleged sense of humor. Cody wants an example."

"You're working at the barn?" Townes said. "Why?"

"Why?" said Simon. "He needed a job is why—it happens in the real world."

"The real world, Simon?" Townes came out from behind his desk. Simon licked his lips, surprised Cody by finding nothing to say. "Here's an example of Ike humor," said Townes. "He was eating a peanut butter sandwich and one of his teeth came out—you've seen his teeth. He dug around in his mouth for

218

the tooth, licked it clean, and said, 'Thank God I got a witness. Now I can sue the pants off Skippy.'"

No one laughed. "Maybe he was serious," Simon said.

"Of course he was serious," Townes said. "That's what makes it funny." His gaze went to Cody. "Anything else? I've got work to do."

Anything else? For sure, but hard to put into words—and not now. He had to think. Cody noticed a big poster on the wall, labeled POISONOUS SNAKES OF THE WESTERN DESERT. Did *Edenic allusion* mean something about the Garden of Eden?

He and Simon backed out of the room and closed the door. In a sneaky way that should have made him feel ashamed but didn't, Cody rubbed his shoulder on the whiteboard, obliterating Clea's message.

NINETEEN

CODY AWOKE IN THE NIGHT, his first night in the cabin near the barn. Through the window he saw the thin crescent moon, now low in the sky, about to disappear behind the treetops. He switched on the bedside light, reread Clea's poem, "Bending," for the hundredth time. Was the bubbling snakelike thing Townes, and the face above his own? Or was it the other way around? Or was the explanation something else completely? He had the crazy idea that if he heard Ms. Brennan reciting it in her scratchy old voice, the meaning would be clear. Cody switched off the light and closed his eyes.

But he couldn't get back to sleep. For one thing, he couldn't find a comfortable position for his knee. His knee was getting better all the time—he no longer got the feeling it could come apart again at any moment—but it still swelled up and felt sore in the night. For another, the walls of the cabin were thin, and once or twice he heard Ike groaning in his sleep, somewhere down below. Most of all, he couldn't help going back to the moment when Bud reared up on the trail. Was it because he sensed Sergeant Orton hiding nearby, or because whatever had happened to Clea had happened close by, and Bud remembered? Cody went back and forth on that, tossing and turning in his tiny room, then recalled the new attitude he was taking to wasted time.

He rose. Time was passing and Clea was out there somewhere; and even—he tried to face the possibility—even if the worst had happened, then what difference did that make? He still owed her his best. Cody got dressed—his sneakers, left by the woodstove, were nice and warm—grabbed the keys to the barn, and left his room, descending the stairs very quietly, pulling the outer door closed behind him with just the tiniest click of the latch.

He walked to the barn, sneakers squeaking a bit on the packed-down snow of the path. The sky was dark but not black; the only true blackness to be seen was the mountains, looming all around. Cody went to the small side door that led to the tack room and stuck the key in the lock. What was this? The door swung right open, meaning Ike hadn't locked it, hadn't even closed it properly. Cody reached around on the inside wall, switched on the light; and saw at a glance that he'd been too quick in blaming Ike. He'd locked the door all right—Cody could tell from the bolt, set in the sticking-out position. The problem was that someone had knocked the whole brass lock right off its screws, splintering the doorjamb at the same time. Cody froze, listened hard. He heard nothing.

A flashlight hung on a hook just inside the door, a big, hefty one. Cody reached for it, at the same time switching off the overhead light. He let his eyes adjust to the darkness, and the layout of the tack room slowly took shape, dimmed way down. Ahead he saw a big fuzzy rectangle, the entrance to the main part of the barn. He moved to it, his sneakers now silent on the smooth old floorboards; silence to hear, dimness to see, and horse smell, dominating the other senses.

Cody left the tack room, walked between the two rows of stalls. Weak pinkish light glowed from the exit signs at both ends of the barn, got reflected in the eyes of the horses. They were all on their feet. Cody knew that horses slept on their feet; did they also sleep open eyed? He didn't think they were asleep, not from the way all those eyes seemed to be watching him. He felt their alertness; something about the feeling made him switch on the flashlight. Cody quickly aimed the beam into all the dark corners, spotting no one, nor any sign of disorder. He kept moving, toward Bud's stall.

Horses slept standing up, but not Bud. Cody told himself he should have known: Bud had his own ways. Cody looked over the double swinging doors of the stall, panned the beam around, saw Bud lying in the straw. Lying down and eyes open; at least, the eye that Cody could see.

"Hey, Bud," he said, very softly. No reaction: that would be Bud, totally zonked out. Cody moved on, shining the beam into all the corners, probing every shadow, satisfying himself that there was no one else in the barn.

He returned to Bud's stall, bothered by some impression, faint and fleeting, in his mind. What was it? He shone the light into the stall. Yes, that was it, the awkward way Bud had one of his back legs bent up underneath him. "Hey, Bud." Bud didn't stir, also didn't seem to mind the light in his eye, an eye that in sleep didn't look as liquid as usual, actually more dusty. "Bud, wake up." Cody panned the beam around. What was this, in the straw by Bud's head? A little wet pool? Wet and red? Cody flung open the stall doors. From behind came a voice.

"What the hell's goin' on?"

Cody whirled around. At that moment, the overhead lights flashed on, and he saw Ike coming toward him, Ike in pajamas, boots, and his ridiculous plaid hat; and also with that whittling knife in his hand. Cody backed into the stall, his feet bumping into Bud. There was nowhere to go.

Ike kept coming, bowlegged and fast. "I said what the hell's goin' on?"

"Did you hurt Bud?" Cody said.

"Somethin's wrong with the horse?" Ike said, pulling up.

"I think so."

Ike came closer. "What did you do?" he said.

"Nothing," Cody said. "Someone kicked in the tack room door—didn't you see that?" And that meant—Cody suddenly putting facts together in a way he wasn't used to—that Ike hadn't hurt Bud. Why would Ike kick in the door? He had a key.

Ike shook his head, his mouth falling open slightly.

"And I've got a key," Cody said.

Ike nodded slowly, and slowly lowered the knife. Cody moved aside. Ike saw Bud, dropped the knife, and fell to his knees. He dipped a finger in the red pool and tasted it. Then, very gently, he raised Bud's head and turned it a little. Cody knelt beside him. There was no missing the round hole, ragged at the edges, just behind Bud's ear.

"Someone shot him?" Cody said.

Ike didn't answer. He wrapped his arms around Bud's neck and held him close. Tears streamed down Ike's ugly face, dripped on that diamond-shaped blaze. Cody shifted around and patted Ike on the shoulder. He spotted a shell casing lying in the straw.

○ ○ ○

An hour later there were lots of people in the barn: Sergeant Orton and some other cops; a vet; Mrs. McTeague; the head-master of Dover Academy, whose name Cody didn't catch, and whom the sergeant addressed as "sir" the only time they spoke. That was when the headmaster asked if Bud might have been killed by a stray bullet, fired by some drunken hunter out in the night, for some reason, and Sergeant Orton said, "No, sir." He held up the shell casing. "Revolver or semiautomatic pistol's what fired this." The headmaster spread his hands as if to say *So?* "Hunters don't use handguns," the sergeant said, "drunk or not, sir."

"I simply don't want any unnecessary panic," the head-master said. "The student body is quite shaken as it is. Rumor spreads so quickly, sergeant. Once the parents get wind of this new—" His cell phone rang, and he moved away to take the call.

The cops snapped pictures. An animal ambulance drove into the barn and the ambulance workers, plus Cody and Ike, got Bud—so heavy—onto a big stretcher, and lifted him inside. After that, Sergeant Orton took Ike into the tack room and had a long talk. Soon Cody was alone with the headmaster in the main part of the barn.

"Sorry," the headmaster said. "I don't know your name."

Cody told him.

"How long have you been working for us?"

"Just started."

"Terrible," said the headmaster. "Terrible. I understand you heard a noise and came to investigate?"

Cody nodded.

"Was it the gunshot?"

"I'm not sure."

The headmaster glanced at the empty stall, then at Cody. "How old are you, Cody?"

"Almost seventeen."

The headmaster's eyebrows—wild and bushy, although the rest of him was perfectly groomed—rose. "You look older." He took a deep breath. "Thank you for all your help. We'll get through this."

Cody didn't say anything. Getting through this wasn't what he wanted. He wanted to find Clea; and also now find whoever had shot Bud. At that moment Sergeant Orton poked his head out of the tack room and called, "Cody?"

The headmaster held out his hand. Cody didn't know why this was a handshaking occasion, but he did the expected.

Sergeant Orton was alone in the tack room, no sign of Ike. "Take a seat." Cody sat on a stool. The sergeant leaned against the workbench, big dark smudges under his eyes. He gave Cody a long look. "I learn more and more about your abilities all the time." Cody kept his mouth shut. "Now it turns out my mole has sharp hearing, sharp enough to hear, what? The break-in or the shot, from all the way over in that cabin, probably a quarter mile from here. Or was that just a little mole story, to protect your cover?"

Cody nodded.

"Ever think about a career in law enforcement?"

"Hell, no," said Cody.

Sergeant Orton frowned, possibly insulted. "So what little scheme brought you out here in the middle of the night? And I don't want to hear you were planning another test of Bud's memory."

Cody gazed back at the sergeant, defiant.

The sergeant gazed right back, small red blotches appearing on his face. "You're persistent, if nothing else."

Cody didn't like that. He was tired of getting talked down to. "What does it matter, anyway, what I was doing? What matters is who shot Bud and why."

"You telling me how to do my job?"

Why shouldn't I? You're not getting it done. Cody kept that to himself but couldn't contain his anger completely, and ended up again looking Sergeant Orton right in the eye, a look he kept up until—surprise—the sergeant dropped his gaze. Cody pressed on. "Somebody didn't want me and Bud searching for Clea." And if that was true, then whole idea of the search was a good one, might even have succeeded.

"Very goddamn persistent," said the sergeant. He seemed to think for a moment. "But I don't buy it. This looks more like sending a message."

"A message to who?" Cody said.

"Have to figure that out, won't I?" the sergeant said, his voice rising in impatience. He rubbed his eyes and went on in a more normal tone. "Meanwhile we'll get cracking on ballistics, see what kind of gun we're looking for." He pushed himself away from the workbench with a tired little sound. "Get some sleep."

Cody stayed where he was. "What's the message?"

"We'll work on that, too."

"But it has to be about Clea, right? This can't be a coincidence."

"Don't jump to conclusions," the sergeant said.

● ● ●

Fifteen minutes later, Cody was back in bed, as tired as he'd ever been in his life. But his eyes wouldn't stay closed. The big muscles of his back and down his legs still seemed to be feeling Bud's heavy dead weight on the stretcher. The enormous waste of such a beautiful living thing: Cody couldn't stop thinking about that. Don't jump to conclusions, Sergeant Orton had said. Did that mean they had to walk to conclusions, creep to them, inch to them? How did that make sense? Time was running out, if it hadn't run out already. Sergeant Orton had it backward: Jumping to conclusions was the only way.

Cody sat up in bed. The night was quiet again, as though nothing had happened. He rose, again got dressed, again went quietly down the stairs, again closed the door softly behind him; but this time he really didn't care whether Ike heard him or not. He took the snow shovel leaning by the door and followed the path to the barn, planning to get the flashlight, but suddenly realized he was seeing things quite well; and glanced up to see faint light in the east, like milk seeping into the night sky. Cody turned, walked past the riding ring and onto the loop trail, the shovel over his shoulder.

The sky was pale blue by the time Cody reached the Upper Mountain Crossover, the air clear and cold. He found the spot where Bud had reared up—one particular hoofprint had frozen perfectly in the snow, every detail sharp. What had spooked Bud: some memory of Clea, or the hidden presence of Sergeant Orton?

Cody started digging. He dug up the snow where the two trails met, then the snow under and around the big spruce tree where the sergeant had hidden with his snowmobile. After that he dug around all the nearby trees and up the crossover trail, working quickly, flinging snow, baring the ground, finding nothing.

"Goddamn it," he said, or maybe shouted, but the woods muffled the sound, seemed to take the fight out of it. Warm now, except for his hands and feet, Cody leaned on the shovel, sweat dripping off the tip of his nose. Bud had sensed Sergeant Orton hiding behind the tree. Cody knew he had to accept that obvious explanation. He also knew he didn't want to go back to the barn. A feeble thought came to him: Maybe in this clear early-morning light he'd spot something he—and everyone else—had missed before. He slung the shovel over his shoulder and started up the crossover trail.

Cody walked, long past the point when the warmth from shoveling had worn off. He alternated hands to keep them warm, one on the shovel, one in his pocket. Buying himself gloves, and maybe a hat? Why hadn't he done that? He laughed at himself, laughed out loud. Other than that one gloves-and-hat thought, his mind was empty. He came to the warming hut without having spotted anything new, anything that didn't belong in the winter woods.

Cody entered the warming hut. Everything the same as before: potbelly woodstove, table, chairs, bench, stool, split wood in the corner, notice on the wall:

A little heat would be nice. Cody picked up a split log, opened the feed door, where last time he'd found the empty Bud Light bottle, the one he'd tossed to Townes. *Should have fired it at his fuckin' head,* Cody thought, glancing over to where the smashed glass had lain by the wall. Someone had swept it up.

Cody lit a fire. The woodstove heated up quickly. He held his hands over it, warmed them. He had a crazy thought: he and Clea in a hut like this, just the two of them; the two of them and time, not endless amounts of it, just a chance to be together. *Clea, where are you?* As he'd done so uselessly before, he took out his cell phone and dialed 11. Like all the other times, it rang and then came her voice. "Hi, this is Clea. I'm not—"

But what was that? Had he heard something else? Cody clicked off, dialed again. And again heard the ring of Clea's phone, except not just that: Somewhere, faint but near, an actual phone was ringing, a ring tone he recognized, like that of an old-fashioned phone. "Hi, this is Clea. I—"

Cody clicked off, dialed again, again heard that ring tone— and followed the sound to the woodpile. He swept the logs aside—they flew across the hut like twigs—and there, at the bottom, lay a little red cell phone he knew well. Cody picked it up, held it carefully in both hands.

TWENTY

CODY OPENED CLEA'S CELL PHONE. Evidence, solid red evidence. Clea had been here in the warming hut. Had she ridden Bud all this way, sometimes pretty steep and rough? Cody didn't remember any hoofprints on his first search on the crossover trail. And wait: Why was he assuming Clea's presence in the hut? Her cell phone was here: That was the only indisputable fact.

He turned the cell phone over in his hands, saw nothing unusual. Some hiker would have discovered it eventually, when the woodpile was getting low. Or maybe before that. The cell phone could have been found already, saving so much time, if only someone had been in the cabin when Cody had made one of his calls. He took a guess at her PIN, entering B-U-D; and got into her voicemail on the first try. He checked the messages.

Beep. "Hello, Clea, it's Dad. The answer to your question is that the contents of your trust fund will be transferred to you in three stages, starting at age twenty-one. Why do you ask? Give me a call."

Beep.

"Hey, it's Alex. Drop by after riding—my mom sent a care package. I think I can promise jujubes galore."

Beep.

"Pick up, goddamn it. We need to talk." That was Townes.

Beep.

"It's me. I—are you all right? You're in the paper but I just can't believe . . . Call if you—when you get this. I hope everything's . . ."

Beep.

"Clea, I'm on my way."

Beep.

Beep.

"I'm here. Let me help."

Beep. No more messages. Cody listened to them all three times. He had the phone, the first real evidence, but somehow Clea seemed farther away than before. He walked around the

233

warming hut, checking places already checked, trying to piece together some kind of story, a story that would explain how Clea's cell phone ended up down at the bottom of that woodpile. A crazy notion entered his mind: If he could find the answer to that question, he would also learn everything that had happened before and after, the whole chain of events. But, standing by a frost-covered window, staring at nothing, Cody got nowhere. Did he have to be so slow?

Cody gazed down at the phone; he liked the feel of it in his hand. About to listen to the messages yet once more, he was struck by another idea: photos. Clea wasn't one of those kids who snapped cell-phone photos of every little life moment, but he had a memory of her taking at least one, a picture of Junior at someone's party.

Cody went to Clea's menu, clicked on pictures. There were nine. The very first one was that party, a party that had taken place, Cody now remembered, at Dickie van Slyke's on a night his parents were out. Junior had a big grin on his face and a keg of beer on each shoulder.

Picture number 2: Bud, looking vacant.

Number 3: Clea offering Bud a sugar cube. She was laughing, looked totally happy. Cody remembered taking that one himself, but couldn't remember what he'd said to make her laugh.

Number 4: The stone gates in front of the main road leading onto the campus—Dover Academy, 1886. Sky blue, trees green, a few kids wearing shorts in the background; had Clea snapped this one the day she arrived?

Number 5: Alex, Larissa, and Townes, arms around each other and smiling; something, maybe a bit of popcorn, was caught in Alex's braces; everyone looked happy.

Number 6: Townes on his horse.

Number 7: Townes and Clea on Townes's horse, Clea behind him, arms around his waist, both of them smiling.

Number 8: Townes sitting at a bar, watching a football game on a big-screen TV. He had a cocktail glass in his hand and an intense expression on his face, maybe even anxious.

Number 9: An extreme close-up of a wrist—a man's wrist—and the base of the palm of his hand. The angle was weird, as if the picture had been taken from a strange sideways position. One other thing: There seemed to be a tattoo on the inside of the man's wrist. Cody was squinting at the screen, trying to identify the tattoo, when the battery died. Kind of amazing it had lasted this long, but Clea's phone was top of the line, with a power-saver mode feature, and also had been lying under the woodpile, closed and unused; and maybe luck was involved, too. Cody hoped so: He knew from football what luck could do—although Coach Huff hated luck, good and bad, and allowed no mention of it. Cody flipped open his own cell phone, took Sergeant Orton's card from his pocket, and called the number written on it.

○●○

"What's that look like to you, Vin?" said Sergeant Orton.

They sat in a trailer behind the North Dover police station—Cody, the sergeant, and Vin, the tech guy. Vin peered at the screen on Clea's cell phone, now charged and running again. "Tattoo, sarge. Tattoo of some kind."

The sergeant gave Vin an impatient glance that Vin missed but Cody caught. "Any possibility of blowing it up on a big screen?"

"Nice idea," said Vin, and less than a minute later he had the wrist photo displayed on a big screen. "Looks like a fish," Vin said.

"Maybe one of those dolphins," said the sergeant.

"It's a shark," Cody said.

The two men had another look. "Yeah," said Vin. "A shark, but kinda crude."

"Prison work," Sergeant Orton said. "See how that's his left wrist? Most likely did it to himself." They gazed at the shark tattoo. "Vin," said the sergeant. "Send an e-mail to all staff, anybody come across some ex-con with a shark tattoo."

Vin turned to a keyboard, muttered along as he typed,

"Any-body come a-cross some ex . . ." His voice trailed off.

"So it's a kidnapping?" Cody said.

"Can't say," said the sergeant. "All we got for sure is the phone in that hut, and this picture."

"The last picture," Cody said. Sergeant Orton had no reply. Cody stared at the screen, memorizing every detail of that wrist—strong and thick, with a bulging vein—and of the shark tattoo.

A uniformed cop entered, handed the sergeant a sheet of paper. "Transcripts, sarge," he said.

The sergeant ran his eyes over the page, then turned to Cody. "Hungry?" he said.

"Not really."

"I am," said the sergeant. "You can watch me eat." He rose. "And when you're done, Vin, start checking inmate descriptions in the databases of all the state prisons for, I don't know, past five years."

"For an itty-bitty tattoo like that?" said Vin. "I've seen them screw up on missing limbs."

The uniformed cop laughed. "Missing out on missing limbs," he said. "That's a good one." Sergeant Orton gave him a look and his mouth closed. Vin's fingers moved to the keyboard.

Sergeant Orton, wearing street clothes—he looked smaller out of uniform—drove Cody in an unmarked car to a dough-nut shop just over the town line and went inside. He came back with coffee and a bag of pastries—cheese Danishes, crullers, bear claws. Cody bit into a Danish, found he was hungry after all.

"Try those bear claws," said Sergeant Orton, mouth full.

Cody tried a bear claw: delicious.

"Best bear claws in the state," said Sergeant Orton. He sipped his coffee, wiped his mustache on his sleeve. "Any bear claws where you come from?"

"No," Cody said. "But I had one in San Diego."

"When was this?"

"Long time ago."

"Your family travel much?"

"No."

"Got any brothers or sisters?"

"No."

The sergeant reached into the bag for a cruller. "So it's just the two of you? You and your pop?"

Cody nodded.

"What happened to your mom?"

Cody stopped eating. "She died."

"How?"

"Cancer." The bear claw was getting sticky in his hands but he didn't want it anymore. "Shouldn't we be doing something right now?"

"Like what?"

"Looking for Clea," Cody said. "With this new evidence."

"Crime scene's out at the warming hut as we speak," the sergeant said. "And we're working on the tattoo, as you know. Not much you and I can do." He paused—was he giving Cody a chance to talk about his family? Cody thought so. He said nothing. "Suppose we could go over the transcript," Sergeant Orton said at last. He took the paper from his pocket, put on his glasses, cleared his throat. "'Contents of your trust fund.' Any idea what kind of money we're talking about?"

"I don't know about any trust fund." Cody didn't even know exactly what a trust fund was.

"She never mentioned it?"

"No. Clea's a normal kid."

"What do you mean?"

Cody shrugged.

Sergeant Orton turned to him, his voice sharpening. "I need you to do better than that."

A little jet of anger spurted inside Cody and he almost said Tough shit. He decided at that moment, once and for all, that Sergeant Orton was nothing but a user, never to be trusted.

But was there any way of getting Clea back without his help? Cody forced himself to find words, the right ones.

"You wouldn't know she's rich," he said. "Not from her herself."

"But from her house, her parents, things like that?"

"Yeah."

"Fran is actually the stepmom?"

"Yeah."

"Where's the mom?"

"She died a few years ago."

"How?"

"A skiing accident," Cody said. "In Switzerland, I think."

"Interesting," said the sergeant.

"Huh?"

"The similarity and all—what with your own mom."

Cody set his coffee cup on the floor; he wanted his hands free. "So?"

"Just filling in the blanks."

Cody sat back, folded his arms across his chest. His mom's death was nobody's blank. The sergeant went back to the transcript. After a while Cody picked up his cup, drained what was left.

"I put in a call to Mr. Weston, of course—about this trust fund," Sergeant Orton said. "He's still in a coma." The sergeant tapped the transcript sheet with his finger. "The question is—why was she asking about it in the first place?"

Cody shrugged.

"She into drugs?"

"I already answered that."

"Does she owe anyone money?"

"Why would she borrow? She always has enough."

The sergeant folded the transcript, stuck it back in his pocket. "How'd you feel about that?"

"About what?"

"Her always having enough and you not."

"I always had enough too," Cody said.

The sergeant turned to him, seemed about to say something, but then his police radio crackled. He took it off his belt, pressed a button. "Yup."

"Sarge?"

"Yup."

"Got a preliminary out of ballistics. We're lookin' at a thirty-eight."

"Start checking permits."

"Already on it."

Sergeant Orton clicked off, turned to Cody. "One little thing. These—don't want to call them breaks in the case, let's just say developments—"

"The phone and the ballistics?"

The sergeant nodded. "We keep that news to ourselves for now."

"Meaning you think whoever we're looking for is close by?"

Sergeant Orton closed his eyes in a strange kind of way, longer than a blink; almost like a little kid who didn't want to see what was happening, if that made sense, and how could it? "Didn't say that," said the sergeant.

●●●

Back in the barn, Cody found Ike on his hands and knees in Bud's stall, scrubbing the floor with a stiff brush. "Otherwise," he said, looking up, "they'll pick up the smell of blood, spook 'em forever."

"The other horses?"

"Who else? Can you smell blood? Gotta take care of the horses."

Cody glanced at the horses. They didn't seem spooked, anxious, or even attentive; all of them just standing in their stalls, doing nothing except twitching their tails or shifting around. Cody walked over to Townes's horse.

"This one Midnight?"

Ike rose, picked up his bucket. "Yeah. Champion of the barn."

Midnight was big and black, with a shining coat and a glossy mane. "How much would a horse like this cost?"

Ike came over, stood beside Cody. "More'n you or me can afford, tell you that."

"Just out of curiosity."

"Ten grand. Maybe thirty."

Cody took a quick sideways look at Ike, trying to see if Ike was ragging on him or something. No sign of that; maybe Ike had even less feel for math than he did. But at that moment Ike surprised him. "We could look up the exact figure, we had a mind to."

"Yeah?"

"Just so happens Midnight got sold not so long ago."

"Townes doesn't own him anymore?"

"What I just tol' you," Ike said. "Don't believe me, I can prove it—show you the books."

"I believe you," Cody said. "But I'd like to see the books."

"Curiosity killed the fuckin' cat—you don't know that one?"

"I never believed it."

Ike gazed at him. "Maybe you're right." He checked his watch. "Slow day, what with the snow. We can spare a minute or two."

They went into the office, a small space off the tack room. Ike sat behind the desk, took a big leather-bound book from a drawer, licked his finger, paged through. "Here we go," he said, turning the book so Cody could see.

He studied a page labeled INVENTORY, all the writing in

blue ink, small and neat. There were two columns, on the left the names of the horses, with a brief description—Bud, for example: "chestnut gelding, age 9"; on the right, names of the owners: "Mr. Win Weston, Little Bend, CO." The horses were listed in alphabetical order. Cody ran his eyes down to Midnight. "Black stallion, age 13." And in the right-hand column, "Townes DeWitt, Dover Academy." Under that, another notation, dated three weeks before: "Papers transferred to LB Corp., North Dover."

"It doesn't say the price."

Ike turned the book, moved his finger on the line, followed it with his eyes, lips moving. "No, it don't. But ten grand at least, take my word for it."

"What's LB Corp.?"

Ike shrugged. "Some business deal." Ike closed the book and put it away.

LB Corp. Cody had a flash of inspiration, maybe the first of his life, a three-part inspiration, kind of complicated, but it made sense. One: LB stood for Little Bend. Two: Something had gotten Clea interested in her trust fund. Three: LB Corp. had to be some—what was the expression? holding company?—belonging to the Westons, set up in North Dover for some reason, the important point being that Clea, or Mr. Weston, or both of them, now owned Midnight. But why?

TWENTY-ONE

NO RANSOM DEMAND, but all of a sudden money was in the picture. Why had Clea been asking about her trust fund? Did it have something to do with buying Midnight? How could her interest in the trust fund relate to any kind of ransom? That would put things in the wrong order: The kidnapping had to come first.

Cody sat in the office at the barn, trying to organize everything he knew on a sheet of paper. He was alone; Ike had driven off to the feed store, would be gone for a stretch, as he'd put it. For the first time in his life, Cody made lists, drew connecting arrows between this and that. He got nowhere. He couldn't escape the feeling that no more facts were needed, just more brainpower. After a while he crumpled up the sheet of paper, tossed it in the wastebasket.

Cody walked into the main part of the barn, past Bud's empty stall, stopped in front of Midnight. Midnight, so tall, gazed down at him, nostrils widening. Cody reached out to pat his face. Midnight turned his head, shied away.

Cody returned to the office, took out the ledger, checked that inventory page again. Midnight: Formerly owned by Townes DeWitt, now owned by LB Corp. Why would Clea want to buy Midnight? She already—at least back then, three weeks ago—had a horse, a horse she loved. Cody gazed at the inventory page for a long time before it occurred to him to flip the Midnight question around: Why would Townes want to sell him?

On a blank sheet of paper, Cody wrote:

Reasons for selling M:
1. T was buying a new horse.
2. Wanted C to have M.
3. Got tired of M.
4. Needed the $.

Any more? Not that Cody could think of, and even this brief list seemed padded. Townes needing money, for example, the kind of money Midnight was worth, up to $30,000, according to Ike: What sense did that make? He almost stroked it off the list, but while his pen hovered over the page, he realized that checking out number one wouldn't be hard. A bunch of phone numbers, including Ike's cell, were written on a chalkboard over the desk.

"Ike? It's Cody."

"Somethin' wrong?"

"No."

"Then what're you callin' me on my cell for? It's roamin'."

"Just a quick question—has Townes bought a new horse, or is he planning to?"

"Think you're talkin' to a mind reader? Who knows who's plannin' what?"

"Did he buy a new horse, then?"

"Why'd anybody want to do that?"

"I don't understand."

"Season's over till spring—you'd just be payin' stable fees for no reason. And this is costin' me." *Click.*

Cody crossed number one off his list.

2. Wanted C to have M.

Cody went through the desk drawers, found a Dover Academy student directory. No Alexes listed, but there were three Alexandras, one of them from Boston: Alexandra O'Rourke.

Cody dialed her number. She answered on the first ring.

"Cody?" she said. "I was just going to call you. Is it true—someone poisoned Clea's horse?"

"Shot him."

"To death?"

"Yeah."

"Oh my God—why would anyone want to do that?"

"I don't know," Cody said.

"This is horrible."

"Yeah. Maybe you could help me out with something—did Clea ever say anything about Midnight?"

"Townes's horse?"

"Yeah."

"Not much—just that he's a great horse, that kind of thing—why? Jesus, did he get shot, too?" Alex's voice rose a little; Cody heard real fear.

"No, nothing like that. He's fine."

"Are you at the barn?"

"Yeah."

"Alone?"

"Yeah."

"Is that safe?"

"Why wouldn't it be?"

"Because something bad is going on—there's already talk

of parents coming to get their kids until . . . until whatever's going on stops."

"Seems a little over the top," Cody said.

"It does?" Maybe it was his imagination, but Cody thought he heard less fear in her tone, as though he'd calmed her in some way; a pretty unlikely notion.

"Yeah," said Cody. "That's all Clea said about Midnight, that he was a great horse?"

"What else would she be saying?"

"Nothing about wanting him?"

"Why would she want him? She loves—loved—Bud."

Cody stroked number two off the list. *3: Got tired of M.*

"Got to go to class," Alex was saying. "You around later?"

"Around where?"

"How about the Rev? Five or so?"

Through the window, Cody saw Ike drive into the parking lot. "See you then," he said. He fetched the wheelbarrow, went out to help Ike with the feed.

"You're not a bad worker," Ike said when they were done with unloading and had walked the horses. "Ask too many questions, is all."

"Here's one more," said Cody, guiding the last horse— Dusty, a little brown mare, very gentle, already one of his favorites—into her stall. "Did Townes get tired of Midnight?"

"Huh?" said Ike, leaning a pitchfork against the wall.

"Bored with him or something?"

Ike's mouth opened, closed, reopened. "Can't believe you did that—right up and asked a question, not two seconds after—"

"And what's the answer?"

"Can't believe you did that when I just—"

"Ike! Answer the question!"

Ike's eyebrows rose. He looked shocked. "What's so goddamn important?"

Cody stole Alex's line, so undeniably right. "Something bad is going on."

Ike licked his lips; his tongue was yellow and scaly. "Bud getting shot?" he said.

"And Clea disappearing," Cody said, and, suspecting that Ike was missing an obvious point, added, "A human being."

"Human being," said Ike in a sarcastic way.

Cody thought: *Weirdo.* And at the same moment remembered Larissa's take on Ike: *Looks like an ax murderer.* But could a weirdo, a murderer, have cried over Bud the way Ike had? Maybe. Some people had to be badly fucked up inside—otherwise how could any of this be happening?

Cody glanced at the pitchfork leaning against the wall, a stride or two closer to Ike than to him. "Did you have some problem with Clea?" he said.

Ike's lower lip, cracked and chapped from weather, started to tremble. "Me?"

"Uh-huh."

"I see through you," Ike said. "You're just like him."

"Like who?"

"Orton."

"I'm like Sergeant Orton?"

Ike nodded. "Sneaky. Two-faced. Asking lots of questions. Accusing Ike first for no good reason."

Cody shifted sideways—yes, maybe a little sneaky—toward the pitchfork. Ike was a strong, rawboned guy, and he might have that whittling knife on him.

"What did Sergeant Orton accuse you of?"

"Just like you are—doing bad. When the truth is Ike could never harm a living thing."

Did such people exist, who could never harm a living thing? Cody doubted it; and if they did exist, he himself certainly wasn't one of them. He gazed into Ike's red-rimmed eyes and said it again: "Did you have some problem with Clea?"

Ike's hand, huge and gnarled, shot out with a quickness that took Cody by surprise and grabbed his right wrist, squeezed it in a grip that felt like fire. "My problem is two-facers like you and Orton."

Cody tried to free his arm, could not.

"Somethin' wrong with you two-facers, thinkin' anything bad about Ike and that kid, nicest kid in the barn, not like some others I could mention. Want proof? Give you proof, same as I gave Orton—I had Dusty over to the vet that whole afternoon, two to six." He paused, chest heaving, breathing heavy, a little spit showing at the corners of his lips. "Don't believe me? Call the vet."

Cody did believe Ike, flat-out; at the same time realized that Sergeant Orton must have verified Ike's story—how else could he be walking around, a free man? "I believe you."

Ike let go. Cody overcame the urge to rub his wrist. Ike glanced at his own hand, stuck it in his pocket. "Just want a fair shake is all," he said.

Cody caught a look deep in Ike's eyes, a look of pain: and somehow knew that Ike had suffered a lot in life. "I know," he said.

Ike turned away. "Answer to your question is no," he said. "Who'd ever get bored with Midnight? Champion goddamn horse in the stable."

In his mind, Cody crossed out number three, leaving only 4. *Needed the $.*

○ ○ ○

"Other than that—and I know this sounds callous," Alex said at a Rev corner table, after Cody had finished telling her about finding Bud's body, "how's the job?"

Cody gazed at Alex for a moment, then laughed. There was a lot to like about that face—soft, smooth skin, lively eyes that made her seem older, those braces doing the opposite, and almost always, in his brief acquaintance with her, an expression of being right there, her mind not somewhere else. Clea had that too; no surprise they'd become friends. "Not bad," he said.

"Whew. You're not offended."

"Nope."

"I know it's awful. No one knows what's going on. But doesn't it have to be related, Clea disappearing and now this?"

"Like how?"

"I don't know how," Alex said.

"Think of a possible connection," Cody said. "You're smart."

Alex didn't deny it. She sipped her hot chocolate, a faraway look appearing in her eyes. "Did you ever see *The Godfather*, part one, I think it is?"

Way too many times: It was Junior's favorite movie, along with *Fight Club*. "You're thinking about the scene with the horse?"

"Just the head, wasn't it?" Alex said.

"And?"

"In that case it was a threat," she said.

Sergeant Orton's idea: sending a message. "Who's being threatened here?" Cody said. "Why?"

Alex gazed into her hot chocolate, shook her head.

Cody stuck to his own theory: Someone had been afraid of Bud, of the possibility that Bud might remember—how else to put this?—the scene of the crime, and lead searchers to evidence of it. In fact, something close to that had happened—he'd found Clea's cell phone; not a fact he was allowed to disclose.

"What?" said Alex. "You were about to say something."

Cody shook his head. She gave him a look. Suddenly and to his surprise unable to meet her gaze, he bent over his Coke, took a sip. He wanted to tell Alex about the cell phone, knew he needed help from someone smart, someone his own age, a friend. Did he trust Sergeant Orton? No. But at the same time, things the sergeant said seemed to make sense. For example: the importance of secrecy. *Whoever they were looking for was close by.*

"Can I ask you a funny question?" Alex said.

"Sure," Cody said, sounding anything but in his own ears.

"Have you got a lot of friends?"

"Yeah."

"Really?"

"What's the big surprise?"

"No surprise. It's not that you're not att"—Alex blushed—"perfectly presentable, but—"

"Glad to hear it."

Alex laughed, blushed some more. "It's just that you seem like a bit of a loner. I mean in a good way, the stranger who rides into town."

"I'm a lousy rider," Cody said.

"I didn't mean literally."

Discussing his friends couldn't lead anywhere good. Cody tried to change the subject, could only find a clumsy way. "But I hear Townes is a good rider," he said.

"I guess so," Alex said. "Doesn't it help that he has the best horse?"

"Who told you Midnight was the best horse?"

"Clea. Isn't it true?"

"That's the word," Cody said. "What else did she say about Midnight?"

"What I said before, how powerful he was—and, oh yeah, how he and Townes were this perfect team."

"Perfect how?"

"In competition, moving as one, that kind of thing. That's what got her interested in Townes, the first time she saw him ride."

Something seemed to twist inside Cody's chest. He felt

Alex's gaze, busied himself with his drink. "That's how they got together?"

"Yeah, through riding," Alex said. "The next thing I knew they were off to New York for Columbus Day weekend, doing the bar scene."

"How?"

"That's the kind of thing Townes can pull off. I think he's got fake ID, but lots of places are pretty lax about carding. Even in this little burg—Big Len's, for example."

"The bar on Governor Street?"

"Supposedly," Alex said. "I've never been, but Townes took Clea a bunch of times."

Cody came close to saying: But she doesn't even like beer.

Alex seemed to read his mind. "She developed this thing for margaritas. But it didn't last long—Big Len's turned out to be kind of grubby." She dipped a finger into the hot chocolate, licked it off. "The whole thing didn't last long, not for her."

"What whole thing?"

"With Townes. She was planning to break up with him."

"She was?"

Alex nodded. "Kind of weird, just me having this little fact. Clea told me the day before she disappeared. She was up really late, working on the Princess Di report. I could hear her through the wall, reciting the speech out loud, so I stuck my head in the door, just to tell her to relax, it was going to be all right, and she turned to me and said, 'I'm going to break up with Townes.' Just popped right out. And I was like, 'How come?' And she promised a tell-all for tomorrow, meaning last Wednesday. But of course that didn't happen."

"Do you think she did it, broke up with him?"

"Wondered about that," Alex said. "I doubt it. Really wasn't time—they were in different classes all day, and dumping him during riding practice wouldn't be her. Makes me feel kind of strange, knowing what he didn't know, watching him on those searches, hacking through the woods like a madman."

But Cody couldn't help thinking: *Maybe she did tell him. Maybe he didn't like hearing it.* He tried to make the facts line up behind those ideas and couldn't. For example, where did the sale of Midnight fit in?

"Did Clea ever say anything about buying Midnight?"

"No."

"Or wanting to own him?"

"No. Why?"

"Just wondering," Cody said.

The waitress—not Deirdre, who didn't seem to be around—brought the check.

"I'll get it," Alex said.

"Not fair," said Cody. "I had the burger and all you had was that little salad." He took the check, added in the tip according to Frank Pruitt's foolproof formula. When he looked up from his calculations, he found Alex watching him.

"Can I ask you another funny question?" she said.

"Yeah."

"Are you going out with anyone?"

The true answer was no, but Cody said yes.

"Oh," said Alex. And then, after a moment: "Anyone I know?"

The logic of the lie now made the true answer yes, but Cody said no.

Conversation didn't come easy after that. They left the Rev, Alex heading back to campus, Cody on his way to Big Len's Sports Bar on Governor Street.

TWENTY-TWO

CODY HAD NEVER BEEN in a bar before. There was plenty of underage drinking in Little Bend, but not in bars. Everybody knew everybody, and it just didn't happen. He opened the door to Big Len's Sports Bar and walked in.

Cody found himself in a dark place, the exact size and dimensions hard to determine. A bar ran the length of the left side, with tables and chairs on the right. Most of the light shone from three TVs, a big one behind the bar, two smaller ones in the table-side corners.

Big Len's was mostly empty. A few men sat at the far end of the bar, hunched over mugs of beer; an old couple was sharing a pitcher at one of the tables. Cody took a stool at the near end of the bar. No sign of a bartender. SportsCenter was on TV, the commentator going over the spreads for upcoming NFL games. Down at the other end of the bar, one of the men said, "Fuckin' eight and a half points?"

"So?" said another man. "Take the under and stop bitching."

"I'm not bitching."

"You bitch more than my wife."

"No one bitches more than her."

"What'd you say?"

"You brought her up."

"Fuckin' watch your mouth, talkin' about my wife."

"Dudes, chill," said another man. And then, raising his voice: "Len. Customer."

A door opened behind the bar at the far end; Cody glimpsed some sort of storage room, cartons, a cooler against the back wall. A man emerged, first in silhouette, and then, as the storage-room door closed, just dimly lit. Tall, broad shouldered, barrel-chested, with long lank hair and a bandito mustache: Big Len. Big Len wore a tight, long-sleeved T-shirt, a studded leather vest, jeans; had a thick gold chain around his neck. He came forward, eyes on Cody—intelligent, experienced eyes, not friendly. Did Big Len recognize him from that time in the parking lot behind the bar—a distant sighting? No recognition showed on his face, not even for an instant. Cody was just another customer to him, but on the young side. Next would be a request for ID, some fumbling excuse, Cody on his way out.

Big Len gave him a slight nod. "What'll it be?"

"Uh," said Cody. "Maybe, like a beer?"

"Like, any special kind?" said Len.

"Bud Light," Cody said, his mind blanking on all other brands.

Without taking his eyes off Cody, Len reached down for a bottle, snapped off the cap, set the bottle on the bar. "Run a tab?" he said.

Cody's mind blanked again; whatever Len had just said didn't even sound like English.

"I'll run you a tab," he said. "Cash, Visa, MasterCard." Len smiled. He had big white teeth, maybe a little too white to be real. "Cash is always the nicest." At the other end of the bar, one of the men laughed.

Len moved away, wiping off the bar with a not-very-clean rag. Cody took a sip from the Bud Light bottle. It didn't taste like anything. First time in a bar, getting served no problem, and he had no desire to drink. A funny story to tell Junior; Cody wouldn't have minded having Junior beside him at that moment—Junior was one person he could trust, maybe the one person.

Down the bar, Len poured another round. "Eight and a half, Len," said one of the men. "How they come up with that?"

"Don't like it, stay away," Len said. "No law says you have to bet."

The man laughed. "Then where would you be?"

Len gave him that bright white smile. "Right here," said Len. The man stopped laughing.

Cody took another sip. Up on the big screen they were now showing highlights of big hits from last week's games. Not all the kids liked the hitting in football, but Cody did: The hitting was what made the game so special. *Like the way you play football, son. Ever been to Pennsylvania?* Deep down—and this was something Cody would never say aloud, would really not even admit to himself—he had a dream of playing in the NFL, had still not abandoned it. Kind of crazy, since he wasn't even on a team, and had this—maybe not a bad knee, but not as good as the other one. Would it ever be? He looked down at his left knee, straightened it, flexed it.

"Like football?"

Cody glanced up. Big Len was back.

"Yeah," Cody said.

"Got a favorite team?"

"Broncos," Cody said.

"Yeah?" said Len. "Don't get too many Bronco fans around

here." He reached down—*snap*—and set another bottle in front of Cody, even though the first one was half full.

"I didn't—"

"On the house," said Len. "Always good to see a new face."

"Um, thanks."

"Name's Len," Len said. He had pale eyes—hard to say the exact color in the weak light of the bar—made all the paler by his black hair. "Len Boudreau."

"Cody," Cody said.

Len stuck out his hand. They shook. Len's hand was big and strong—bigger and stronger than Ike's—and he squeezed pretty hard, but just for a split second before letting go.

"New in town?" he said.

"I . . . no," Cody said. "I've been around."

"Yeah?" said Len. He reached down, snapped open another Bud Light; but this one was for him. He tilted it to his mouth, took a big hit, almost half in one swallow. Len wiped his mouth on the back of his sleeve. "What the doctor ordered, right, Cody?"

"Yeah."

"But beer sometimes needs a little pal." He reached behind him, took a bottle off the shelf without looking, set it on the bar with two shot glasses. "How's bourbon sound?" Len said.

Cody had tried bourbon only once—a night out with some of Junior's older cousins, all real big like Junior, even the girls—had ended up totally wasted, and the next morning had sworn off bourbon forever. "Uh, wouldn't really—" he began.

"Take that for a yes," Len said. "Who turns down a free shot of JB? Only the limp-wristed types, right?" Cody didn't answer. Len filled the shot glasses, clicked his against Cody's. "Here's to football," he said, and raised his glass. Cody hesitated. Len made a little glass-raising gesture. Cody raised his glass. Len drained his shot in one swallow. Cody did the same. Len refilled the glasses. "Been around, huh?" He took another big hit of Bud Light, again wiped his mouth on his sleeve. "Funny—don't recall seeing you around."

"Well," said Cody, "here I am." Not a bad reply, just popping out at the right moment, perhaps slightly alcohol fueled.

Len laughed, a loud laugh, quickly cut off. "Unless you're a ghost," he said. "Not a ghost, are you, Cody?"

Cody felt a bit like he was in a football game. In football you got pushed and had to push back. "Don't believe in ghosts," he said.

"Me neither," said Len. "Or black cats or four-leaf clovers or any of that shit. You believe in any of that shit, Cody?"

"No."

"Puts us in the minority," Len said. "Tiny minority." He raised his shot glass. "Here's to minority rights." Len downed this second shot just like the first, in one gulp.

Cody did the same. Was there a choice? None that he could see. His throat burned for a second, and a little buzz started up in his head: pleasant, but this was not the time. He heard movement behind him, glanced around, and saw the old couple shuffling toward the door, leaning against each other.

When he turned back, Len was watching him. "Good customers," he said. "But not players. You a player, Cody?"

"I don't know what you mean."

"Aw, come on. You're a bright young man. Don't know what a player is? Somebody who likes a little wager from time to time, say on those Broncos of yours—that's a player."

"I'm not into that," Cody said.

"They're giving away three and a half this week," said Len. "Might be a good time to start."

Cody shook his head.

"Maybe you're not as big a fan as you make out," Len said.

Cody shrugged.

Len had another big swallow of Bud Light. "Drink up."

Cody took a sip.

"Know any players?" Len said.

"No."

"Hard to believe," Len said. "Unless you don't get around much."

"I get around."

Len nodded. "Sure you do," he said. "You been around and you get around." He paused; silence, except for a crunching hit on the big screen. "So you must know some of the—don't want to say kids, do I?—young people from around here."

"Yeah." No other answer made sense.

"Like?" said Len.

"Just, you know, ordinary, um, kids."

"For example?"

"You wouldn't know them."

"Try me," Len said. He leaned across the bar, his head above Cody's, only a couple feet away. Their eyes met. Len smiled. "Go on—I don't bite."

"Clea Weston," Cody said.

Big Len's head snapped back. His smile vanished, just like that. He took a long look at Cody. "Some kind of humor on your part?" he said.

"No," said Cody.

Big Len glanced down the bar; the men were bent over their mugs, in silence again. His gaze returned to Cody. Cody could feel Big Len's mind working. He opened his mouth to say something. But at that moment the door opened, and in walked Deirdre, the Irish waitress from the Rev.

She looked around, clutching an envelope in both hands; her face pale, her eyes like two black ovals. Deirdre saw Len and approached, but slowly, as though moving through some thick medium. If she recognized Cody—or even noticed him—she gave no sign.

Len shifted a few steps away, laid a coaster on the bar. "Deirdre," he said. "A sight for sore eyes. What'll it be?"

"If I could just—" Deirdre began, then stopped and tried again. "A moment of your time, please." Cody saw she wasn't wearing her eyebrow stud; because of that, or some other reason, she looked much younger, not much older than him.

"Phil," Len called down the bar. "Mind the store for a few minutes." One of the men got up, walked around the bar, stood on the other side, opposite his stool. Len came around the other end, faced Deirdre. "My office suit your needs?" he said.

"Yes, I'm sure that's—"

"After you." He touched the small of her back. She moved deeper into the bar, toward a door in the rear wall. Len glanced at Cody, his eyes narrowing. "Phil," he said, "drinks on the house for this gentleman. Make sure he's happy." Phil nodded. Len followed Deirdre, through the door and out of sight.

Phil, a fat guy with watery eyes and the silvery glints of a two- or three-day beard on his face, made his way over. "Get you something?"

"I'm okay for now," Cody said. "Where's the men's?"

Phil pointed at a door in the back corner, near one of the

267

smaller TVs, and returned to his place down the bar. Cody waited for a minute or so, then rose, crossed the floor, and went through the doorway in the back corner.

He found himself in a dark, narrow corridor, lit only by a flickering overhead bulb. Three doors: men's, ladies', and one unmarked. He went into the men's, stood at a urinal, one of those urinals with framed reading material on the wall above it. Cody read:

To: Len Boudreau
From: North Dover Christmas Parade Committee
Dear Len,

Many, many thanks for your generous support of this year's parade, the best ever in the opinion of just about everyone who participated—to say nothing about the numerous spectators! The committee is very grateful. An official charitable contribution receipt made out to your corporation will be sent under separate cover.

Sincerely,

[Illegible Signature]

All at once Cody got the idea there was something important in that letter, important to him. He read it again; the important thing, if there at all, remained hidden. There was no glass on the frame, making removal of the letter a snap. Cody removed it and put it in his pocket.

He left the men's room, moved into the narrow corridor. Voices came through the wall, the low rumbling sound of a man, high vibrations of a woman, maybe a scared woman. Cody went silently to the unmarked door, put his ear to it, heard nothing. He turned the knob—slow and careful, not making a sound—and pushed the door open.

The corridor continued on the other side. Cody followed it, past a door with an exit sign over it—a door with a round window, looking out to the parking lot—and to another door, closed and windowless. A thin door: Len's voice came through, very clear.

"Counted this money twice, sweetheart," he said, "and I'm still coming up two grand short. And the thing is, math was always my best subject."

"Mi—Mick needs another week," Deirdre said, her voice high, the words coming too fast. "Just seven days, maybe less. He's just waiting for—"

Len cut her off. "Know what pisses me off the most? He doesn't even have the balls to come himself, hides behind a woman. What kind of man does that?"

"He's a good man," Deirdre said. "It's just that the other chef's sick and—"

There was a loud thump, maybe Len pounding his fist on a desk. "Don't want to hear it," Len said. "He's a fag, period." Then came a long silence. "Maybe if I count one more time, it'll end up different. What are the odds on that?" Deirdre said nothing. Len counted, in no hurry, "One hundred, two, three, four . . ." stopping at four thousand five hundred. "Nope," he said. "Comes out the exact same. Damn." Cody heard him take a deep breath, the exaggerated, regretful kind. "Know what happens now?"

"Oh, please not," said Deirdre.

"Sorry, sweetheart. Got to follow through—that's just good business."

"Please don't hurt him."

"Only hurts till they get him on the pain meds," Len said. "From what I hear, anyway—the leg breaking, all that shit, I contract out."

"Just a week, Len. I'm begging you."

"Hey," said Len. "Believe that's the first time I've heard you say my name. Do it again."

A long silence. Cody backed away, opened the exit door, went into the parking lot. His hands were balled into fists, so hard and tight they hurt.

○ ○ ○

Cody looked around the parking lot, saw the big black pickup with the Smith & Wesson sticker, plus six or seven cars, including a dark sedan at the back with the interior light on and a man behind the wheel. The light went off, and the man became invisible.

Cody walked back to the Rev, where he'd left his car. He got in, drove toward the campus. The night was cold, the streets deserted. As Cody went by the village green, unlit and shadowy, headlights shone in the rearview mirror. He glanced up, thought he saw the outlines of a sedan. Cody sped up. Within seconds, the other car—yes, a sedan—was right behind him; right behind him and with a blue light flashing on the dashboard. Cody pulled over.

TWENTY-THREE

THE BLUE LIGHTS STOPPED FLASHING. In his side mirror Cody watched a man get out of the sedan and come forward. He didn't appear to be in uniform, wore a long winter coat with lapels—underneath Cody could make out a white shirt, a knotted tie. Not a particularly big man, but his head was big. And his face was round: Had Cody seen him before? Maybe at the Rev? He wasn't sure.

The man tapped on the window with his gloved hand. Cody hesitated; a blue light on the dash didn't make you a cop. The man reached into his coat. A single thought—just a number, but it made sense, leaped into Cody's mind: .38. His car was still running; he put his hand on the shift, ready to bang it in gear and hit the pedal. But no gun appeared. Instead the round-headed man flashed a badge—didn't flash it, really, more held it to the glass, giving Cody plenty of time to read.

Above the badge was a state seal, showing lots of trees and a cow. Below that, a name: Ronald C. Brand, and an unsmiling photo of the round-headed man. And at the bottom: Special Agent, Office of the Vermont Attorney General, Public Corruption Unit. The man—Special Agent Ronald C. Brand—tapped on the window again, not hard. Cody slid it down.

"License and registration," said Agent Brand. He had a soft voice, not at all authoritative. Cody handed over his license and registration. "Sit tight," Agent Brand said.

Cody sat tight. Things were happening fast. He needed time to sort out all his confusion. Sitting in the car, waiting for Agent Brand to return, Cody didn't know where to start. He remembered Clea talking about some amazing poem that began with a man losing his way in a dark forest. Beyond the village green, over the rooftops of North Dover, he could see a real, nonpoetic forest looming in the night.

Tap tap on the window. Cody hadn't seen Agent Brand coming. He slid it down again. "Cody Laredo?" said Brand. "Resident of Little Bend, Colorado?"

Cody nodded.

"This your car, Cody?"

He nodded again.

"What I've got here is a Colorado registration. That correct?"

Uh-oh. Problem on the way. All these systems, designed by adults, generations and generations of them, to trip you up: Cody was realizing how well they worked.

"Yeah," said Cody. "Correct."

Agent Brand nodded. "See the problem with that?" he said.

"Vermont plates," said Cody.

Brand laughed; just a short, soft sound, maybe surprised. "Care to explain?"

Cody took a good look at Agent Brand. He had a round face, didn't seem threatening at all, looked honest, whatever that meant. Was there such a thing? For example, Ike didn't look at all honest, but Cody had almost no doubt that he was. *Hard to know who to trust.* "Can I see that badge again?" he said.

Without a word or the slightest sign of annoyance or anger, Brand took out his badge and handed it to Cody. Cody examined it again: a five-pointed gold star, probably gold-plated or even brass; but official looking, at least to his eyes.

"If you think it's a fake," said Brand, passing a card through the window, "that's the AG's office line—he works late."

"The attorney general?" Cody wasn't one-hundred percent sure what the job was, but he knew it was important.

"This is Vermont," said Brand. "We don't stand on ceremony."

Cody gave back the card and the badge, tried to make up his mind. Sergeant Orton had said to keep the mole arrangement just between the two of them, but how was that possible now? And what could be the harm in another law enforcement guy knowing? "Why don't you call Sergeant Orton?" Cody said. "He can explain."

"Sergeant Orton?" said Brand.

"Yeah. Ted, I think his name is. From the police. The North Dover police." He gestured at the night. "Here."

"Heard of Orton," Brand said. "Can't say I really know him."

"Well, he, um . . ." Where to begin?

"Happy to talk to him," Brand said. "But why not hear your side of it first. Mind if I get in?"

"Um."

"Or we could sit in my car," Brand said. "It's cold out here, son, being the point."

"Okay," Cody said. Brand walked around the car, got in, removing a fast-food wrapper from the seat and dropping it on the floor.

"Nice wheels," he said. "First car?"

"Yeah."

"Moment I got my first car," Brand said, "I went for a spin, ended up driving all the way to Canada. Know that feeling, the open road?"

"Yeah."

"Those were the days," Brand said. He reached in his pocket, took out—what was this? Some kind of digital recorder? "Any objection to me taping this?"

"Taping what?"

"Our little chat."

"But why?" Cody said. "Why tape it?"

"In the interest of justice," Brand said. "Helps build a proper case."

"A case against who?" Cody said.

Brand laughed again, that soft sound of surprise. "Excellent question. The answer is—too soon to say. But no reason it would be you." He paused for a moment or two, then added: "Is there?"

"I haven't done anything wrong," Cody said.

"Sounds good to me," Brand said. "Walk me through it."

"Through what?"

"This plate discrepancy," said Brand. "Why we're here."

Cody glanced at the digital recorder, and Brand's round

face, the face of . . . what? A teacher, maybe, the kind of teacher kids liked. "If I was the, um, target, then you'd have to read me my rights."

"Ever thought about law school?" Brand said.

Of course not. Cody shook his head.

"Yes, I'd have to read you your rights, if I was playing by the book. And, for many reasons, that's the way I play."

"Give me one," Cody said.

"One what?"

"Of the reasons why you play by the book."

"Because I like to win," Brand said. "An honest case tends to hold together in front of a jury."

Cody nodded. "The plate thing was Sergeant Orton's idea," he said.

"What was the purpose behind it?" Brand said.

"You know about Clea Weston?" said Cody.

"The missing girl."

"Yeah. The thing is, she's from Little Bend, too." Cody glanced at Brand. "Did you know that?"

"No."

Was he lying? Not that Cody could see. And why would he? Cody couldn't think of a reason, but that didn't mean there wasn't one. "You're not working on the disappearance?"

"I wasn't," Brand said.

But now he was? A special agent from the state attorney general—how could that hurt? "We used to go out, me and Clea," Cody said. "So when I heard the news, I came."

"Simple as that."

"Yeah. And when Sergeant Orton found out, he thought I'd make a good mole."

"Mole?"

"Like a spy. But Colorado plates would have blown my cover, so he gave me the Vermont ones."

"Got it," Brand said. "And what did the mole dig up?"

Did Cody hear a little sarcasm in his tone? "Her cell phone, for one thing."

"Yeah?" said Brand; no sarcasm now. "Go on."

Cody told his story: the cell phone, what was on it, Bud getting shot, Sergeant Orton's theories. It grew more and more disorganized, all these details mixing in—like his job at the barn, the "Bending" poem, Clea's trust fund, the ownership of Midnight getting transferred and how he'd figured out that LB Corp. had to be the Westons—but Brand just listened, not once opening his mouth.

Cody came to the end; maybe not the end, but he stopped talking. They sat in silence. After a while Brand said, "LB Corp.—Little Bend. Very clever on your part." He took out his wallet, peeled off some bills. "Here."

"What's this?" said Cody, not taking the money.

"Five hundred bucks," Brand said. "We have a fund for situations like this. Call it traveling money."

"Traveling money?"

"Time to go home," Brand said. "Back to Little Bend."

"Huh?" said Cody. That made no sense.

"The mole thing is over—and I'm talking tonight," Brand said. He switched off the recorder. "Right now, this minute, we're going to the barn, pack up your stuff, change those plates back, and then I'll escort you out of town."

"No way."

Brand gazed at him for a moment, his face suddenly not quite so round and friendly, the hard bone structure somehow showing through. "I know it's tough," he said. "You're a brave kid, and a competent one. But I can't risk you getting caught in the switches."

"What does that mean?"

"Means you're in danger, Cody. I can't protect you, so you can't stay."

"Protect me from who?"

"I'm not at liberty to get into that."

Cody shook his head. "I'm not going anywhere."

"Don't turn this into a power struggle."

"I'm not turning it into anything. I'm staying, that's all."

Brand sighed. "The last thing I want to do is arrest you, lock you up, start getting complicated with the Colorado State Police."

"Arrest me for what?"

"Attaching illegal plates, underage drinking, a few others I'll think up if I have to."

So much for honesty and playing by the book. Anger awoke in Cody, turned hot very fast. "But I told you about the plates."

"That you did. You can stay in a cell while I check out the story."

Cody's voice rose. "And you can't prove I had anything to drink—you were outside."

"First," said Brand, "I can smell it on your breath. Second, Phil is on my payroll."

"Phil?"

"The substitute bartender."

Cody went silent. Very slowly, things began to realign in his mind, possibilities rising and falling, but nothing locking into place. He tamped down his anger.

"Be reasonable," Brand said, holding out the money.

Could Brand really make all that trouble, locking him up, bringing in the Colorado State Police? Cody had no reason to doubt it. "Okay," said Cody. "But I don't want the money."

"Take it, please," said Brand. "Otherwise you'll just be

handing me a nasty accounting problem."

Cody took the money—ten times what Sergeant Orton had given him, if that meant anything. Phil—fat old drunk at the end of the bar and part-time bartender—was on the payroll of the attorney general's office. If nothing was what it seemed, then he, Cody, had to be like that too.

○ ○ ○

Brand followed Cody to the parking lot by the barn, waited while he got his things. Cody went up to his little room, threw everything into his duffel, walked down the narrow stairs and back outside. Ike was standing by the door, his face yellow under the overhead light.

"Goin' somewheres?" he said.

"Yeah."

"Like where?"

"I'm leaving town."

"How come? You just started."

"It didn't work out. Not because of you."

"Because of the academy people? Don't pay no attention to them—off in the clouds."

"That's not it either," Cody said. A snowflake wafted down between them.

"Suit yourself," Ike said. "Don't think Ike can't manage on his own."

"I know you can," Cody said. He started moving away, paused. "Do you know Len Boudreau?"

"Know to stay clear of him," Ike said.

"What is it he does, exactly?" Cody said. "Besides owning that bar."

"What don't he do, more like it." Ike spat in the snow; then his head jerked up abruptly, as though he'd been struck by a thought. "Don't tell me you're in shit with Big Len."

Cody shook his head.

"'Cause if you are," Ike said, "then best leave town for sure."

"Does he lend money? Is that it?"

"Lend? He don't lend nothin'."

But something to do with money, because Deirdre's boyfriend was into him for over six grand. "Is he a gambler?"

"Hell, no," said Ike. "He don't gamble. Bein' a bookie's a sure thing."

All that talk about point spreads, overs and unders, eight and a half, three and a half: The realignment that was going on inside Cody's head sped up a little. "He's a bookie?"

"Big-time," said Ike.

"Big-time? In a small town like this?"

Ike's eyes narrowed; he looked offended. "Plenty of money in North Dover, goin' back to earliest days."

"Enough to support a big-time bookie, just from football bets?"

"Football, basketball, whatever—lots of folks got a sickness, case you ain't heard." From the barn came the faint whinnying of a horse. Ike went still for a moment or two, then said, "Nothin' to worry about—just Dusty havin' a bad dream."

* * *

Cody carried his duffel down the path to the barn. He remembered that strange line from Clea's letter: *It's hard to know who to trust sometimes. Like rolling the dice—a cliché that turns out to have real meaning.* For a moment he thought he was about to put everything together, total understanding just seconds away; but it didn't happen. A wind rose, very light; Cody felt a snowflake touch his face, and then another.

Agent Brand was waiting by Cody's car; he'd changed the plates, held the Vermont ones in his hand. "What happens with them?" Cody said.

"I'll take care of it," said Agent Brand, opening the door for Cody. Cody tossed in the duffel. "Just follow me," Brand said. "I'll lead you as far as Route Two. After that it's a straight shot across the state line to the Thruway."

"I can find my own way," Cody said.

"This is better," Brand said. "Don't worry—I'll be in touch."

"About what?"

"Clea Weston. The moment we find anything, you'll hear from me."

The wind rose a little higher, rattled the treetops. "Do you think she's okay?" Cody said; a stupid, childish question, but Brand was smart, worked for the attorney general of the whole goddamn state, and Cody couldn't keep it in.

"Every case is different," Brand said.

"No bullshit," said Cody, his tamped-down anger suddenly bursting out. "Tell me the truth."

"The truth in disappearances like this," said Brand, his voice still mild, "the statistical truth, is that after the first twenty-four hours the odds go way down. After forty-eight, they go down some more, and then it's pretty much a flatline situation."

Cody nodded. There was at least one similarity between Brand and Big Len: They worked the odds. He got in the car.

Brand led him down the road, past the tennis courts and the hockey rink, to the Dover Academy gates. Cody's headlights swept across a figure leaning against one of the stone pillars. Was it—yes, Townes DeWitt. Townes glanced at his watch, perhaps waiting for someone, as Cody drove by. Cody checked the rearview mirror, thought he saw Townes putting his cell phone to his ear. Then he rounded a corner and Townes was gone.

A few minutes later they crossed the town line, Brand's sedan first, Cody four or five car lengths behind. They drove south, winding through dark hills, snow falling but still light, almost not present at all. A crossroads appeared: Route 2. Brand pulled over, stuck his hand out the window, waved Cody on. Cody passed him, hung a right onto Route 2, headed west. Brand flashed his lights. Cody sped up, drove over a long rise and around a corner, came to a lookout. He turned in and stopped the car.

Going back right away? Probably not smart: Brand might be waiting, just in case. Cody sat there, lights off. After a while he took out the letter he'd lifted off the men's-room wall at Big Len's, the one from the Christmas parade committee. He switched on the interior light, read it a few times. Then he found a pen on the floor, went over the letter one last time: the letter to Len Boudreau, promising to send his corporation a charitable contribution report for tax purposes. Cody lowered the pen to the paper, circled the *L* in Len, the *B* in Boudreau, the *corp* in corporation. *LB Corp.* Nothing to do with Little Bend, Clea, or the Westons. Big Len now owned Midnight. Cody had jumped to a conclusion. Who had warned him against that? Sergeant Orton; Sergeant Orton, who had enlisted Cody's help, while Agent Brand had tried to get rid of him. Did that make Sergeant Orton the one to trust?

Cody wasn't sure. He just did what he'd been intending anyway—had never even considered anything else. Headlights off, he swung the car around and headed back, east on Route 2. No one waited at the crossroads. Cody switched on the headlights and kept going.

TWENTY-FOUR

CODY DROVE BACK into North Dover. Everything looked different—Spring Street, the Rev, the village green, all changed. Crazy, but for the first time in his life he was really seeing, seeing the way things were. For example, the man-made part of the visual world—buildings, lights, roads—was no more than a pitiful veneer, could all be gone in a flash. For some reason that made him feel powerful, as though he were connected inside to the might of the great dark earth itself. His sticking-place: some deep anchor in the bedrock. He was the loner, the stranger, as Alex had said, who rides into town. A good feeling, and Cody took some moments of enjoyment from it before he returned to normal. "Get a grip, boy," he said aloud, and turned up Mountain Road, the gateposts of Dover Academy two dark verticals up ahead.

Cody drove through, his headlights sweeping over two figures standing near some bushes off to the side. Twenty or thirty yards ahead, he pulled to the side, cut the engine and got out. Snow still fell, still very light, like a dry mist. A voice—Simon's voice—cut through the night.

"He said no. What the hell was I supposed to do?"

Cody walked back toward the bushes. No moon or stars, but the sky held a lot of reflected light from the town, much brighter than usual, maybe because of all those fine snow-flakes. Two figures by the bushes—about an arm's length apart—easily recognizable: the shorter, thinner one, Simon; the big one, Townes.

"You whine a lot," Townes said. "Anyone ever bring that up?"

"Don't talk to me like that," Simon said, with a firmness in his tone that Cody admired. "I was trying to do you a favor."

"You fucked it up."

"It's a lot of money."

"Ten grand? Bullshit."

"But enough so he asked questions."

"And what did you tell him?"

"What we agreed—our plucky little start-up tale, those

file-sharing widgets, whatever the hell it was."

"'Plucky little start-up tale'? Do you ever listen to your-self?"

"No. I haven't reached your heights of solipsism."

"What the fuck are you talking about?"

"Look it up."

Cody—maybe there was something in this new way of seeing after all—knew what was coming next, but Simon did not. "You flamer," Townes said, throwing an overhand punch square at the middle of Simon's face. Simon fell straight back in the snow.

"Hey!" Cody said, coming forward.

Townes whirled around. He looked surprised, but no more than that, and only for a second or two. "Get the hell out of here," he said.

Cody went right by him, bent over Simon. Back in Little Bend, he'd been in a fight or two, and witnessed some others, seen guys knocked cold by a sucker punch, but Simon's eyes were open. "You all right?" Cody said. Simon didn't say anything, just moved his hand gingerly over his face. Blood trickled from his nose and mouth. Cody reached down to help Simon up; at the same moment a heavy hand landed on his shoulder. Cody turned.

"You a little slow?" Townes said. "I told you to go—this is

none of your business."

"You don't know what you're talking about," Cody said.

"The fuck I don't."

An idea, a really good one, popped into Cody's head. "Let's see your wrists."

"Huh?" said Townes.

"The left one. Pull up your sleeve."

"Are you on drugs or something?"

"I'm going to have a look at your wrist, one way or another."

"In that case," said Townes, "I'll make it easy for you." His gaze suddenly shifted, aiming over Cody's shoulder. But Cody knew a little about fighting, was at least partly ready for the sucker punch that came next, and it glanced off his temple instead of smashing him in the face. A glancing blow, but still powerful; Cody staggered sideways. Townes was strong—maybe not as strong as Junior, but much quicker. Cody didn't even see the second punch, left-handed, which caught him flush on the jaw. A bell-ringer; but Cody had had his bell rung before, more than once on the football field. The important thing was not to panic. Even if you were getting the shit kicked out of you, panic was bad. Junior had kicked the shit out of Cody plenty of times when they were little. Boys who grew up in Little Bend—boys like Cody, anyway—learned to take some hits. Cody backed away, shrugged off the pain—you could do that literally with pain, up to a point—and got his hands up.

Townes came barreling in, a big strong guy, throwing punches with both arms; big, strong, and aggressive, but maybe not that knowledgeable about fighting. Cody took most of the punches on his shoulders and upper arms, kept his gaze on Townes's enraged face, saw an opening, and threw a punch of his own.

Townes's head snapped back. For an instant he looked shocked, and then came fury, his lips jutting out, spit spray flying and a whirlwind of flailing blows. Some landed and some did not, but none did much damage: It was all a wild attack designed to induce panic, surrender, flight. Cody didn't flee, moved the other way, in the unexpected direction, stepping inside and driving his left fist right into Townes's gut. Townes doubled over. From down under, twisting up with all his strength—he hated Townes, no doubt about that—he caught Townes on the point of the jaw with his right fist. But maybe not quite that accurate, Townes turning his head at the last instant, then falling forward, or diving, or some combination, a move that ended with Townes tackling Cody and falling on top of him.

Townes clawed his way up to a straddling position on Cody's chest. Panting, bleeding, he glared down at Cody, then grabbed a big double handful of snow and mashed it into Cody's face. Cody squirmed, tried to move, to get out from under, could not. He couldn't even breathe, felt like he was going to drown: panic time now. Townes pressed down on Cody's face with all his weight and power, shoving snow up his nose, into his mouth. Cody tried to wriggle away, got his head averted just a bit. Townes made a growling sound, changed the angle of his arms slightly to keep the heavy pressure on Cody's face. That little movement allowed Cody to jerk one arm free, strike Townes in the neck with the side of his hand. Townes grunted in pain and all at once didn't feel quite so strong and heavy. Cody sliced up at his neck again, this time hitting him right on the windpipe. Townes made a choking, gagging sound and sat up straight, clutching his own neck. Cody twisted out from underneath, scrambled to his feet. Townes rose too, panting harder—they were both panting—his breath whistling in his throat. Cody saw rage in his eyes, murderous rage, and was sure his own eyes looked the same. He raised his hand, made a little gesture with his fingers, meaning *Let's go*. Townes cocked his right fist, charged forward, threw a tremendous punch at Cody's head. Cody ducked, just a few inches—actually feeling the breeze as Townes's fist flew by—and hit Townes with just about all he had left, this time right on the button for sure. Townes went down and stayed down.

Cody bent over him, fumbled back Townes's left sleeve, and found no shark tattoo on his wrist, no tattoo of any kind. Just in case Sergeant Orton and Vin the tech guy had made a mistake, Cody checked the right wrist, too, also sharkless. He let Townes's arm go. It flopped back in the snow, limp; but Townes was breathing all right.

From behind came a groan. Cody turned, saw Simon getting to his feet. His nose was bleeding and crooked; his eyes were wide.

"Did you kill him?" Simon said.

"Of course not," Cody said. "What were you fighting about?"

Simon touched his nose. "I think it's broken."

"Looks like it," Cody said. "Answer the question." Simon shrank back. Afraid? Afraid that Cody was going to get into it with him, too? "Come on, Simon. I need your help."

"For what? I'm not processing very well right now."

"I'm looking for Clea," Cody said.

Simon, so smart, probably the smartest person Cody had ever met, seemed confused. "But we all are. Everybody is."

Cody made an impatient gesture with his hand, sweeping that remark aside; Simon shrank back some more. "What were you fighting about?" A car came through the gates, headlights passing over Simon for a second. His face was covered in blood.

"Was Townes trying to borrow money from you? Ten grand?"

Simon nodded. "From my father," he said. "I don't have that kind of money of my own. Not that I can get my hands on, I mean."

"Trust fund?" Cody said; he was getting better at seeing how things really were, no doubt about it.

Simon nodded again. "My father refused."

"Why?" Cody said. "You said he's a genius at making money. Ten grand can't be that much for someone like him."

"I suppose he didn't buy the cover story."

"What cover story?"

"That Townes and I needed seed money for an Internet start-up." Simon gazed down at Townes. "My father, always full of the wrong kind of surprises, turned out to have a number of complex, technical questions, actually demonstrated what seemed to be a deep knowledge of the subject matter, totally factitious subject matter, but irony's no help at times like that."

A lot of that went right by Cody, but he got an insight into Simon's father's moneymaking ability. "What's the real story?" Cody said. "Why did Townes need the money?" More realignment in Cody's mind, even the first faint clicking into place. "Is he a gambler?"

Simon looked surprised. "Mostly just on football—how did you know that?"

"How much does he owe?"

"He never told me."

"But he's rich. Did his father turn him down, too?"

"Did I not mention Pegasus Partners?" Simon said.

Cody had a vague memory of it. "Yeah, but—" he began, then saw flashing yellow lights from the direction of the main Dover Academy buildings.

"Campus security," Simon said. "This might be a challenge to explain."

"Christ," said Cody. He glanced at Townes, now stirring in the snow, then back at Simon. "What else do you know?" he said. "About Clea, I mean."

"Clea? Is there some connection?"

"Answer the goddamn question."

"Nothing," Simon said.

"That better be true," Cody said, but he doubted it was. The flashing lights came closer, security on the way. Cody could foresee many ways for things to go wrong with them. He ran to his car, got in, spun it around, and sped away.

●　●　●

Pegasus Partners. For that Cody needed a computer. He drove to the barn. He'd forgotten to turn in his key; Cody took that for a good sign. He let himself into the office, switched on the computer. A few minutes later he'd learned that Pegasus Partners was a recently defunct hedge fund that had been run until its demise by Nedland W. DeWitt, "former golden boy of the derivatives world." Due to "bad bets in the subprime securities market" and "heavily leveraged put positions in precious metal commodity futures" plus several other reasons also not understood by Cody, Pegasus Partners had gone under on the Friday before the Columbus Day weekend, resulting in huge losses for its investors and also in dozens of lawsuits against Nedland DeWitt, who was selling off all his possessions—including his yacht, his collection of Persian art, his houses in Aspen and Easthampton—and filing for bankruptcy.

Cody switched off the computer. Townes, a bettor like his dad, was no longer rich, couldn't pay his debts, had fallen down the economic ladder to Cody's level, a level that didn't bother Cody, but it was the only level he'd ever known; a big difference.

In his mind, everything stopped realigning and clicked into place at last. Among other things, he now knew, almost for certain, that Big Len had a .38. He, Cody, did not, meaning this was the time for the mole to surface. A fistfight was one thing, a gunfight another. He took out the card Sergeant Orton had given him and called the number.

TWENTY-FIVE

SERGEANT ORTON WAS WAITING for Cody at the doughnut place across the town line, where Cody had eaten the bear claw. The doughnut place was closed, no lights showing, nobody around. That strange light snowfall was still happening, almost not a snowfall at all, and the starless, moonless sky still held that strange glow. Sergeant Orton, not driving the cruiser tonight but in an unmarked, soccer-mom–style minivan, waved Cody over. Cody parked beside him, left his car, got into the minivan.

The sergeant wasn't in uniform, wore an old parka with sewing-repair stitches on the upper arm of one sleeve, same spot where a uniform badge would be. There was something wrong with him, visible even in the weak light that came from the dashboard instruments. Cody couldn't put it into words, but he saw it right away. Somehow the sergeant looked older, bonier, and his bushy mustache—up to now a jolly kind of touch—seemed like just a dismal add-on. He gave Cody a quick glance. "What happened to your face?" he said, his tone oddly dull, as if he actually didn't want to know the answer.

"It's nothing," Cody said.

"Whatever you say," said the sergeant. "Said you had something for me. What's up?"

"I . . . I think I understand the whole thing," Cody said. "What happened to Clea."

Sergeant Orton's eyes closed for a moment. He opened them, turned to Cody, now spoke with more energy, the corners of his lips turning up in what might have been a smile except that his eyes didn't join in. "Sounds promising. I'm all ears."

"It turns out you were right," Cody said. "One of your theories, or part of it, at least. This is all about gambling."

Sergeant Orton nodded, the barest little movement.

"Is that what you thought all along?" Cody said.

The sergeant reached forward, turned up the heat. "Go on," he said.

There was something modest about Sergeant Orton; Cody

liked that. He was getting a fix on the man at last. "Do you know Len Boudreau?" Cody said. "The guy who owns Big Len's, the bar on Governor?"

"Heard of him," the sergeant said.

"Guess what," Cody said, sounding, even to himself, like an excited little kid. But he was excited, couldn't hide it. "Big Len's a bookie. A big-time bookie."

Sergeant Orton fumbled in the pocket of his parka. He took out cigarettes and matches, lit up, cracking the window an inch or two. No reason the sergeant wouldn't be a smoker, but it surprised Cody just the same. Maybe he read Cody's mind, because he said, "Trying to quit." He took a deep drag. "Bookie, huh?" he went on. "What makes you think that?"

"I don't think—I know," Cody said. "I've even seen him in action."

"How do you mean?"

"Taking the money," Cody said, leaving out Deirdre and the rest of it. Any reason Sergeant Orton had to know that about her? Not that Cody could see.

"Where was this?"

"Right in the bar."

"You were in the bar?"

"Big Len served me himself."

"Booze."

"Yeah."

"Underage," Sergeant Orton said. "I could pop you for that."

"Huh?" Agent Brand had said the same thing; what was with these cops and their obsession with underage drinking? Best to leave Brand out of this. Brand wanted him long gone, believed he was long gone; no good could come of him getting together with Sergeant Orton.

The sergeant tapped ash out the window, turned to Cody, this time with a smile that looked real. "Just jerking your chain." He squinted at Cody's face. "Big Len do that to you?"

"No," Cody said. "That part doesn't matter. What matters is that it's a gambling thing, NFL point spreads. Len made a big mistake—he thought Townes was rich."

"The boyfriend?"

Yes and no. According to Alex, Clea had been about to dump Townes; there was a slight chance she had dumped him, that Wednesday afternoon at the barn. A complication, but of the personal kind, almost certainly having nothing to do with the case. "Yeah," Cody said. "The boyfriend. My guess is he did some betting last year, back when he was rich, and either won or paid up when he didn't, so Big Len got the idea he'd always be good for the money. But now the money's gone, Townes must have made some bad bets, gotten in deeper—and couldn't pay."

"Fucking idiot," said Sergeant Orton.

"Townes, you mean?" Cody said; no reason he should have been surprised by the sergeant's language, but Cody was; and even more surprised by his sudden anger.

"Just tell your goddamn story," Sergeant Orton said. He took a deep breath, went on more mildly. "Sorry. This is a bit of a shock, that's all. If true."

"Oh, it's true," Cody said. "I can even—" Cody felt a strange sensation, a sort of brainpower surge. Weird and unaccustomed: He didn't want to trust it.

"You can even what?" Sergeant Orton said.

"Maybe this sounds crazy," Cody said, "but I think I can predict that Big Len owns a .38."

Sergeant Orton took another drag. "Yeah?" Exhaled smoke swirled like a sickly green cloud in the dashboard lights.

"That's what he shot Bud with," Cody said. "And you were right about that, too. It was about sending a message, not stopping me from taking Bud out."

"What message?"

"That Clea was in danger if Townes didn't pay up fast."

"Lost me."

"Don't you see? It's a kidnapping, but not exactly like any of the kinds you mentioned. Big Len took Clea hostage. Because he thought—" Forget that. *Focus.* Whether she was

301

still Townes's girlfriend or not didn't matter at all. "Because she was his girlfriend. You see what this means?"

"Tell me," said Sergeant Orton, ramping up the heat a little more.

"She's alive," Cody said. Wasn't that obvious? "Big Len will free her as soon as Townes pays him back. And Townes—" Maybe not a totally bad kid: At that moment Cody realized the kinds of threats Big Len must have made to keep Townes from going to the police. "—And Townes is trying to come up with the money. That explains Midnight."

"Midnight?"

"Townes's horse, the best horse in the stable—Big Len owns him now," Cody said. What else could that be but a partial payment? "But he won't wait forever—that's the message of what happened to Bud."

"Getting me a little confused with all these horses," the sergeant said.

"What's so confusing?" That question, sharp and irritated, just came popping out and Cody didn't regret it. Big Len wasn't going to wait forever.

"Seems simple to you?" the sergeant said.

"Not simple, but—"

"Nothing simple about it."

"What do you mean?"

Sergeant Orton just shook his head, remained silent for a few moments. "The part about Len Boudreau owning the horse—how did you figure that out?"

Cody explained—all about the inventory book at the barn, and the framed note from the Christmas parade committee.

"Very nice," said Sergeant Orton. "Passed this scenario on to anyone else?"

"No," Cody said. "But it's not just a scenario—it's what actually happened, just has to be."

"No offense," said Sergeant Orton. "Bad choice of words on my part. Have to check all the details, but I'm inclined to believe you—which is why I need to know who else you've told. Can't be putting myself in a position of ignorance with any potential interview subjects. No way to conduct an investigation—one of those things I learned the hard way. Nothing worse than seeing some scumbag walk on a technicality."

That made sense to Cody. "I haven't told anyone. You're the first."

"Sure about that?"

"Yeah."

"Then let's roll," Sergeant Orton said. He spun his cigarette butt out the open window, its red end pinwheeling into the darkness. Snow fell, perhaps a little denser now, and harder.

"Want me to follow you?" Cody said.

"Better stick together for now," said the sergeant. "Your car'll be safe here." He paused. "In fact, maybe I should have the keys—I can send a patrolman over, pick it up for you."

Cody handed over his keys. "Where are we going?" he said.

Sergeant Orton drove the minivan out of the doughnut place lot, crossed back over the North Dover town line. "First," he said, "we might as well swing by the barn."

"Why?"

The sergeant's window slid closed. "Pick up that ledger you mentioned," he said. "Can't risk having evidence disappear on us, can we?" Cody, unsure, tried to figure that one out. "Not when we're this close to cracking the damn thing wide open," Sergeant Orton went on. Cody nodded. Cracking the damn thing wide open: He couldn't wait.

○ ○ ○

Sergeant Orton parked by the barn, unbuckled his seat belt. "I'll go in with you," he said. "Just to be on the safe side."

Safe side of what? But then Cody remembered Agent Brand: *You're in danger, Cody.* He saw that Sergeant Orton had his gun strapped on, even though he wasn't in uniform, and felt safe.

Cody opened up the office, reached for the light switch. "No need for that," the sergeant said, switching on a pencil flash. The beam roamed around the room, came to rest on the desk. "In there?" said Sergeant Orton.

"Yeah."

They moved to the desk. Sergeant Orton held the light. Cody opened the top drawer, didn't see the ledger. He riffled through some papers and folders; no ledger. Cody tried the other drawers, then the file cabinet beside the desk, finally a stack of documents by the copier, all without success.

"What the hell's going on?" said Sergeant Orton.

"I don't know," Cody said. "It was here, in the top drawer."

The sergeant shone the light in Cody's face. "You making any of this up?"

Cody held up his hand, shielding his face. "No," he said. "Why would I?"

"That's a tough one," Sergeant Orton said, lowering the light.

They went outside and got in the minivan. The snow fell more heavily now, and the wind was rising. Sergeant Orton put the minivan in reverse, twisting his head to see out the back. The headlights swept across the barn, and as they did, Cody saw Ike's face in one of the windows. Cody glanced at the sergeant, still peering out the back. Should he say something? Cody didn't know. Sergeant Orton wheeled out of the parking lot, onto the road, and the moment passed.

The sergeant looked at him. "Something on your mind?"

305

The answer was that image of Ike's face in the window; but Cody said, "Did you want to go question Townes?"

"That's on the list," the sergeant said. He turned onto Spring Street, passed the Rev, closed for the night. "Townes do that number on your face?"

Cody shrugged.

"Bet he ended up worse," Sergeant Orton said. "If I was a betting man." Cody didn't answer. "You a betting man, Cody?"

"No."

"Stay like that." He turned onto Governor, drove past the boarded-up gas station, the run-down houses, the vacant lot. For a moment Cody thought they were headed to Big Len's, but Sergeant Orton didn't slow down. As they went by the bar, the door opened and Phil—substitute bartender but also on Brand's payroll—stepped outside. He shivered, zipped up his jacket, glanced at the minivan. "Only so much trouble you can handle in life," the sergeant said.

"Um, what do you mean?"

"Talking about gambling," Sergeant Orton said. "Takes over some people's lives." He hung a left onto a side street, poorly lit and rutted, junk in some of the front yards. Cody had been here before, the night he'd followed the big black pickup with the Smith & Wesson bumper sticker. "Gets in their god-damn dreams," the sergeant said. It took Cody a few seconds to realize he was still talking about gambling. Snowflakes

306

swirled in the headlights; Sergeant Orton increased the wiper speed and hunched over the wheel.

"Where are we headed?" Cody said.

The sergeant gazed straight ahead. "Time to play a hunch," he said, "maybe speed things up a little."

"You have a hunch where Clea is?"

"Didn't say that."

But Cody believed it anyway. His heart seemed to beat harder in his chest; he even thought he could hear it.

● ● ●

The houses by the roadside, dimly lit or not lit at all, grew more ramshackle and farther apart. Dense forest rose on either side; a faded sign read: LEAVING NORTH DOVER. They climbed into the mountains, no other traffic on the road, the tall minivan getting buffeted by the wind. Sergeant Orton glanced over. "Hey! Buckle up."

Cody buckled his seat belt. They rounded a bend, then another. "How far is it?" Cody said. "Wherever we're going."

"Not too far," said the sergeant. "What I'd like to get straight is how come Boudreau thought Townes was rich when he actually wasn't."

"They were rich until recently," Cody said. "But his father lost all their money in a hedge fund. I think Townes kept that to himself."

"Then how do you know?"

"One of the other kids figured it out."

"Which one?"

"Simon. I don't know his last name. Don't even know what a hedge fund is, exactly."

"Can't help you there," said Sergeant Orton. "Some complicated form of gambling would be my take." He lit another cigarette, talked around it. "What'd you tell Simon?"

"About what?"

The sergeant's voice sharpened. "Gambling, hostage, Len Boudreau—this whole brainstorm of yours."

"Nothing."

The sergeant blew out some more of that sickly green smoke, this time from his nose. "Good at keeping things to yourself, aren't you?" he said.

Cody shrugged.

"I'm six months from retirement, eighty percent pension plus benefits," said the sergeant. "You realize that?"

"What are you going to do?" Cody said.

"Do?"

"With all your free time."

Sergeant Orton laughed, a strange laugh, not at all amused. He choked on his cigarette smoke, gasped once or twice, tossed the cigarette out the window. "Maybe I'll take up knitting," he said.

"Are you, um, married?" said Cody.

"Was," said Sergeant Orton.

The headlights found a ruined farmhouse standing close to the road. Cody remembered it; not far ahead he'd lost sight of Big Len's pickup and spun out. Sergeant Orton passed the farmhouse and then slowed down. Two or three hundred yards later, he almost came to a stop before turning onto a narrow track Cody hadn't noticed that first time, if he'd come this far at all.

The track wasn't plowed, but two deep ruts cut through the snow and Sergeant Orton followed those. They led over a shallow rise, down the other side, through a dense orchard—the trees black and twisted against the snow—to a lopsided hut or cabin with a chimney on top.

"What's that?" Cody said.

"Old cider house," the sergeant said. "Out of business."

"Abandoned?"

"Yeah, abandoned."

Clea was in there: Cody knew it beyond doubt. Sergeant Orton parked by a rusted-out tractor. They got out of the van. No lights showed in the cider house, but Cody smelled smoke. They walked to the door, a crooked, windowless door, the paint peeled off. Sergeant Orton knocked, one of those coded knocks—*tap; tap tap tap; tap; tap tap tap.*

The door opened. Backlit in the doorway by a lantern hanging from the ceiling stood Big Len. His gaze went from Cody to Sergeant Orton.

"What the hell's this kid doin' here?" said Big Len.

Sergeant Orton drew his gun. "This kid, as you call him," said the sergeant, "knows everything." He stepped behind Cody and stuck the gun in his back. "Get inside."

TWENTY-SIX

ORTON KICKED THE CIDER-HOUSE door shut with his heel. Cody took in a big dusty room with a cider-pressing machine, cobwebs all over it; old barrels stacked in the corner; tar paper over the windows to keep light from showing. "Sergeant Orton?" he said. "What's going on?"

Orton's features—big nose, small eyes, bushy mustache—hadn't changed but somehow he no longer looked like himself; now not just an older version, but no version at all. He made a little gesture with the gun. "Shut up," he said. That gun: exactly like Cody's father's gun, the one in his bedside table—a Smith & Wesson .38. What was going on? Cody was standing still—they all were, nothing moved in the abandoned cider house—but in his mind things were happening at impossible speeds.

"You?" he said. "You shot Bud?"

"I told you to shut up."

"What do you mean—he knows everything?" said Big Len.

"Are you paying attention, for Christ sake?" Orton said. "Didn't you just hear him?"

Big Len glared at Orton. "Then why the fuck did you bring him here?"

"What was I supposed to do?"

"And when you did bring him here, why the fuck didn't you throw a bag over his head?"

Orton's mouth opened and closed.

Big Len's gaze left Orton, shifted to Cody. "This is the old boyfriend? The one you had under control, quote? Back at the bar, sarge old buddy, I knew for goddamn sure he was out of control. Like totally."

"Out of control?" said Orton. "Look who's talking. If you hadn't been out of control in the first place—or, it turns out, if you'd run a simple credit check—none of this—"

"Zip it."

Orton zipped it, even though he was the one with the gun. At that moment Big Len's cell phone rang. He grabbed it, said, "Phil? What's up?" He listened for a moment, said, "Can't talk right now—I'll get back to you."

And then, just as he was clicking off, Cody yelled, "Brand! Brand!"

Big Len shoved the phone in his pocket. "What the hell? What's Brand?"

Cody didn't answer.

Big Len turned to Orton. "What's Brand?"

Orton shrugged.

Len took a step closer to Cody. "What's that mean, Brand? Tryin' to pull something?"

Cody kept his mouth shut. Big Len smacked him hard right across it with the back of his hand, a heavy, heavy hand. Cody staggered back but kept his balance and didn't say a thing.

"Who knows about this kid?" said Big Len.

"How do you mean?" Orton said.

Big Len glared at Orton again. "Use your head."

"Nobody knows, not really," Orton said.

"So he could be a drifter?"

Orton's mouth opened, as though to bring up an objection, but he ended up just nodding his head.

Len's gaze—pale and intelligent—returned to Cody, examined him in an unhurried way, almost as though Cody weren't a living, breathing thing. "Maybe we can do even better than that."

"Like how?" said Orton.

Len's eyes remained fixed on Cody. "Comes a time when you get out of the game, cut your losses."

"What game?" said Orton.

"'What game?'" Len said in a high, mimicking voice. "Suck it up, sarge. Him bein' here—a big mistake, and all yours."

"What was I supposed to do?"

"You already said that. It didn't help. Say something that helps."

"Cut your losses—Christ. How did you think this was ever going to work?"

A vein bulged in Len's forehead, big and blue. Cody thought he was going to shout, but instead his voice dipped low. "Nobody cheats me," he said. "That clear by now? I'll burn their fuckin' house down, blow up everything, down to the ground." He stared at Orton until the sergeant dropped his gaze.

Orton moved toward the fireplace, a blackened fireplace filled with ashes. It was cold in the room, and Orton made a breath cloud when he spoke. "He's got a car."

"Yeah?" said Len. "Here?"

"Not far," said Orton.

"We'll need the keys," Len said.

Orton took Cody's car keys from the pocket of his parka, held them up.

"Well, well," said Len with a smile. "You're way ahead of me after all."

Orton shook his head, a vigorous side-to-side motion, as though that suggestion was unthinkable.

Len laughed.

"What's funny?" Orton said.

Len stopped laughing. "Not a goddamn thing." He picked up a roll of duct tape that lay on the floor by the cider press. Len had to stretch a little to do it; the movement made his sleeve slide up past the wrist, revealing the shark tattoo. "What's the cop expression?" Len said. "Secure the prisoner?" Orton hesitated. Len made a gimme motion with his hand. "I'll hold the iron for you." Orton took two or three steps across the room, gave the gun to Len. Len didn't quite have it when Cody wheeled around, grasped the door handle, shifted it the wrong way—*come on, come on*—then the right way, finally throwing the door open. He bolted outside. Or started to bolt outside: Cody hadn't even completed one full stride—not his usual explosive burst, his knee still unready for that—before something hard and heavy came crashing down on the back of his head. He sagged to his knees in the snow, tried to get up— maybe even rising a little—and thought for an instant that he was going to stay conscious, but did not.

●○●

"Is someone there? Who are you?"

Cody dreamed he heard a voice.

"Can you talk? Are you all right?"

The best of all possible voices. Down where he was, under the pain, he settled in for a long listening session, but the voice went silent, leaving nothing to hear but a throbbing, very close, and, farther off and faint, the occasional crack and pop of burning wood.

Cody opened his eyes. He saw nothing at all, total blackness. He tried to reach up with his hands, explore the space around him; but his hands would not move. They were bound behind him: *duct tape*. Everything came back to him, and with memory came the full force of the throbbing pain in his head. His body sent other signals—like he was lying on a cold floor, kind of twisted up. He tried to rise, found that his legs were taped together from just below the knee down to the ankles.

"Is someone there?"

That voice, not a dream voice, but real, the source close by but muffled, maybe by an intervening wall: Clea's voice. He called out, "Clea!" Or tried to; they'd taped his mouth shut too, muffling the Clea sound down to something between a grunt and a groan.

"Cody?"

Cody made the sound again, more of just a grunt this time, the kind of grunt that said yes.

"Oh my God—Cody. It's you."

He grunted again.

She moaned, a soft, despairing sound, but he could hear. "What did he do to you?"

Cody tried to grunt in a reassuring way. Where was he? Where were Orton and Big Len? He looked around, every movement igniting stabbing pains in his head, and saw nothing. Were his eyes taped, too? He blinked; he could blink, no problem. Would that have been possible with duct tape over his eyes? No.

Cody wriggled a few inches across the cold floor, bumped up against something solid and vertical, a wall or door. He rolled the other way, used his momentum to get up on his knees. Not very high, but high enough to make him dizzy. Blackness spun around him and he lost his balance, tilting sideways, falling into that solid vertical, headfirst. He cried out in pain, a cry that didn't get out, got bottled up in his throat, and slumped to the floor.

"Cody? Cody?"

Cody lay on the floor, inhaling air through his nose, finding he couldn't get quite enough. Did he feel liquid in there? Was his nose bleeding, drowning him in blood? Cody rolled over onto his stomach, heard a faint drip drip on the floor. Yes, his nose was bleeding, but now he could breathe better.

"Cody? Cody?"

He breathed, tried to get himself together. He was in some

unlit space—most likely in the cider house—separated from Clea by a wall, meaning she was in an adjoining room. Where were Orton and Big Len? He'd been making noise, noise they would have heard. At that moment he remembered something Big Len had said: *We'll need the keys.* Oh, God. He rolled onto his side, kicked out with his taped-together legs, struck something solid.

"Cody?"

He grunted.

"That's the door. You're—he must have put you in the closet. I can't see, but I heard the sounds of it."

She couldn't see? Had they—Cody couldn't even allow himself to have the thought.

"He—he never lets me see him. But it's Len, isn't it—from the bar?"

Cody grunted. How much time did they have? Bear claw place and back: His mind was foggy, refused to make calculations. But in a closet? Had to get out. He squirmed around, rolled a bit, rose again to his knees, again felt a wave of dizziness and pain. This time he fought it off. Cody curled his toes up under him, rocked back, forced himself to his feet. More dizziness, more pain. He leaned against the wall; or maybe door—he could feel the doorknob pressing against his thigh.

Cody tried moving his fingers. They moved; the duct tape

didn't extend that far. He shifted around, got his back to the door, felt for the knob with his fingertips. He tried turning it. The knob turned, despite the awkwardness of his grip, but the door didn't open.

"Cody?"

Balancing against the door, Cody got down on his knees again, tricky with his lower legs taped together. His attempt to ease himself onto the floor ended with a sideways fall and another head bang, this one on the side but a pain igniter just the same.

"Oh, Cody."

Had he made another one of those throat cries of pain? That had to stop. *Focus.* And not a hard floor, anyway, but a dirt one as he was now realizing, kind of late; so no more fussing.

Cody rolled onto his back, arms jammed beneath him, and raised his legs. His feet touched a wall. He changed positions, rotating his body, his feet touching another wall—and then the doorknob. Cody felt around, found the door frame, shifted his feet—bound together, yes, like the end of a battering ram—just to the other side of the knob, away from the frame, and drew his knees back until they must have been almost touching his face, had he been able to see them. Then he kicked out with all his strength.

A loud thump; the door didn't give. Cody battered it again,

and again, and again, giving everything he had, grunting with the effort, ignoring the pain that awoke in his bad knee. Again and again and—*crack. Crack!* Something splintered. Cody bashed at it once more, and the door swung open.

"Cody? Are you out? I'm over here."

Cody knew where she was. He could see her. The night sky, visible through two high windows, shone with a dark kind of light, illuminating a cellar full of shadows and one shadow in particular, the shadow of a human figure, seated in a corner. A human figure with her arms behind her back and a black bag over her head. And not only that: Cody could see the dull gleam of chain links, running from a ring in the wall to a shackle around her ankle. He wanted to kill.

Cody rose up on his knees, tried to move toward her, found he could barely inch along. Much faster to roll: He dropped down, rolled across the cellar floor, bumped up against her leg.

"Oh, God," she said.

He kind of stroked her leg with his head, almost like a dog, but it was all he could do. Clea pressed her leg against him.

"Cody," she said.

He grunted, an urgent, demanding sort of grunt.

Clea understood. "My fingers are free," she said.

Cody squirmed around behind her, saw her wrists tied

320

together with rope, her fingers facing out. He lowered his face to her right hand. She felt around. "Duct tape?"

He grunted.

Clea felt around some more, probing with her fingernails. "Okay," she said after a few moments. "My thumb's under the seam." Cody heard a brief ripping sound. "There. I've got a grip. Try turning your head."

Cody turned his head. More ripping. He changed his position, moving sideways to her now, turned his head some more. Rip. He shifted again. This time when he turned his head, she turned her body the other way, and they made a much longer rip. "That's it," she said. Now they were working quickly, like a team that had practiced a difficult trick many times.

Rip, rip, rip. The pressure of the duct tape over Cody's mouth began to ease. One last rip and the tape drooped and fell away. Cody rose to his knees and then his feet. He got a corner of the black bag over Clea's head between his teeth and pulled. The bag came off. Cody spat it from his mouth.

Their faces were close together. Even in the shadowy darkness, Cody could see how bad she looked, face so hollow, eyes two black pits. He saw, but tried not to show anything, instead just gave her a quick kiss on the cheek, almost shy. For a moment he thought she was going to cry, but she did not. "Crazy," she said, "but I thought you'd come. I thought it a lot." Her voice broke and then tears did come, hers and his mingling on their faces.

"Not much time," he said. Clea nodded, stopped crying at once.

Almost without words, they knew what to do. Cody turned. Clea began digging with her teeth at the tape around his wrists. She found a corner, bit down. Rip. She jerked her head back. Rip rip. The tape loosened. Cody worked at it with the fingers of one hand, then squeezed his other hand free and tore off the rest of the tape. A few seconds later, he'd freed his legs. He felt for his cell phone: gone.

Cody hurried behind her, started on the rope around her wrists. "Is there light here?"

"Just when he brings the lantern."

Cody fumbled with a knot. "You've been like this the whole time?"

"Mostly just the chain," Clea said. "If he comes down he wears a mask. But tonight before they—are there two of them now?"

"Yeah."

The knot loosened. "Before they brought you down, he tied me up and covered my head. I . . . I hate that." She started crying again.

"Everything's all right," Cody said, probably a pretty stupid

322

thing to say. But she stopped crying. "Wriggle your wrists."

Clea wriggled her wrists.

"Pull."

She pulled. One hand came free. Then the other.

Cody drew her to her feet. They held each other. Over her shoulder Cody saw a seatless toilet close by, within reach of the ankle chain. To kill: oh, yeah.

He bent down, examined the shackle around her ankle, found the keyhole.

"Where does he keep the key?"

"I only saw it once, after he knocked me off Bud and brought me here," Clea said.

"Outside that warming hut?"

"That's where he brought me first. Before he tied me up, I tried to sneak a picture of him and hide my phone, but I guess it didn't work out. Is Bud all right?"

"Yeah."

Cody followed the chain to the ring in the wall. He tugged on the ring, then pulled at it, then kicked the wall; all useless. "Is there an ax or anything?"

"Not that I've seen."

"Maybe upstairs."

"Don't go."

Don't go: last words of the "Bending" poem. Cody didn't

323

go. Instead, he hurried around the cellar—once bumping into the hot side of a woodstove he hadn't noticed—finding nothing useful. But then a spade, lying in a wheelbarrow.

Cody grabbed the spade, straddled the chain, attacked it with the pointed blade over and over, using the spade as a pile driver. No good. He moved to the wall, a wooden wall, the ring bolted in place. Cody started smashing at the wall with the spade, all around the ring, at first getting nowhere, but then a crack appeared, and another. He went a little crazy, fury overcoming him, entered a savage state, trying with such intensity to destroy that wall, destroy the whole cider house, that he almost didn't hear Clea.

"Cody!"

He glanced up, saw yellow light in the two high windows, yellow beams there and gone: headlights. Cody took a huge backswing, swung the spade with all his might at that iron ring. A two- or three-foot section of the wall caved in and the ring fell free, bolt and all. Cody scrambled around, got his hands on the bolt and chain, thrust it all into Clea's hands.

"Quick," he said. They started up the stairs, Cody first, carrying the spade. He opened a door at the top and they hurried into the cider-press room, still lit by the ceiling lantern. Cody glanced around, saw only one way out: the front door. He was reaching for the handle when the door opened: Big Len, with Orton right behind him. They looked shocked, but only for a moment. Cody raised the spade. Orton drew his gun and said, "Drop it."

Cody dropped the spade.

Big Len turned to Orton. "That's what you call securing him? You're fuckin' useless." He picked up the spade, gazed for a moment at the blade. "But this'll do the job."

Orton, behind him, closed his eyes for a long moment, that way he did, like someone not wanting to see. "Has to be some other way," he said.

"Dream on," Big Len said. He motioned with the spade. "Outside."

Cody touched Clea's shoulder. They went outside, Cody and Clea first, Big Len and Orton right behind. Cody's car stood by the black pickup. Cody felt the spade nudge him in the back, directing him toward his car.

○ ○ ○

The wind had died down, the snow had stopped falling, and that strange glow in the night had vanished. Cody stood by the car with Clea, one arm around her, facing Big Len and Orton.

"What happens now," said Big Len, "is an unfortunate accident on one of our many dangerous roads. The real kidnapper, trying to escape the forces of the law, pedal to the metal—hey, not bad. I was thinking of the hairpin bend over the Mohawk

325

Ravine—good for three or four fatalities a season, right, sarge?"

Orton didn't answer.

"Everyone knows about teenage drivers," Big Len said. "Story sells itself. You careless kids forgot to buckle up." He hefted the spade, then turned toward Clea. She raised her hands and backed against the car, letting go of the chain; it fell to the snow. "Don't make this harder than it has to be," Len said.

All at once, the clouds parted and the moon, bigger than the night before, shone through. Cody saw that Clea was wearing the jade earrings. He stepped in front of her.

"Wait a minute," said Orton.

"Huh?" Len said.

Orton, gun still pointed at Cody, moved sideways, closer to the rear of the car. "He's got the Colorado plates on."

"So?"

"I gave him Vermont plates," Orton said. "Need them back."

"Why?"

"Why? Goddamn connection is why." He took out the pencil flash, shone it in Cody's face. "Where are they?"

The answer was that Agent Brand had them. Was that the right answer for this moment, right now? Cody thought of a better one. "In the trunk," he said.

Orton took out Cody's keys, popped the trunk, shone the light inside. "Don't see 'em," he said.

"Way at the back," Cody said.

Orton leaned into the trunk, pencil flash in one hand, gun in the other. "Where?" he said.

"Under all those rags."

"What rags?"

"Right there," Cody said, stepping forward.

"Hey," said Big Len, sticking out the spade, trying to block Cody's passage.

But not quick enough. Orton started to straighten up, also not quick enough. Cody got both hands on the trunk lid and flung it down as hard as he could. The edge struck Orton on the back of his head, jamming his face into the locking mechanism. He slumped to the ground, the gun flying from his hand, and lay still.

Cody dove for the gun. Big Len hit him with the spade while he was in midair, a tremendous blow that knocked the wind out of him. Cody landed on his back in the snow, hard enough to bury the gun somewhere beneath him. Big Len jumped on Cody, knelt on his chest, raised the spade in both hands, blade pointed straight down at Cody's face, his eyes bestial.

"Run!" Cody shouted.

But Clea didn't run. Instead she darted in from behind and looped the free end of the chain around Big Len's neck, once, twice, so fast. He gasped, let go of the spade, which fell beside Cody, grabbed at the chain, tried to get his fingers underneath, could not. Clea pulled on the free end. Big Len squirmed and threw an elbow at her, but she was right behind him, out of range. He struggled, face bloating, eyes bulging. Clea just pulled harder, heaving on that chain. Big Len made gurgling sounds. His tongue hung out. From down at the bottom, Cody had a clear view of the expression on Clea's face. It scared him, scared him as much as anything that had gone before.

Then the sky filled with flashing blue, and sirens sounded, an angry blare that seemed to come from all around. The arrival of Special Agent Brand, accompanied by Phil and a squad of state troopers, saved Big Len's life. It took two of the troopers to pull Clea off him.

○ ○ ○

After that, Cody just wanted to jump in his car with Clea and take off for home. Instead they had to go to a hospital for a few hours to get checked out—the same hospital where Orton and Big Len now lay, cuffed to their beds. Then came a day or two of talk, with Agent Brand, the state attorney general, lots of other officials Cody couldn't keep straight in his mind.

He and Clea hardly left each other's sides, not even at night.

Maybe the adults didn't like that, but somehow they'd lost their moral authority, if only for a while. The very first thing, the very first night, Clea said, "I have bad judgment sometimes."

"Who doesn't?" Cody said.

"I was an idiot. I got . . . swept up. Then all of a sudden he just wanted the money."

"Me, too," said Cody. "This minute."

"I've got other plans for this minute."

From all the talk, Cody learned that Phil had acted right away on his cry of "Brand, Brand." Brand had hurried to the barn, where Ike described seeing Cody and Orton coming out of the office. Ike had hidden the ledger in his room just after he and Cody had checked it, because he "couldn't trust nobody." A state trooper had spotted Cody's car on the road from the bear claw place to the cider house, and called in.

Betting slips turned up that proved Orton had fallen deep in debt to Big Len, although he made no admission and Len was saying nothing. Townes was arrested on conspiracy charges. His big-time lawyer, an old friend of Townes's father working for free, vowed those charges wouldn't stick. The attorney general's spokesman said the state would prove that Len had learned of Clea's post-practice rides in the woods from Townes. The big-time lawyer denied that and claimed Townes was one of the victims. One thing Cody knew: Townes searching the woods like a madman—that was unforgivable.

Cody's own father arrived, together with Fran. Cody's father was quiet, seemed smaller than usual, patted Cody on the back a few times and accepted congratulations from many strangers. Once or twice, Cody caught his father glancing at him in a new way, kind of proud and amazed at the same time. Fran passed on the news that Clea's father had opened his eyes, even spoken a bit, first some gibberish about his country club, but then as his mind cleared a single word: "Clea?"

Larissa organized a candlelit ceremony for Bud. Clea held Cody's hand the whole time. Lots of Dover Academy kids came, including ones like Alex and Simon, whom Cody had gotten to know a little bit. They all looked at him differently. Cody preferred the old way. The only person who looked at him the old way was Ike.

Fran made arrangements for shipping Cody's car home; over his objection, but it happened during one of the frequent times in that period when he could hardly keep his eyes open, so he didn't put up much of a fight. That ended the driving-back-across-the-country idea, just the two of them. Cody, his father, Clea, and Fran flew home on the same flight. Cody and Clea sat together, the armrest pushed back, sharing a blanket. They slept the whole way.

EXTRAS

REALITY CHECK

A Letter from the Author

Hello, Reader.

If you aren't just skipping ahead to the Extras but actually read *Reality Check*, then you know that Cody Laredo, the main character in the story, is (or was, considering what happens to him in the game against Bridger High) a high school football player. I love writing about sports and they've played a role in almost all my books. In the Echo Falls series, Ingrid's a soccer player, and there's some football, too—her brother Ty is the only freshman on the varsity team. Other sports I've written about are baseball, hockey, tennis, skiing, snowshoeing and free diving (the kind where you hold your breath). Baseball is a factor in *Bullet Point*, my next YA novel.

Sports are intense, emotional, full of conflict, and often come with a handy premade dramatic structure of their own: all very attractive stuff for the novelist. In competition, people often reveal aspects of their character you don't see in their off-field lives. Cody, Dickie, Jamal, Junior, Coach Huff, Martinelli—just from the action, you learn something about what's inside all of them. For some kids, sports are the most important part of their high school experience. Part of the reason has to do with the need to be physical. Don't lots of kids feel cooped up in the classroom from time to time? I know I did. And then there's the intensity. Many high schoolers get more of a charge from sports than anything else in their lives—anything adult-sanctioned, that is.

And memories are formed from sports you play as a child and teenager, memories you won't forget, I guarantee it. Here's something that happened to one of my sons when he was a kid. Bottom of the last inning, his team losing 3–0, and he comes to the plate with two out and the bases loaded. (There's that premade dramatic structure I was talking about.) What happens? He hits an inside-the-park grand slam and his team wins, 4–3. They carried him off the field. I can still see it, clear in every detail.

Sincerely,
Peter Abrahams

Enid's Laws

My mother was a writer and taught me a lot when I was very young. A few years ago, I wrote down what she'd taught me in the form of Enid's Laws. There are six of them:

1. **Organization is everything.**
   If the story isn't organized, what have you got? A mess. To be organized, you have to make some big decisions from the get-go, such as: What's the POV? One character? Multi? Tell it in first person? Third? How about the tense? Tone? I've got a nice beginning but will it lead to an end? Getting stuck without an end is bad. Make sure an ending is possible, and "the world blows up" doesn't count. There are maybe 10,000 decisions in writing a novel. Accept that.

2. **Fiction is about reversals.**
   Just like high school or college wrestling (meaning real wrestling). It's much more fun to watch a back-and-forth match than a blowout.

3. **Torment your protagonist.**
   Or, flipping it the other way, don't fall in love with your characters. And the main one—perhaps a hero, perhaps not—needs to be tested.

4. **Push everything as far as you can without contriving.**
   Get everything you can from your ideas—don't leave the gold mine only partly dug. But stop before you do anything

that makes the reader feel your behind-the-scenes presence and think that terrible thought: That couldn't happen.

5. **Always advance the story.**
Sometimes when you're writing you'll come up with a lovely little passage, a description of sagebrush at sunset, say, and a white dove gliding low. Does it move the story forward? No? Then out it goes. Shoot that dove!

6. **Be original.**
On every page! In every paragraph! No boilerplate! Ever!

Later I added a seventh law: Be playful.

I think you'll find plenty of examples of Enid's Laws in *Reality Check*. But this isn't a test—just read the book for fun. And speaking of fun, here's a scene where I was keeping that seventh law, the playful one, in mind. The truth is I never have to make myself obey this rule; I actually just can't help it. The scene is from *Into the Dark*, book three in the Echo Falls Mystery series, starring Ingrid Levin-Hill.

The history teacher didn't show up Wednesday morning, which meant, one: a sub, in this case Mr. Porterhouse, gym and health teacher, and two: an automatic extension on the Whiskey Rebellion paper, a lucky break for Ingrid, who'd forgotten all about it once, remembered in the picnic area at the falls, and then somehow forgotten again.

"What," said Mr. Porterhouse, reading from a note card, "is the significance of the Boston Tea Party?"

No hands went up.

"C'mon, you sports," said Mr. Porterhouse; he called everyone "sport." "The Boston Tea Party—dawn's early light, rockets' red glare, big big big."

Ingrid, who thought she'd had a pretty good grip on the Boston Tea Party until that moment, now wasn't sure.

Still no hands. Mr. Porterhouse fingered the whistle that always hung around his neck. Was he going to blow it? "Know what they say about them that—those that forget history?"

No hands.

"They're totally—" Mr. Porterhouse stopped whatever he was going to say, backed up. "They're in the cra—in the toilet, is what." He paused to let that sink in. "So, Boston Tea Party, significance of."

Brucie raised his hand. Mr. Porterhouse didn't see him. Brucie waved his hand around like a red-carpet celebrity. He was invisible to Mr. Porterhouse.

"'Kay," said Mr. Porterhouse. "Baby steps. Where did it happen?"

Where did the Boston Tea Party happen? Was that what he was asking? Ingrid sat up; this was starting to get interesting.

Mr. Porterhouse suddenly whirled and pointed straight at Dustin Dratch, sitting beside his twin brother, Dwayne; easy to tell them apart—Dustin had the cauliflower ear. They were the biggest kids at Ferrand Middle by far, partly because they were fifteen, having been held back twice despite the social promotion rule in Echo Falls schools.

"Tell the people, Dustin," said Mr. Porterhouse.

"What people?" asked Dustin.

Dwayne made a snorting noise, its meaning unclear.

"These people, Dustin," said Mr. Porterhouse. "Your fellow scholars."

Dustin looked around the room, squinting a bit, as though trying to spot something cleverly hidden. "Tell 'em what, again?" he said.

"Whereabouts of the Boston Tea Party," said Mr. Porterhouse.

From where Ingrid sat, she could see Dwayne nudge Dustin under desk level, and maybe whisper something quickly too, although they might have just relied on twin telepathy. Whatever the message, Dustin passed it on to the class. "They had it in a restaurant," he said. "Like, where else?"

A Sneak Peek at

BULLET POINT

COACH BOUCHARD MET all the baseball players after school that day in the gym. The coach was a little white-haired guy with big hands and cold blue eyes that never seemed to blink. He'd coached baseball at East Canton High for forty years, won many district championships and six state championships. But before that he'd had a long career in the minor leagues, finally making it to the majors for the last week of his last season, and going one for seven at the plate, that one being a triple, as Wyatt and the whole team knew from looking him up online.

The players sat in the stands, Coach Bouchard on his feet before them. "Any of you guys not heard the news by now?" he said. No one spoke. "Pretty straightforward—we got the ax. Not just us, all sports, all what they call extracurriculars." The coach had a way of dragging out certain big words, like extracurriculars, resulting in a tone Wyatt thought was sarcastic. "Excepting for the marching band—that got saved at the last minute. What're they gonna march for, that's my goddamn question." Coach Bouchard glared at the team, like they'd done something wrong. "How about you guys? Any

9

questions of your own?"

The boys were silent.

"This ever happen to you before?" the coach asked. "Don't think so. Then there gotta be some questions."

A kid said, "Why? Why is this happening?"

"Town's broke," said the coach.

"How can the whole town be broke?" said another.

"State's broke, too," the coach said. "School budget comes part from the state, part from property tax here in East Canton. But when folks is in foreclosure—you all know what that means? Foreclosure?" Nods here and there. "When the bank's taking your house away—that's foreclosure." Wyatt knew already: he'd seen it happening on his own street. "And when folks are in foreclosure, do they keep on paying their property tax?"

"Why should we?"

Wyatt glanced back up in the stands, saw that question had come from Willie Garcia, a senior, the backup middle infielder. He didn't remember ever hearing Willie speak before, never seen much expression on his face, either. Plenty of expression now: he looked angry.

"I hear you," said Coach Bouchard. "And it's not just folks' houses. When a business goes under, say a business like Baker Brothers, then they stop paying taxes, too. Not many businesses that size in East Canton. Town can go broke in a hurry." He gazed at the boys. "Any other questions? If there ain't, those of you what got equipment belonging to the team, go on and keep it, far as I'm concerned. Other'n that—"

"I've got a question," Wyatt said.

"Shoot," said the coach.

"Where are we going to play baseball?"

Coach Bouchard closed his eyes and shook his head slowly from side to side.

The coach left the gym, walked down the hall to his office, and went in, leaving the door open. The boys hung around for a few minutes, saying how fucked-up this all was, and how much the school sucked and the town sucked, "and the whole stupid planet," Willie said. And because that was funny, or maybe because Willie was suddenly talking, everyone started laughing, and they left the gym, pushing and shoving a bit, but in a better mood. As they went down the hall, Wyatt, toward the back of the crowd, glanced in and saw that Coach Bouchard was packing stuff in boxes. He looked up at Wyatt.

"See you for a sec?"

Wyatt nodded, entered the coach's office.

"Close the door."

He closed the door.

"I'd say take a seat," the coach said, "but Herman already took the chairs." Herman was one of the janitors.

"Where are you going?" Wyatt said.

"Home."

"I mean how come you're packing up?" No more baseball, but coach doubled as a health teacher.

"Handed in my resignation, effective"—he checked his watch—"eleven minutes ago."

Wyatt gazed at him, didn't know what to say.

"Thinkin' I'm a rat?" the coach asked. "Deserting a sinkin' ship?"

A rat? Wyatt could never think of Coach Bouchard that way. The coach wasn't exactly what you'd call a warm person, but he was straight up, gave each kid a fair shot—no one ever complained about favoritism—and besides, he'd taught Wyatt so much: how to be patient at the plate, wait for his pitch, even set the pitcher up a bit, plus all the intangibles like being relaxed and alert at the same time, and putting the team first, and playing hard until the last out. "Oh, no, Coach, I wasn't thinking that. I was thinking, you know, what about health class?"

The coach paused, his hand on a trophy he was taking from a desk drawer. "Not gonna help them sugarcoat this," he said.

Wyatt didn't understand. Who was "them," for starters? He remembered something from history class, how even the Great Depression had finally come to an end. "The economy's going to get better, right, Coach? What if it gets better soon, like by the summer? Then we could have a team again next year."

The coach gazed at him. Those cold blue eyes didn't look quite so cold. "Yeah, sure, anything's possible. And I'm the last one to run my mouth on any of this. But we got complicated problems, maybe more complicated than people can handle."

"But people made the problems in the first place, didn't they, Coach?"

The coach smiled. His teeth were yellowish plus a couple were missing, but there was something nice about his smile. "Got a head on your shoulders," he said.

Wyatt didn't get that at all. Except for math—and not that he was great at math, B's, yes, but he wasn't in the top stream—he was an average student, maybe below.

"You're a smart kid, is what I'm saying," the coach explained, perhaps because Wyatt was standing there with his mouth open. Wyatt came pretty close to arguing the point. "Want some advice? About playing ball, I mean. An old dumbass like me ain't qualified to opinionate about nothin' else."

What was going on? Wyatt had never heard the coach talking like this; he was always confident, teaching the team, Wyatt figured, how to be confident by example. "Yeah," he said, "sure."

"Reason I'm tellin' you this," Coach Bouchard said, "is you've got some talent for the game, maybe the kind, if it keeps developin' and you grow some more, that'll take you to a college. Not sayin' D-One, you understand, no promises on that score, and notice I'm not breathin' a word about pro ball, but— somewheres. Meaning scholarship money, son, and the chance to get a real education. You follow?"

Wyatt nodded. College: that would be something. How much more did he have to grow? Wyatt was a hair over five ten and built solid, weighing one seventy-five.

"My advice," said the coach, "is for you to get out of here fast."

"Get out of where, Coach?"

"This school, this town. Got to establish residence in some other town, a town that's got a high school with a good baseball program."

Establish residence? What did that mean? He named the only team from their district that had given them trouble last season. "Like Millerville High?"

The coach snorted. "Think Millerville's in any better shape than us? Same thing could happen there, if not this month then next, or next year. No, where you gotta go is someplace more prosperous, the kind of town that'll have baseball no matter what, even in a crappy economy."

Wyatt tried to think of towns like that. He hadn't traveled much, had been out of state only once, last year when the four of them—he, Cammy, Linda, Rusty—had taken a trip to Disneyland. He'd seen prosperity on that trip—they'd spent an hour or so driving around Beverly Hills—but the coach couldn't be meaning somewhere like that. Was there even a high school in Beverly Hills? That would be like transferring to the moon.

"I'm thinkin' Silver City," the coach said.

"Silver City?" It was at the other end of the state, four hundred miles away.

"Know any folks down that way?"

"No."

"Not an issue—I got some contacts at Bridger High. I'll make some calls—just say the word."

"So, I'd be, like, living in Silver City?"

"Exactly. Living there. Residing. Can't just parachute in and suit up. That's only in The Show." Coach Bouchard laughed.

Wyatt didn't get the joke. "But, uh, Coach, living with who?"

"Some family that likes baseball. Boosters, kind of thing. Coach down there's Bobby Avril—should be able to set you up, no problem. Bobby sent a kid to Tulane last year, full ride, and another one to Arizona State."

Full ride: sounded like words to make a magic spell. This was all so much. Wyatt tried to line it up in his mind the way the English teacher did on the blackboard, using—what were those marks called? Bullet points? Yeah, that was it. Wyatt lined up the most obvious bullet points, like living in a new place, a booster family, Bobby Avril, and leaving home.

"Well?" said the coach.

Wyatt took a deep breath. "Yeah," he said. "I'll do it."

"Smart man," said the coach. "All you got to do is keep doin' what you're doin'. Play hard, stay relaxed."

Wyatt nodded. Yes, he could do that. He was going to miss things, his mom, of course, and Dub and the team, and other kids at East Canton High, but: yeah. And Cammy. He was going to miss her, too. Wyatt held out his hand. "Thanks, Coach, thanks a lot."

"Don't thank me," the coach said. They shook hands. The coach's hand was hard and rough, the big fingers twisted. Wyatt turned to go. He was almost at the door when the coach called him back. "One more thing," he said. Wyatt walked back into the room. The coach opened a filing cabinet under the window, searched through the bottom drawer. "Here you go," he said. "Might as well have this. Everything's just gonna end up in boxes in my garage, moldering away." He gave Wyatt a photograph, six by nine or so.

"What's this?" Wyatt said. A black-and-white photo and obviously kind of old, the edges yellowish and turning up, it showed two guys in baseball uniforms with East Canton on the chests, although the lettering was different from the lettering on the uniforms now. One of the guys, the unsmiling, older one, had a salt-and-pepper mustache. The other was a kid, maybe about Wyatt's age, a good-looking kid with a big white smile on his face. Wyatt didn't recognize either of them.

"Who are these guys?"

Coach Bouchard jabbed his finger at the older one. "That's me, for Christ's sake."

"Oh," said Wyatt. "Sorry." The mustache had fooled him, plus how young the coach looked; his face—now deeply grooved—had hardly any lines at all. But those cold eyes were the same; he should have seen that. "Who's the other one?"

"Take a guess."

Wyatt had no idea. "The team captain, maybe?"

"Woulda been, if he'd stuck around for another season."

"Uh-huh," Wyatt said. Why did the coach want him to have this picture?

"No idea who that is?" Coach Bouchard asked.

"Nope."

"Look closely."

Wyatt looked closely, shook his head.

The coach gave him a long stare. "Maybe this ain't such a good idea," he said. He reached for the photo, got a corner of it between his fingertips, but Wyatt didn't let go.

"Why not?" he said. "Who is this guy?"

Coach Bouchard sighed. "Ah, Christ," he said. "It's a slick-fielding shortstop I had way back when. Name of Sonny Racine."

The photo trembled slightly in Wyatt's hand. "My father?" he said. "My real father?"

The coach sighed again. "Biological, I guess they say these days, 'stead of real."

Dad may not have been framed after all.